HAUNTING
LICENSE

Books by Carol J. Perry

Haunted Haven Mysteries
Be My Ghost
High Spirits
Haunting License

Witch City Mysteries
Caught Dead Handed
Tails, You Lose
Look Both Ways
Murder Go Round
Grave Errors
It Takes a Coven
Bells, Spells, and Murders
Final Exam
Late Checkout
Murder, Take Two
See Something
'Til Death
Now You See It

Anthologies
Halloween Cupcake Murder

HAUNTING
LICENSE

CAROL J. PERRY

Kensington Publishing Corp.
www.kensingtonbooks.com

KENSINGTON BOOKS are published by

Kensington Publishing Corp.
900 Third Avenue
New York, NY 10022

ISBN: 978-1-4967-4361-9 (ebook)

ISBN: 978-1-4967-4360-2

First Kensington Trade Paperback Printing: July 2024

10 9 8 7 6 5 4 3 2 1

For Dan, my husband and best friend

Sunny Places, Shady People.
Florida Happens.

(from my 2018 Bouchercon convention T-shirt)

Note to readers:

The ideas and words in this novel were generated entirely by the author without use of any AI application.

Chapter 1

Maureen Doherty suppressed a smile as George and Sam wrestled their awkward burden up the front stairs of the Haven House Inn, one man at each end of the vintage, round-topped steamer trunk. "What did the old woman have in this thing?" Sam grumbled as the trunk bump-bumped up the stairs.

"Feels like rocks," George complained, pausing to wipe his brow.

The two men were part of the inn's household staff and "the old woman" Sam had referred to was the late Penelope Josephine Gray, the mysterious benefactor who'd made Maureen sole heir to Haven's century-old hotel. After leaving her job as a sportswear buyer for a now-closed Boston department store, Maureen had been in Florida for less than a year. It was early morning in the middle of June, and the twenty-seven-year-old Massachusetts native was about to experience her first summer in the Sunshine state.

"Do you guys think you can fit the trunk into my office?" Maureen asked. "It might be a little tight."

"Sure, Ms. Doherty," Sam promised. "We can jam her in there somehow."

"Why does anyone want an old box that weighs a ton?" George muttered. "It's just more of the stupid stuff the old woman hoarded." Maureen had to admit that George's assessment of the contents of the unwieldy piece of luggage was quite possibly correct. Penelope Josephine Gray had, without a doubt, been a serious hoarder. The contents of a king-sized storage locker had recently proven that. She also had to admit that amid the debris they'd unearthed in the locker, there'd been some treasures too. Penelope Josephine had planned to write a book, and Maureen had been told that the material the old woman had gathered for it was stored in a big steamer trunk.

"Feels like rocks," George declared again.

But it might be treasure, Maureen thought.

Molly and Gert, two more members of the inn's housekeeping staff, sat in rocking chairs on either side of the top step. "Come on, boys, you can move faster than that!" Molly teased.

"Yeah," Gert agreed. "What's a'matter? You two getting old?"

Maureen smiled. The four—Molly, Gert, Sam, and George—senior citizens all, had more or less come along with her inheritance of the inn. The previous management had exchanged room and board for their services, and Maureen hadn't had the heart to change the arrangement. Besides, she'd come to love them all.

After some huffing and puffing and not a few minor cuss words, the trunk was situated in the first-floor office—wedged between a four-drawer metal file cabinet the previous office manager had spray-painted yellow and a white wicker table with a copier on top of it. This was one of the areas awaiting a serious redo. In Maureen's top desk drawer was a professional portfolio of drawings of what the Haven House Inn *could* look like—*if* the place could ever bring in enough money to pay for it.

Maureen had already managed to make over the inn's dining room and had begun construction of a gift shop on a corner of the broad porch. She looked forward to the upcoming return visit of interior decorators, Trent and Pierre, the designers of the portfolio, anticipating how pleased they'd be with her progress so far. Plans had been in place for several months for the two to return to Haven to celebrate Trent's June birthday.

She was tempted to dive into the trunk immediately, but she'd learned in the short time she'd been an innkeeper that the needs of the inn had to come first. She checked her watch. There were already good smells of breakfast wafting from the dining room. *Coffee? Bacon? Cinnamon rolls?* There'd eventually be time to see what Penelope Josephine's most recently discovered hoard might yield, but for now she needed to finalize the next week's lunch menus with executive chef Ted Carr, contact an electrician about repairing the aging neon VACANCY/NO VACANCY sign that had lately taken to randomly blinking on and off, and perhaps most urgently, taking her golden retriever, Finn, for a walk. Breakfast could wait.

She thanked the men for their efforts, tipped them each generously, and headed for the elevator. The Haven House elevator was quite a piece of work. Shiny brass accordion-style doors opened into a polished wood and scrolled metal interior. She got in and pressed the UP button, watching through etched glass windows as the cage ascended two stories within its brick-walled enclosure. As soon as she stepped out onto the soft, rose-colored carpeted third floor, she heard Finn's welcoming "woof" from behind a white paneled door. "I'm coming, Finn," she said, inserting the key.

Finn greeted her with happy kisses and tail wagging. "Did I keep you waiting, poor baby?" Maureen knelt on the floor beside the golden, scratching behind his ears.

"It's about time you showed up." A familiar, feminine voice came from the direction of the long blue couch. Not too long ago Maureen would have been quite startled by the

voice and the shimmering form beginning to take shape before her, but she'd reluctantly accepted the fact that she
shared her apartment with the ghost of a long-dead movie
starlet.

Maureen stood. "Oh, hi, Lorna," she said, facing the beautiful, fair-haired apparition who always appeared in black
and white—just as she had in the many 1930s movies she'd
made as Lorna DuBois. "Busy morning. I'll take him for a
nice run on the beach to make up for being late."

"That's good," Lorna said. "I was beginning to think I'd
have to take him myself, and I'm not dressed for dog walking." She performed a model-like turn, displaying the satiny,
strapless, form-fitting, slit-to-the-thigh gown. "Like it? Edith
Head designed it for Audrey Hepburn in *Funny Face*."

"It's lovely," Maureen agreed. "and dog walking isn't a
good idea for you anyway. You're kind of transparent, you
know? People would notice."

"I know," she agreed. "Haven doesn't like us ghosts running around in public."

Lorna was right about that—and she was surely not the
only ghost in town. It hadn't taken Maureen long to learn
that the city of Haven was *very* haunted indeed! She'd also
learned that the citizens of Haven vehemently denied that
fact to anyone who asked. There was no desire to have
"ghost hunters"—and the attendant TV mobile units, ceme-
tery vigils, audio equipment, night-vision cameras, and the
swarms of people who followed that sort of thing—disturbing
the pleasant pace of their off-the-beaten-path hometown.

Maureen took Finn's leash from a hook behind the kitchen
door and attached it to his collar. "I'll see you later, Lorna,"
she said, heading for the door. Taking the stairs instead of the
elevator because Finn was more comfortable that way, they
made their way to the ground floor.

Once on the sidewalk, the two picked up their pace, the

woman in an easy jog, the dog fairly prancing toward the beach at the end of the boulevard. Most of the shops on Beach Boulevard hadn't yet opened. It was a peaceful time of day that Maureen always enjoyed. They approached the Beach Bookshop and Maureen waved to shop owner Aster Patterson, who sat in a hot-pink Adirondack chair with bookshop cat Erle Stanley on her lap. A folding tray table held a chintz-patterned teapot, several teacups, and a matching platter full of round white cookies. Aster was an early riser. She got up before sunrise every morning to bake those cookies.

"Come join us, Maureen," the woman called, gesturing to a striped folding beach chair. "I have a nice pot of Irish breakfast tea and a plateful of Peter's favorite shortbread cookies all ready to enjoy." The bookshop was one of the few un-haunted businesses on the boulevard, and Aster baked those cookies every day, hoping to entice the late Peter Patterson's spirit to visit her.

Maureen had become accustomed to Aster's unusual outfits—today the woman wore red-plaid Bermuda shorts and a black-and-white-striped hockey referee's shirt. A very large pink eyelet sunbonnet covered white hair. Finn stopped midprance and tugged Maureen toward the woman. "Okay, Finn," Maureen told the dog. "We'll stop, but only for a minute. We have a busy day ahead of us." She sat, facing Aster. Finn, with an agreeable "woof," put his head on Aster's knee and gave Erle Stanley a friendly lick on the nose.

Aster poured steaming tea into one cup. Using silver tongs, she added one lump of sugar. "There you are, darling. Now tell me, what's in it?"

"What's in what?" Maureen accepted a shortbread cookie.

"The big old trunk the boys delivered from the historical museum, of course. What's in it?"

Word gets around fast in Haven.

"I don't know. I haven't opened it yet."

"They say that's Penelope Josephine's trunk and that it's locked." Aster passed the cookie platter again. "Have another. These were Peter's favorites, you know."

"Who's *they*?" Maureen wanted to know, accepting the delicate treat.

"Oh, you know. Folks. People. Everybody at the Quic Shop." Aster referenced Haven's only grocery store, "gossip central" for the town, another business that opened early every morning. "I heard it's so heavy, it could be full of rocks."

"So George says," Maureen agreed. "But I don't mind telling you, if the folks—people, and everybody at the Quic Shop want to know—I believe it's only full of material Penelope Josephine collected because she'd planned to write a book someday. The Historical Society gave it to me because, after all, I'm her only heir."

"Do you have the key?"

"Probably. She left a big ring full of keys. We haven't figured out what half of them go to." Finn gave a little whiney woof, tugging at the leash. Maureen stood. "Thanks for the tea, Aster. Finn's anxious for his run on the beach." The two resumed their jogging pace along the boulevard, slowing when they'd reached the shoreline. While Finn took care of business, Maureen looked left and right, smiling, realizing that they had the beach almost to themselves. A few waders were mere dots far down the beach, someone on a Jet Ski zoomed around in the distance. There was a sailboat on the far horizon. Finn would be able to run free. She bagged the doggy-doo and deposited it in the nearby receptacle, then, squinting in the sunshine, moved closer to the water's edge, peering into the gently lapping waves.

The body was facedown, moving in a slow, rolling motion with the incoming tide.

Chapter 2

Ever curious, Finn moved closer to the thing, nose twitching. Maureen yanked back on the leash and stood, once again looking left, then right, not smiling this time, wishing there was someone—anyone—nearby, some fellow human to validate the thing that was lolling among tiny white bubbles, mere inches away from the toes of her running shoes.

Call somebody, she told herself, taking a step back, reaching for the phone in her pocket and tapping the numerals 911. An operator answered immediately, asking the nature of her emergency. "A b-body on the beach," she stammered.

"What is your location?" was the next calm, reasonable question. Maureen looked around for the closest landmark. "I'm right behind the Haven Casino," she said, identifying the sprawling white building where Haven held weddings and dances and trade shows and baby showers.

"Is the person male or female?"

"I . . . I don't know. It's face down in the water. The tide's coming in."

"Is there anyone else with you?"

"No, I'm all alone. There's no one nearby at all."

"No swimmers? No one?"

"No one. There's a sailboat in the distance, and I saw a Jet Ski out there, but it's gone now."

"I'm notifying your local police. Do you feel safe where you are now?" the calm, reasonable voice asked.

"I . . . I guess so," Maureen said.

Local police. That means Frank Hubbard.

"Woof," Finn offered. "Woof woof."

"I hear a dog. Is the dog with you?" the voice wanted to know.

"Yes. My dog is with me."

"I'll stay on the line with you until help arrives." The voice was steady, reassuring. "The police station isn't far away."

"I know. Thank you." Maureen realized that her own voice was far from steady.

Come on, Frank. Hurry up! What if the tide starts to take this thing away? I'm not going to touch it.

There was a sound. A welcome one. "I hear sirens. The police must be on their way."

"Yes. Will you be all right now?"

"I will," Maureen said. "Thank you so much. Here they come." Stuffing the phone into her pocket, Maureen tugged on the leash, moving herself and Finn toward the white building and away from that nameless, faceless body rocking ever so gently in shallow waves.

Maureen had been correct in assuming that the first responder on the sad scene would be Officer Frank Hubbard, Haven's top cop. He drove a blue Ford, lights flashing, siren howling, up onto the sidewalk in front of the Casino, followed by an ambulance and the black van she recognized as the St. Petersburg medical examiner's vehicle. Once the siren noise had faded away and the red, white, and blue light show had dimmed, Hubbard climbed out of his cruiser and approached Maureen. Wordlessly, she pointed to the spot she'd just left, and two EMTs, who'd already donned boots and gloves, a stretcher between them, hurried toward the shoreline she'd indicated.

"Well, Ms. Doherty," Hubbard said. "What have you gotten yourself into now? Found a body, have you?"

Maureen knew she was being recorded on his bodycam. "Yes, sir," she said.

"Come along, then. Follow me." He followed the EMTs and she followed him. Finn lagged behind and she tugged the leash gently. "Is the deceased anyone you know?" Hubbard asked.

"I don't know. He—it's face down in the water." She slowed her steps, watching as the men lifted the body, placed it on the waiting stretcher, and carried it onto dry sand.

"Let's take a look then, shall we? He shrugged his shoulders. "Let's hope he hasn't been in the water too long—and that none of the sea critters have been chewing on his face. Know what I mean?"

She knew exactly what he meant and didn't want to think about it. The man on the stretcher—and she could tell as they drew closer that the body was that of a man because of his gray beard—wore khaki shorts, the kind with many pockets, and a T-shirt adverting Fin-Nor fishing reels. "A fisherman," she whispered as they drew closer.

"You know him?" Hubbard almost snarled the question.

"I'm not sure." Standing beside the stretcher, she looked down at the man's face, glad that it was unmarked by sea critters. The EMTs stood by, one of them holding a blanket, ready to cover the body. "Quite a few of the fishing charter boat crews eat at the inn," she said, "and most of them dress that way."

"I know him," Hubbard spoke in a monotone. "His name is Eddie Manuel. He captains the *Tightline*. Six-pack charter boat out of the Haven Marina. Ring any bells?"

"I've heard his name before," Maureen recalled. "Some of the guests at the inn have chartered that boat. Isn't he . . . wasn't he . . . sort of famous around here?"

"A highline fisherman. One of the best." Hubbard signaled the EMTs to cover the man's face, then dropped his voice. "He was an old friend of mine."

"Oh, Frank, I'm so sorry." Maureen gave Hubbard's arm a sympathetic pat. "I had no idea."

"When your call came in, I hoped it wasn't him." The EMTs carried the captain of the *Tightline* across the sand toward the black van. Maureen and Hubbard remained at the shoreline, still facing the blue-green gulf water, Finn sitting quietly between them. "Eddie's wife called me this morning. The boat was all tied up at the dock, but he hadn't come home last night."

"You knew he was missing?"

"Not technically missing. Just a few hours late coming home from work, you know?" He shook his head. "Not like him. Not at all."

"I'm so sorry," she said again. "Frank, I have to get back to work. If you need me for anything, just call."

"Sure. You run along, Doherty," he said. "I'll send an officer by to take your statement about seeing the . . . seeing him in the water like you did."

"Okay. Come on, Finn." They hurried across the sand toward the Casino. "You didn't get much of a run, did you?" she asked the golden. "We'll take a proper one later." She watched as the black van moved slowly onto the boulevard, then glanced back at where Hubbard still stood alone. "Poor Frank. He's very sad." Finn gave a soft "woof," and raced ahead, pulling her along.

When the two reached the inn, the four members of the housekeeping team—Gert and Molly, George and Sam—were seated in rocking chairs at their usual spots on the porch, two of them on each side of the staircase. Maureen dropped the leash so that Finn could run up the stairs, greet his friends, and receive the expected pats and scratches and "good boys." Those formalities attended to, Finn lay down beside George, and four pair of eyes focused on Maureen.

"So you found old Eddie Manuel." Gert followed the statement with a *tsk-tsk* sound.

"Drowned, was he?" Molly rocked her chair forward.

Maureen hadn't thought about the cause of death, and the question caught her by surprise. "I don't know," she said. "I suppose so." *News via Quic Shop already?*

Molly answered the unspoken question. "My cousin Bertha's husband plays golf with the brother of one of the EMTs who picked up the body. She called me as soon as she heard."

"You okay, Ms. Doherty?" Sam asked. "That's no fun, finding a dead body."

"Not her first time either," George added. "Right, Ms. Doherty?"

George was right. Maureen had been in Haven for only a few hours when she'd discovered a dead man on this very porch. "I'm all right," she fibbed. Finding another body didn't make it any easier. "Did you all know him?" The four heads nodded in unison.

"Great fisherman," Sam declared. "He used to have breakfast here sometimes when he had an early charter."

"Ted knew him," Molly offered. "Eddie was an old friend of Ted's family."

"I guess Eddie's kid will take over the business—running the *Tightline*," George said. "Though nobody's going to be as good at it as Eddie."

"Well, that's not fair," Gert said. "The kid's barely twenty. It takes time to learn."

"It'll take a good long while for that one to learn half of what Eddie knew," Sam scoffed.

"Yeah," George agreed. "Like forever."

"Huh, men!" Molly gave Sam a punch on the arm. "You

just watch. Tommy will be fishing rings around old Eddie in no time. You guys are just narrow-minded."

So Eddie Manuel has a son named Tommy who can take over the business. "Everybody has to start somewhere," Maureen frowned, siding with Gert and Molly. "The boy may surprise you."

"It'd surprise us if Tommy was a boy." Sam laughed. "But she ain't."

Molly punched Sam's arm again. "Tommy is Eddie's daughter. Her real name is Thomasina after a grandfather named Thomas. But she likes to be called Tommy. And she's a licensed captain, just like Eddie was."

Sam rubbed his arm. "Hey, take it easy. I'm already lame from slinging an old trunkful of iron frying pans around."

"Rocks," George interrupted.

"It's neither one," Gert insisted. "What *is* in it, Ms. Doherty?"

In an amazing display of topic hopping, the conversation had moved from a dead fisherman to the qualifications of a girl boat skipper to Penelope Josephine's locked trunk—all in the space of a few minutes. Maureen gave the same answer she'd given to the question of how Eddie Manuel had died. "I don't know," she said, and pushed the green door open. She grabbed a quick cup of coffee and a still-warm cinnamon bun from the buffet table, returned Finn to her apartment, and prepared to face the rest of this strangely begun June day.

Chapter 3

With a stack of fresh-from-the-copier menus under her arm, Maureen once again opened the louvred door leading to the dining room. Admiring the way the new beach-inspired color scheme and the completely refurbished vintage bar blended with the inn's original round tables and snowy white linen tablecloths, she was sure that Trent and Pierre would be delighted with the way she'd interpreted their design.

Moving through the room, she pushed open the door leading to the kitchen where, with all traces of breakfast cleared away, the usual before-lunch activity was happening. Confident that everything in the Haven House Inn's kitchen would be moving along perfectly under the direction of her one-time bartender, now "executive chef," Ted Carr, Maureen spoke a quick "good morning" to Ted's assistant Shelly. The young woman paused in directing two new hires on the correct way to chop vegetables, and nodded toward the tiny space in the corner of the immaculate room, laughingly referred to as "Ted's office."

Ted stood, smiled, when she approached his desk. "Hey," he said.

"Hey, yourself. How're you doing?" Maureen asked, placing the menus on his desk. "Want to take a quick look at next week's lunch menus before I send George and Sam out to distribute them?"

"Sure. Have a seat," he said, sitting, and indicating the chair next to his. "I understand you've had an eventful morning. You okay?"

"I was going to ask you the same thing," she said. "You knew the fisherman?"

"Since I was a kid." He spoke softly. "I should have been with you instead of running earlier. Maybe we should start running together again." The two had developed a habit of taking early morning runs on the beach together along with Finn, but had recently stopped, attempting to quell rumors that the inn's owner and the bartender she'd promoted to executive chef were somehow romantically involved. Ted reached for the top menu on the stack. "I miss you."

Maureen missed him too, more than she cared to admit even to herself. If they weren't romantically involved, she knew that they were darned close to it. The long kiss they'd shared one morning on the beach had proven that. Determined to keep the relationship—or whatever it was—on the down-low, they'd stopped the morning runs, but not the knowing looks from the staff or the whispers from the grocery store. She wanted to say "I miss you too," or "I wish you'd been with me"; instead, she tapped the stack of menus. "Any mistakes?"

He didn't look at the papers, but directly into her eyes. "No mistake."

She knew he meant the kiss and not the roast beef sandwiches or the red beans and rice. "You sure?"

"I'm sure." Only then did he glance at the sheet with its color photos of main dishes and desserts, its prices and daily specials. "This looks okay too. See you and Finn on the beach tomorrow morning?"

"To run?"

"Of course. To run."

"Do you want to talk about your friend? About Eddie Manuel?'

"Maybe tomorrow."

Still smiling when she returned to the lobby, she handed some of the menus to Jolene, a sometime waitress and an always-willing stand-in front desk receptionist. "Next week's menus," Maureen told her. "Everything looks delicious. Talk it up to the guests, please."

"I will." Jolene agreed. "I just wish we had more guests to talk to. The phone hasn't rung so far today."

"I know. Is it always this slow this time of year?" Maureen asked.

"I don't know." Jolene looked thoughtful. "I don't think the old manager kept track of that kind of thing."

"Well, anyway, the Vacancy/No Vacancy sign out front blinking on and off can't be helping the situation." Maureen said. "I need to get that fixed." Returning to the front porch, she divided the remaining menu into two piles, handing one to George and the other to Sam. "Here you go, guys," she said. "Let's see if we can drum up a little extra lunch business around town. I'll be in my office if you need me."

Once behind her desk, Maureen phoned Gaudreau and Son—her trusted go-to duo for all kinds of repairs. Waiting for the call to be answered, she focused her attention on the vintage trunk beside the copier. "I'll get to you next," she promised. Pulling out the bottom desk drawer, she picked up the jangling round ring full of Penelope Josephine's keys, confident that the trunk key would be among them. "Hello. Mr. Gaudreau? Maureen Doherty here. I have a small electrical problem."

Having obtained the elder Gaudreau's assurance that "Sonny" would be there today to fix the sign, Maureen began sorting through Penelope Josephine's key collection. Having learned about the old woman's penchant for hoarding, she was prepared to find out that many of the keys didn't belong to anything at all at the inn, although she'd already discovered that some of them did indeed open doors and cabinets on the property.

Key ring in hand, she scooched down beside the trunk to get a close look at the keyhole. Finding the right key was much easier than she'd expected. The number on the lock, 178, matched the number on a small, squatty key. "Piece of cake," she said aloud, twisted the key in the lock, and lifted the brass-bound lid.

There was a definite odor arising from the trunk—not unpleasant, and somehow familiar. *Old papers, like a closed-up library, maybe,* she thought, *and something else—like fall leaves in Massachusetts, and salt water.*

The top layer appeared to be made up of colorful paper things—brochures, advertisements, greeting cards—all crowded together. This was going to take a while to sort through, she realized when she attempted to pick up a brochure marked "Tiki Gardens." It was stuck quite firmly to another folded advertisement for something called "Pueblo Village." *I'll bet these are some of this area's long-gone tourist attractions,* she decided. *I'll have to try to separate them without tearing them apart. It will be fun to frame them and hang them in some of the guestrooms.*

Carefully now, realizing that the tightly packed contents of the trunk had made paper items especially fragile, Maureen put one finger under the corner of an oblong card, printed in blue on white stock and bearing a photo of a familiar scene. With gentle pressure from thumb and forefinger, she lifted the card and placed it on the top of her desk.

The photo showed a young man holding a giant redfish. The man was a stranger to her, but she recognized the sign behind him. In fact, in a small silver frame in her upstairs office, there was an old photo of herself as a child, holding a much smaller fish, posing in front of that same sign. That sign, faded now but still legible, advertising Haven's fleet of fishing charter boats, still stood in the same spot on the beach. It was in front of that sign that Maureen and Ted had shared their first kiss. It felt to Maureen that finding this particular card at the top of Penelope Josephine's trunk might be more than coincidence. Normally, back in Massachusetts, Maureen wouldn't have entertained such a thought, but living in Haven, hobnobbing with ghosts and keeping a fortune-telling card from a Zoltar machine—along with another Zoltar card she'd found in an old Christmas greeting from Penelope Josephine's hoard as well a coin she perceived as lucky—locked in a secret compartment in her top bureau drawer, had changed her way of thinking about a lot of things. She carefully picked up the card and read the blue-printed copy.

WELCOME ONE AND ALL TO
HAVEN'S FIRST ANNUAL
FISHING TOURNAMENT!
JUNE 16–18, 2000

Does Haven still have an annual fishing tournament in June? she wondered. *How come I haven't heard about it? If there is one, we'd better get on board with it. That would be a perfect way to attract some anglers to stay at the inn for a week.* She opened her laptop and tapped "Annual June fishing tournament in Haven Florida" into the subject line. That produced information about several charter boats, some fishing tackle advertisements, and an article about a September big-game fishing tournament happening in Tampa. Nothing about June fishing in Haven.

She returned her attention to the 2000 card. She read about the prizes offered, both trophies and cash awards. They'd had several different categories too. There were biggest fish awards for several species and even a "catch and release category" that involved measuring and photographing the catch and releasing it back into the gulf.

What a great promotion this must have been—and could be again.

She took another look at the picture of the young man proudly displaying the giant fish. There was a caption below the picture in tiny blue italics: *First Mate Eddie Manuel of the MV Tightline with a Record Catch.*

Chapter 4

How many coincidences can there be in one day? Maureen put the blue-and-white card faceup on her desk and closed her eyes. "Eddie Manuel, what do you want from me?" she whispered. "I found you on the beach and I'm truly sorry about that. But now you've practically jumped out of Penelope Josephine's trunk." Eyes still closed, she leaned back in her chair. "What do you want from me?" she asked aloud again.

There was a dainty tap-tap at the door and Jolene appeared. "Ms. Doherty? Officer Hubbard is here. Do you want to see him?"

Maureen lowered the cover of the trunk. "Sure. Send him in." He'd told her he'd be sending an officer over to question her about finding the body. So now he'd decided to question her himself—and maybe he could answer a few of *her* questions. Frank Hubbard was no Zoltar, but maybe he'd be able to fill in some of the blanks this day had presented so far.

Hubbard was in full uniform, cap with gold braid and all. Unusual. Had this become a big-time investigation or was he on his way to give out an award or something? "Come in, Frank." She gestured toward the chair facing her desk. "Have a seat."

"I have just a few questions about how you happened to find poor Eddie, Doherty," he said. "Then I'll be on my way over to Eddie's mother's house to help her and his wife and kid with the funeral plans."

"I'm sure they'll appreciate that," Maureen told him. "Is there anything at all we can do to help?"

"I'll let you know. We can't plan anything for sure until the medical examiner finishes his work." He took off the cap, dropping it on top of the fishing tournament card, and put a small recorder on the desk. "I'm recording. Okay?"

"Of course."

"You stated when we spoke earlier that there was no one else on the beach when you saw the—um—the deceased in the water. Correct?"

"I didn't say there was no one on the beach," she corrected. "I said there was no one nearby. There were people in the distance—just no one near enough to hear me if I called out—or near enough to see what I was seeing."

"You told the nine-one-one operator that your dog was with you."

"Finn. Yes."

"You said something to the operator about seeing a Jet Ski in the area."

"A Jet Ski . . ." She frowned, trying to remember, to bring back the moment. Once again, she closed her eyes. "A Jet Skier and a sailboat," she said. "They were both far away, though."

"How far?"

"Oh, Frank. I'm not a sailor. I don't know how to judge distances on the water. The sailboat was really far away. I couldn't say what color it was. Just a sail in the distance."

He leaned forward, his elbows on the edge of her desk. "What about the Jet Ski? Could you tell how many people were on it? If they were men or women?"

Her eyes closed again, concentrating hard. "The Jet Ski was one of the big ones. The two-seat kind. I think it was blue with white letters or numbers or something."

"Numbers? What was the name? Or the number?"

Maureen shook her head. "I don't know. It had something written on it. I'm sure of that, but it was too far away for me to read it."

"Could you tell anything about the riders? One or two? Men or women?"

"Sorry. No. Just a shape."

"So you think it was one person?"

"I couldn't swear to it, but, yes, it looked like one person."

Frank Hubbard stood. "That's okay. It's good you remembered the colors and the writing. The thing is, we're thinking that Eddie Manuel might have fallen from a Jet Ski. He hadn't been in the water for long. You know. No evidence of critters. Anyway, we thought maybe he'd had a heart attack or something like that and fell off and drowned. He had a couple of rental skis at his dock, and Tommy says he used one sometimes to check on things along our shoreline. One of them is missing, and it wasn't one they'd rented, so chances are Eddie was using it. It'll drift ashore somewhere. We're on the lookout for it. We're thinking that whoever you saw on a ski when you found Eddie might have seen something. We're checking all the big rental places anyway. It seems like blue-and-white skis are popular all over the place. Thanks, Doherty." He turned off the recorder. "Listen, Doherty, off the record . . ." He glanced around, as though he thought somebody might be listening, and dropped his voice. "I know you have a—a kind of gift for figuring out things about people who've died."

Maureen began to protest. This wasn't the first time he'd said such a preposterous thing about her. "Frank—Officer Hubbard. I don't—"

He put on his cap. "If you think of anything else about that morning, anything at all, give me a call."

"I will," she agreed, deliberately changing the subject. "Do you have another minute to answer a question or two from me?" She looked down at the blue-and-white card advertising the long-ago tournament. *Blue and white,* she thought. *Like the Jet Ski.* Hubbard followed her glance.

"That's Eddie." His voice was hoarse. "Where did you get this? Why do you have this?"

"That's one of the things I wanted to ask you about. It was in Penelope Josephine's trunk. I found it just before you knocked. Do you remember that tournament? Were there any more of them after that one?"

Hubbard sat down again. "That tournament. Must have been twenty-odd years ago. I'd just joined the force. Eddie was mating on his dad's boat. There was some kind of city celebration going on. For the millennial, I suppose. And I think it was Haven's ninetieth anniversary too."

"That would be right," Maureen looked at the vintage map of Haven above her desk. "Haven was founded in 1910."

Hubbard nodded. "Yep. It was a big deal back then. They even had a parade."

"But were there any more June fishing tournaments after that one?" she asked again.

"No. Some bad stuff happened on the last day of the thing. It's a lot of work to put together a thing like that, and nobody wanted to take on the job after the first one."

"I could tell by reading this card that it must have been a chore, but it must have drawn a lot of folks to Haven. Why didn't anyone else want to run it?" Thinking that a tournament would *still* draw a good crowd, and wondering exactly how difficult it would be to put one together, she waited for his answer.

"Bad luck. Bad karma. Somebody died on the last day, and some people thought it could have been murder," he said. "I told you, I was new on the force, so I wasn't much involved in the investigation—such as it was—so I don't really know the nitty-gritty details. I can look it up, though."

"Bad enough karma that they'd give up after the first one?"

"Sure. You know how Haven people are. They don't want the ghost hunters here, messing around looking for ghosts. I don't believe in them, you know, but it's always been that way. Even then, they sure didn't want a lot of attention on a dead body next to the Indian mounds." He dropped his voice again. "A ghost from an old Native tribe was something nobody in Haven wanted to deal with."

"I understand," she said, surprised that, in fact, having lived in Haven for less than a year, she *did* understand how all that worked. "So somebody died over near the Indian mounds?" Visiting the mounds had long been on Maureen's "to do someday" list, but as yet she hadn't taken time away from her innkeeper duties to do it. Some local tour guides even offered a tour of the area, and some inn guests had taken it and enjoyed the experience.

Hubbard paused, then answered, "More than died. Got himself murdered is more likely."

"Who was he?" Maureen wanted to know. "And exactly how did he die?"

"It looked like somebody whacked him on the back of his head with something. He never saw what hit him. He was a fella who went by the name of Sherman. He was from out of town. A Yankee, they say. Nobody knew a lot about him. He came here for the fishing, they say."

"And he fished from Eddie's father's boat? The original *Tightline*?"

"Yep. Eddie remembered him. He told me once that the guy was a good fisherman. Minded his own business. Tipped the mates every trip."

"Did they ever catch whoever killed him?"

"Nope." Hubbard scowled. "It's still somewhere in the cold-case files."

Maureen recognized the scowl. Hubbard didn't like cold cases. He liked all the questions answered, all the facts proven, all the evidence tied up with a nice neat bow. "Are you thinking that Eddie's drowning has anything to do with that fisherman's dying years ago?"

Hubbard scratched his head. "Not exactly. See, Doherty? That's just it. I found out this morning that Eddie didn't drown. No water in his lungs."

"He was already dead before he wound up in the water?"

"That's what the M.E. report says. He could have had a heart attack and fallen in, maybe. He had a bruise on the back of his head, maybe from banging it on the ski. We've talked to everyone who was on the *Tightline* yesterday. He had a half-day charter. An easy one. He took half a dozen birdwatchers over to the Forest around noon, dropped them off, and picked them up before sunset. You know the place?" He didn't wait for an answer. "Just north of here." He pointed at the framed map over Maureen's desk. "That big green blob between the old county road on one side and a narrow strip of beach on the other. It's a damn jungle in there, still the way it was back then. Only now it's a county park. A bird sanctuary. The park department mostly takes care of it. They mow the grass and check the mounds the first of every month, like clockwork. Anyway, nature people like to go in there to take pictures of birds and bees and snakes and all. Sort of like the Everglades, you know, only drier. We talked to all six of them—all solid citizens—and they said that Eddie seemed to be just fine when he picked them up at a little wharf on the beach. Eddie was real familiar with the place. He was working on some kind of project about restoring Florida shorelines. Anyway, he was cracking jokes and trying to talk them into going fishing someday instead of tramping around in the trees. His kid Tommy was mate on the trip. She told us that after they dropped the group off, she and her dad went back to the dock and worked around the boat until it was time to pick the party up. She says Eddie was in a good mood. She went home early and Eddie brought the group back to the dock in Haven by himself. Easy day."

"But by the next morning he was dead on our beach." Maureen spoke softly, picturing again the body face down in the water. "From a possible heart attack. And falling off a Jet Ski."

Hubbard looked up at the map again. "They have to do some more tests. Personally, I don't think it's that simple. The man was healthy as a horse. That's kind of why I was asking you about your—um—your feelings about it."

"I have no feeling about it," she insisted. "I mean, I'm sorry he's dead and all, but I have no special gift for this sort of thing, believe me."

"I know. You always say that." The policeman's tone was annoyingly condescending. "People like you, they don't know they have it."

Maureen shook her head. "Okay. Okay. So what are you thinking? That it's possible that somebody moved the body from someplace else and put him in the water?'

"Hey, it could happen. Maybe the medical examiner's tests will turn up something."

"Do you have any idea *where* he died, then?" she asked.

"There was some dirt and rocks and busted up shells in his clothes. I sent samples over to Tampa to see if they can tell where it came from. See, the thing is, that Yankee, that guy Sherman, he had shells in his pockets when they found him too. It just makes me wonder." He adjusted his cap and stood. "Well, I have to get over to Eddie's mother's place. Call me if you come up with anything else."

"I will. You know I have all those old inn registers. I think I'll look up June sixteenth to eighteenth for 2000, just to see if that Mr. Sherman might have stayed here," Maureen suggested. "If he did, I suppose some of my housekeeping staff might remember him too."

After Hubbard had left, Maureen put the well-worn BACK IN FIVE MINUTES sign on the reception desk, and—checking her watch to be sure of the time—she climbed the stairs to the suite she called her "upstairs office" where the stacks of guest registers were stored. It had once, long ago, been known as Suite Twenty-Three, but there was no longer a number on the door. No one had slept in the suite for many years because it was believed to be haunted. Thankfully, that wasn't a problem anymore, and it made an excellent office. Running up the stairs was significantly faster than taking the elevator. The books were dated on the spine bindings, so it was easy to pull the 2000 edition from the pile and make it back downstairs within the five-minute timeframe.

She'd not only be checking for someone with the last name of Sherman, as she'd told Hubbard, but also to see if there'd been a full house at the inn during that first—and apparently last—Haven fishing tournament. If so, there was a good chance that she might need that NO VACANCY sign in working order fairly soon.

Once back in the lobby, tucking the BACK IN FIVE sign into the drawer, she opened the guest register to June of 2000. The weekend of the tournament ran from Friday, June 16, through Sunday, June 18. That meant people should have started to show up at the inn sometime during the week beginning with Sunday, June 11. She gave a whispered "Wow!" as she counted the lined pages covering those dates. That NO VACANCY sign must have been lighted up for darned near the whole time. There were only a few single first-floor rooms open during the entire time of the event. It didn't take too long to find the name she was seeking. Everett Sherman had written in a bold, back-slanting cursive. So the man whose death had jinxed any future Haven tournaments had been a guest at the Haven House Inn—he'd occupied a suite—which proved nothing. With a sigh, she marked the page with a menu, closed the book, pulled out the BACK IN FIVE sign once more and dashed up the stairs to return the old register to the upstairs office closet.

Once back at the reservation desk, she asked herself an important question: Was it possible to prepare for a fishing tournament on really short notice? She'd become pretty good at short-notice promotions so far as a novice innkeeper. Why not give it a try? "I'm sitting here with a half-empty inn right now," she muttered to herself. Half of the current guests would be gone by the weekend, and so far she only had advance reservations for Trent and Pierre and for a man from a wildlife magazine. Both parties were booked to arrive the following afternoon. "What have I got to lose? First, I'd better find someone to talk to who knows something about fishing." She punched in Ted's number on the aged intercom system.

He answered right away. "What's up?"

"I have a half-baked idea. Have you got a minute to either like it or talk me out of it?"

"I love your half-baked ideas," he said. "I'll be there as soon as today's lunch special chicken pies come out of the oven. About ten minutes."

Ten minutes would give her just about enough time to pull together a few notes so that the idea wouldn't sound *entirely* half-baked to Ted. She began by opening Haven's slim version of the Yellow Pages and looking under Fishing Guides and Parties. Good news. There were fifteen different charter boats listed. If the fishing charter business was as slow as the tourist hospitality business, the various captains involved should be glad to consider participating in the *second* annual Haven Fishing Tournament. She made a copy of the page and then copied both sides of the blue-and-white 2000 card, highlighting in yellow the list of events that had happened back then. She printed out a copy of the current June calendar, and highlighted the last full weekend of the month—June 23–25. She titled the top of the first page with simply the words "June Fishing Tournament." She'd have a little less than two weeks to pull this off. "Nothing ventured, nothing gained," she said aloud, and stapled the pages together so that the admittedly Mickey Mouse presentation would look a little more professional when she showed it to Ted.

Chapter 5

Exactly ten minutes had passed when Ted appeared in the doorway of her office. She'd left the door open so that she could keep an eye on the reception desk while she worked. "Thanks, Ted," she said. "I know you're awfully busy. I'll make it quick. I just need to run an idea by you."

Maureen knew that Ted had been at work in the kitchen since early morning. Breakfast at the inn had become popular with both tourists and local folks, and lunchtime business continued to bring in enough money to keep the dining room in the black even during a slow month. As Ted took a seat opposite hers, Maureen was confident that perfectly browned, deliciously fragrant individual chicken pot pies would be ready and waiting for the noontime customers and each of the round dining room tables would be set for luncheon, with bouquets of wildflowers at the center of each one. But, somehow, Ted looked as if he'd just stepped out of a shower, his snowy white chef's jacket unwrinkled and immaculate, hair neatly groomed, even his shoes looked freshly polished. *How does he do that?* she wondered, pushing a stray lock of hair away from her forehead and trying to hide highlighter-stained fingers on her right hand in her lap. *He's been on his feet since sunup, and he manages to look like a TV cooking-show host straight from central casting.*

As she'd promised, she immediately got to the point. "I
know that you know a lot about local fishing in the gulf, and
I need your honest opinion on something." She handed him
the stapled sheets. "Can we possibly put together a fishing
tournament like this one in just a little over a week? If we're
going to stay on track financially for June, we absolutely
need to attract a lot of paying hotel guests in a short time."

Ted studied the sheets silently, nodding once or twice and
smiling a couple of times. He tapped the copy of the blue-
and-white card. "You have a picture of Eddie," he said. "We
were really young back then. Just kids."

"You remember the tournament well?"

"Of course. I caught a prize-winning kingfish. I think my
mother probably still has the winning trophy. I won a new
Shimano reel. I still have it."

"Do you think we can do it? Or maybe you can think of a
better way to fill up the inn for a week or so." Maureen
sounded hopeful. "It means the difference between finishing
construction on the gift shop or just boarding it up until later
in the year."

"It won't be easy," Ted ran a finger along the list of charter boats. "But these guys will be willing to help us. They're
hurting financially too, you know."

She bit her lip, liking the sound of his use of the word
"us," yet hardly daring to believe the positive tone of his answer. "So you think maybe . . . ?"

He finished the sentence for her. "Maybe we can do this?
Sure we can. I'll bet we can put this together in a week. What
have we got to lose?" He pointed to a breakfast menu posted
on Maureen's bulletin board. "You make my pancakes and
bacon look and sound like *Breakfast at Tiffany's*. Listen." He
held the stapled pages up. "You just make this into a real
proposal with graphics and everything. Tomorrow morning
when we take our morning run, we'll visit the fishing docks.
Those guys are up early, waiting for charters or hanging on

the phones waiting for customer calls. We'll pitch the idea, get them onboard, and start lining up sponsors."

"I'll get right on it," Maureen promised, already visualizing a photo she'd recently seen on Facebook of one of the inn's customers holding a good-sized fish—and at the same time thinking about what Hubbard had shared about the death of Ted's old friend Eddie, wondering what more she could offer that might help with the investigation. She'd meant to do a little research on the local Indian mounds too—the place where the man named Sherman had died.

She and Ted each looked up from the desk when a brief *ding* from the push bell on the reception desk announced that the younger Gaudreau had arrived to fix the blinking sign.

"First things first," she mumbled, and hurried into the lobby while Ted headed back to the kitchen. "Hi, Sonny," she said. "Follow me. I'll show you the problem."

The problem in question blinked its confusing lighted message just beneath the HAVEN HOUSE INN sign on the front railing of the porch. It read VACANCY in bright red letters for about sixty seconds, then changed to the NO VACANCY message for another minute. "I don't know whether the trouble is with the sign itself, or with the light switch on the wall inside," Maureen explained. "It's been doing it for a couple of days now."

"Couple of days," echoed Gert from her front row rocker.

"At least," agreed Molly.

"The wiring in the whole place is old, you know," the younger Gaudreau pointed out. "Could be either one."

"Do you think you can fix it?"

"Probably. It's not as old as everything else around here. My dad says the lady who managed the place before you came had it put in. He says that before she came, the old woman just hung up painted signs for vacancy or no vacancy on those two hooks on the edge of the porch."

Maureen looked up at the hooks. "I always thought those were for plants. We hung poinsettias there last Christmas."

"Whatever works for ya." With a toolbox under one arm, he approached the red-lettered message which at that moment announced NO VACANCY. He stood in front of the sign for a long moment. "Easy fix," he said, lifting the sign, looking behind it, and removing a long screwdriver from the box.

It must have been easy, Maureen decided, because after a couple of taps and a twist of the screwdriver, he stepped back. "Okay," he said. "Go inside and flip the switch. Which is it, anyway? Vacancy or not?"

"Vacancy for sure," Maureen said, reentering the lobby, leaving the door ajar, and touching the top button on a panel beside the registration desk. "Did it work?" she called.

"Yeah. Now try the other one."

Maureen tapped the bottom button. "Does that one work too?" she called.

An "okay" from Sonny and a couple of cheers from Gert and Molly answered the question. By this time George and Sam had returned and added their comments to the chorus. Junior presented her with an invoice, she wrote a check, mentally checked off another chore attended to, made sure that the sign indicated "vacancy," and returned her attention to the hastily designed stapled pages and her half-baked idea of organizing a fishing tournament for Haven.

The rules from the 2000 card seemed to make sense—listing the various species of fish sought and the area to be fished, the starting times and dates, the angler categories—men, women, and youth—and the prizes offered. Artwork and photos wouldn't be a problem—previous guests had been happy to share fishing photos and the internet offered free or inexpensive art. The original title of the event, "The First Annual Haven Fishing Tournament," needed work. Although

this one would officially be the second annual fishing tournament, using that name would surely raise questions about the
sad circumstances of the first one. She wished she'd asked
Ted for suggestions. Leaning back in the chair, she scrunched
her eyes tightly shut, concentrating hard, mumbling to herself words involving fishing. "Salt water? Anglers? Rods and
reels?"

"Excuse me?"

Maureen sat up straight, eyes wide open. The woman smiled
across the reception desk. "Your sign says you have a vacancy
now. I was confused about it when I first drove past your
charming inn a little while ago and the "no" sign was on."

"A little temporary electrical sign malfunction," Maureen
explained. "It's all fixed now, and we do have a vacancy.
Welcome to Haven House Inn. How long will you be staying
with us?"

The woman picked up the faux-quill pen and signed the
register. "I'm not quite sure," she said. "Perhaps a week or
more, if that's possible."

"We have rooms and suites available for as long as you'd
like to stay," she said, handing the woman a rate card, noting
with ready-to-wear buyer's practiced eye the Carolina Herrera sleeveless silk floral dress. "The Joe DiMaggio Suite is
available. It's on the second floor with a view of the gulf."

"The Joe DiMaggio Suite? Did he really stay here?"

"He spent a few days here in February of 1961. It was the
last year the Yankees had spring training in St. Petersburg."
Maureen dropped her voice. "Some say he had Marilyn
Monroe with him, but there's no proof of that."

"Wow. Interesting. I'll take it."

Maureen accepted a credit card and made a copy of the
driver's license—noting that the attractive woman's birthdate
stated that she was over forty, although she certainly didn't
look it. Maureen handed her the room key and directed her

to the elevator. Maureen glanced at the signature in the register. *Dr. Kimberly Salter. She has a Massachusetts license plate. Small world.* "Where are you parked, Dr. Salter?"

"I'm right out in front of the building. Is that all right?"

"It is for the moment," Maureen advised, moving to the front of the counter and handing the woman the key to the suite. "I'll have a houseman help you with your luggage, then you can park in our lot behind the inn. There's plenty of parking space, and there's a lobby entrance from there." Maureen was proud of the inn's parking lot, much bigger than the ones most of the newer hotels had. The original boundaries of Haven House Inn included not just the paved area, but another two acres of what the old-timers called a "wood lot"—an assortment of native trees providing shade—and the assurance that no other business would ever be built behind her property.

The newest guest followed her to the porch. "George," Maureen called as they approached the foursome closest to the front steps. "Dr. Salter will be staying with us. Would you help with her bags, please? She'll be in the Joe DiMaggio Suite."

George stood immediately. "Yes, ma'am," he said, eyeing the sleek, recent model metallic gray Audi e-tron. Gert, Sam, and Molly, interested, each leaned forward in their rocking chairs, watching intently as George removed a turquoise soft-sided carry-on with spinner wheels and a trim Vera Bradley tote from the Audi's trunk. Then the inn's new guest drove cautiously onto the path leading to the parking lot. Within minutes. Dr. Kimberly Salter returned to the lobby via the side door. With a smile in Maureen's direction, she held up the room key and stepped into the waiting elevator. "Would you ask the houseman—George—to bring the luggage up when it's convenient? I think I'll go out and look around at this charming town for a bit."

Maureen pushed open the door to the porch where George stood—in a protective stance—beside the fashionable luggage. "You can take the bags up to the DiMaggio Suite, George. The doctor may be going out for a while."

"You can probably handle it without hurting yourself," Sam teased. "Those bags look pretty light."

"So what?" George shook a finger. "Don't forget. I got stuck with the old woman's trunk full of rocks."

"You two old men are getting soft," Gert declared. "It's probably a good thing we'll have a doctor in the house."

"A successful one, I'd guess, by looking at the car," Molly offered.

"Massachusetts plates," Sam said. "Somebody you know from back home, Ms. Doherty?"

"No, Sam. It's a big state." Maureen laughed.

George pulled the wheeled carry-on with the tote tossed over one of his shoulders. "So she's in the DiMaggio Suite? A Yankees fan?"

"I have no idea," Maureen said.

"She's more than likely a Red Sox fan," Gert proclaimed. "Joe's little brother Dom played for the Sox. You ask her, George. Yankees or Sox."

"If the doctor has driven all the way from Massachusetts," Maureen pointed out, "she might be too tired for small talk."

George, without comment, pulled the green door to the lobby open, nearly bumping into the doctor in question.

"Oh, there you are, George." Her smile was bright. "Would you just put my bags inside the suite? I noticed a bookshop just down the street. I'm heading there for a quick browse, if they're open."

Chapter 6

"The suite is excellent, Ms. Doherty. Thank you for recommending it. Love the photos of Joe." With a flip of the silk Herrera, the click of a high-heeled Jimmy Choo, and a friendly wave to the assembled Haven House staff, Dr. Kimberly Salter hurried down the steps and onto the brick sidewalk below.

"Not a bit tired, that one," Sam whispered. "And a Yankee fan for sure."

"Yep," Molly agreed. "For sure. I wonder what kind of books she'll be looking for down at Aster's place."

"Romances or mysteries," Gert declared. "That's what women like to read when they're on vacation. At least that's the kind of paperbacks I usually find in the rooms after they leave."

"Isn't it about time for Finn's walk, Ms. Doherty?" Molly asked. "You could walk him down past the bookstore and see what she buys. I'm betting on romance."

Maureen shook her head. "You guys are impossible! I mean, Finn is due for a walk, but I'm not about to snoop on a guest."

Molly smiled broadly. "Well, if you happen to notice, you'll let us know. Right?"

Maureen couldn't help laughing. "Of course. I will." She

reentered the lobby, alerted Jolene that she'd be away from the desk for a while, and stepped into the elevator, enjoying, as she always did, the etched glass and polished wood of the interior. Finn's welcoming "woof" greeted her as soon as the brass door slid open and she headed down the hall to her third-floor suite.

"I'm coming, boy," she said, unlocking the door. "Sorry I've kept you waiting."

"I've kept him entertained." It was Lorna's voice. "The cats are here too. We all want to know about Kimberly-what's-her-name." Maureen pushed the door open, not surprised to see two cats on the cat tree and the golden retriever sitting on the couch, but she was surprised to see Lorna—doing a model runway walk and turn in the silk-print Herrera—now rendered in black and white but just as stunning as the original pastel floral print.

"I see you've borrowed her dress already," Maureen said. Lorna had long ago explained her method of borrowing. She had the ability to acquire what she called "the essence" of whatever she wanted—usually clothes. She often wore "the essence" of Maureen's outfits, as well as the designer originals she regularly borrowed from the wardrobe departments of famous movie studios, and occasionally the latest fashions from Macy's or Nordstrom's show windows in Tampa.

"I love her taste," Lorna said. "I can hardly wait for her to unpack her suitcases so I can see what else she has. What do you know about her?"

"Just that she's a doctor and she's from Massachusetts." Maureen got Finn's leash from the hook behind her kitchen door and fastened it to his collar, then tucked a plastic bag into her shorts pocket. "She drives an electric Audi and right now she's walking to the bookstore." She pulled the door open. "Come on, Finn. See you later, Lorna."

She and the dog took the stairway down the two flights and exited the building via the side door, avoiding any further quizzing from the front porch foursome. She quickened her step as they walked along the brick sidewalk. She'd promised the golden a "proper walk" after their morning beach excursion had been so sadly interrupted, and she intended to keep her promise. Her to-do list for this day was far from finished, but she was pleased that she'd at least completed the lunch menus and they'd been distributed along the boulevard. The VACANCY/NO VACANCY sign problem had been solved too. She'd found the key to Penelope Josephine's trunk and had discovered the fishing tournament card, which might very well solve the problem of declining numbers of inn guests threatening the solvency of the place. She'd promised Ted that she'd have a presentable version of the proposed tournament ready in time for their resumed morning run.

Her thoughts turned again to the dead boat captain. She'd asked Hubbard what she could do to help his family. She thought about the many Irish wakes she'd attended in Boston. *People always bring food*, she remembered. *We can at least do that much. I'm sure Ted has already thought of it. I can order flowers from Petals and Kettles too, and sign the card from Molly, Sam, Gert, and George. They'll like that.*

Finn slowed down when they'd almost reached the bookshop. "Woof," he said. "Woof woof." He'd spotted Erle Stanley, Aster's elderly tuxedo cat, all alone, sitting on the table in front of the shop. Finn tugged on the leash.

Maureen tugged back. "Maybe we'll stop to visit on the way back home," she promised. "Look. We're almost at the beach." She broke into an easy jog, Finn trotting happily beside her as they approached the Casino building. She glanced up and down the sandy shoreline. "Not like it was this morning, is it, boy?" There were people sunning on towels, others walking dogs, kids splashing in the water, teenagers glued to their phones.

Stepping onto the sand, avoiding the area where they'd found the dead man, they ran in the direction of the charter-boat docks—the route Maureen and Ted had always chosen on their morning runs. There were a few motorboats in sight and a couple of Jet Skiers too. There were at least two blue-hulled Jet Skis with their brand name lettered in white on each side. Was Frank Hubbard right about the one Maureen had seen in the early morning light being from a particular rental site, or were there hundreds of identical skis in the area?

They halted, resting, at the faded sign where preteen Maureen had once posed with a fish. Thinking of that black-and-white photo, now framed in her upstairs office, reminded Maureen that she needed to choose a similar picture for the fishing tournament proposal she and Ted meant to deliver the next morning. "We have a lot more to do today," she told the golden. "Let's hurry home."

"Woof," he agreed and the two reversed direction, not pausing until they once again reached the Casino. Maureen sat on the steps of the building, emptying sand from her sneakers and taking the plastic bag from her pocket as Finn attended to doggie business. Sand brushed away and bag disposed of in the nearby bin, the two walked at a more leisurely pace along the boulevard back toward the bookshop where Aster had joined the tuxedo cat on the shop's patio. The woman waved and called to Maureen. "Come on and join us. We have nice cold lemonade and cookies."

"Okay. We'll stop," Maureen whispered to the dog, "but just for a minute. I'm thirsty and, anyway, I'd like to hear what Aster thinks of our newest guest."

Finn lay down beside the chair where Erle Stanley pretended to be asleep, and Maureen sat opposite the bookseller, who now wore a Harry Potter–inspired outfit consisting of a T-shirt emblazoned with a HOGWARTS crest and red fleece jogger pants with GRYFFINDOR spelled out on one leg. "One of your guests stopped by today." Aster poured a glassful of lemonade from a vintage Kool-Aid pitcher. "Here, help yourself to cookies. Peter's favorites, you know."

Accepting both drink and cookie, Maureen refrained from asking what kind of books the new guest favored. "So, you've met our new tenant. She seems very pleasant."

Aster answered the unasked question anyway. "Yes. She told me her name is Kim and she bought some books on local history and geography. A very inquiring mind, that one, and," she added, "she has lovely taste in clothes."

"She certainly does," Maureen agreed. "She has a beautiful car too. Her medical practice in Massachusetts must be pretty successful."

"I suppose so," Aster said. "She didn't talk about herself at all. She just wanted to know all about Florida. She bought Gary Mormino's *Land of Sunshine, State of Dreams* and Cathy Salustri's *Backroads of Paradise* and a copy of *Funky Florida Facts*. Oh yeah, she bought Mac Perry's *Indian Mounds You Can Visit*. She said she was going to go back to the inn and put on some proper shoes and sign up for one of the Indian mound tours."

Not a romance or mystery in the bunch, but that's the second time today I've heard about the Indian mounds—and that was about a murder. "I haven't taken that tour myself yet," Maureen admitted. "Have you?"

"Sure. Several times. All the schoolkids have to take the tour anyway, so I needed to know enough to answer questions about it." She shook her head. "Not much to see, you know. It's . . . well, a couple of round mounds. With trees and grass and bushes and stuff. It's a very quiet place. Peaceful-like. The guide talks about the Tocobaga Indians. They're the guys that built them out of oyster shells and sand and broken pottery and arrowheads about a thousand years ago."

"Interesting," Maureen said. "I'm going to do it as soon as I get the time."

"Are you busy down there at the inn? The book business is pretty darned slow," Aster complained.

"I'm just busy trying to think up ways to attract some business. Dr. Salter was my first guest this week. We're lucky that we have the local restaurant business."

"That's for sure. Sam dropped off the new lunch menu. I'll be over for Ted's meatball-vegetable soup special on Thursday." She grinned. "I'm trying to figure out how he makes it and I think I've almost got it. That Ted is a gem."

"I know it," Maureen returned the smile.

"Good-looking, too. I see him in the morning when he goes for his run." Long pause. "Didn't you used to run with him?"

Maureen didn't take the bait. "No doubt about it—early morning is the best time for running on the beach."

"Guess you got a shocker on the beach this morning yourself." Aster's voice was soft. "Maybe you don't want to talk about it."

"There's not much to tell," Maureen said. "I saw the body in the water and called 911. The police are in charge of it now. I'm thinking of sending some food over when they announce services for the poor man. Maybe you could make some of these cookies. Everybody loves them."

"Peter loved them, you know." Another long pause. "I wonder if Eddie Manuel's ghost will haunt the beach. Or maybe his boat."

Eddie Manuel's ghost was something Maureen hadn't thought about for even a second—and didn't want to think about now.

Chapter 7

Once back at the inn, they climbed the front stairs, Maureen noting that the VACANCY sign was shining brightly. She paused to tell the curious foursome that neither mysteries or romances had been among the new guest's books of choice. "Just Florida history books," she told them. "No fiction at all."

"We know," Gert offered. "She showed them to us when she got back from the bookstore. She's going to take that Indian mounds tour some day this week."

"Good. That means she'll be staying with us for a while. We can use the business." Maureen pushed the green door open. "It's great to have a doctor in the house. Maybe she'll help our bottom line get well."

"She's not that kind of doctor," Molly said.

Maureen paused in the doorway, then turned to face the porch-sitters once again. "What do you mean?"

"I mean she doesn't treat sick people. Sam asked her about his arthritis and she told us that she's a doctor who studies about people who lived a long time ago—like even thousands of years," Molly explained. "She's an ant-something-or-other."

"An anthropologist," Gert corrected. "And she just got back from digging up arrowheads and stuff in New York."

Archaeology, anthropology. That would explain the book choices. "Wow. When I was a kid, I read about all the treasures they found in King Tutankhamen's tomb and I wanted to be an archaeologist when I grew up."

"And the only old fossils you found was us," George chimed in, accompanied by hearty laughter from the group.

"I wouldn't have it any other way," Maureen told them—meaning it—and continued into the lobby, Finn at her heels. Jolene was still at the registration desk. "Anything happening?" Maureen was hopeful.

Jolene shrugged. "No room reservations. A couple of calls about the lunch specials. That's all."

"Oh, well. I'm going to take Finn up to my apartment. I'll be right back down to relieve you." Maureen knew that she needed to spend some serious time in the lobby office working on the fishing tournament proposal if she and Ted were going to have it to share with the charter boat guys in the morning. Could they actually pull this plan together in a week? She and Finn hurried up the stairs to the third floor. As Ted had pointed out, what did they have to lose?

Even before she'd reached the door to her suite she heard the sound of Abba's "Dancing Queen." Lorna had learned how to talk to Alexa, and had a fondness for music from the seventies, so Maureen wasn't surprised to see the shimmering ghost relaxing on the couch. Bogie and Bacall, apparently soothed by the music, appeared to be asleep on the cat tower.

"Oh, hi, Maureen," Lorna greeted her. "You look kind of frazzled. What's going on?"

"Not much businesswise," Maureen admitted, "but I have a few projects that need attention. You look great. New outfit?"

"I stopped by the doctor's suite. She's done some unpacking." Lorna stood and did a model-like turn, displaying a short denim skirt and white silk blouse, tooled leather cowgirl boots with stiletto heels. "Simple but elegant, don't you think? The Saks Fifth Avenue tags were still on, the skirt and blouse and the boots are from Bergdorf Goodman. I'm absolutely loving your new guest. I can hardly wait to see what else she's brought with her."

"A very interesting woman. She's an archaeologist."

"Really? That explains the outfit she's wearing today. I wouldn't be caught dead in it—even if I am. It's a khaki thing that looks like it came out of Steve Irwin's laundry bag. Some butt-ugly Crocodile Dundee boots to go with it."

"Aster said that Dr. Salter was going to tour the Haven Indian Mounds."

"That explains it, then. She's dressed for work, so I guess the Lewis and Clark expedition look is okay."

"I've got some work to attend to," Maureen told her. "Gotta run. Here's Finn. Have a nice day." She paused. "You should go somewhere to show off that outfit."

"Nashville," Lorna began to disappear. "Rick Springfield concert."

Maureen took the elevator down to her second-floor office and grabbed a folder of celebrities-who'd-stayed-in-Haven photos from the tall wooden file cabinet—a handsome mid-century relic left by her hoarding predecessor. She vaguely remembered seeing a picture of one of them holding a fish and hoped this was where she'd seen it. It didn't take long to find the lead photo for the proposed presentation. Bingo! It was a clear black-and-white shot of Babe Ruth holding what the attached copy identified as "a nice kingfish."

She headed down the stairs, dismissed Jolene, and with the office door open to keep an eye on the registration desk, got to work. Swiping some copy from the original 2000 blue-and-white card regarding prize categories, she used information from the Haven Charter Boat Association's website about the speed and comfort of the vessels themselves, mentioned special rates for fishermen at the Haven Inn, dropped in a few fishing photos guests had given her, and added clip art of various fish species. She used the working title of "Haven June Fishing Tournament." Within a couple of hours Maureen had produced a creditable trifold brochure to present to the local fishermen. She'd decided to print fifty copies—enough for the charter fleet and a few extras. Printing even fifty copies on the aging printer and hand folding the things would take quite a while, so she handed the finished product to George to take to the nearest quick-print store for completion.

The day's ambitious to-do list completed, she began to straighten out her desktop. Photos returned to the proper folder, and charter boat information added to the tournament document file on her computer. She looked up when the bell over the front door jingled. Lunch was over, and it was too early for dinner customers. She hadn't seen him around Haven lately, but she recognized Jake as soon as he walked in. He was a reporter from a daily paper over in Tampa—a very thorough and super-inquisitive reporter.

"Hi, Maureen," he said. "How're things in the inn biz?" They'd been on first-name terms since Jake had come to Haven the previous year to investigate the murder of the man Maureen had discovered dead in a rocking chair on the porch.

"Not bad, Jake," she said. "How're things in the big city?"

"Not as interesting as they are here, apparently," he deadpanned. "You found another body, huh?"

She chose not to answer the question. "You're a little late for lunch, but I'm sure Ted can heat up a chicken pie for you. Or, can I buy you a drink? We have a special going on Bloody Marys."

"Sounds good," he said. "I need to talk to you, though. I may have dug up something about the dead guy, Eddie, that you ought to know about. Can I have that Bloody Mary here in the lobby?"

"Sure." She tapped the push-bell on the desk. Waitress Shelly pushed open the dining room door. "Can I get you something, Ms. Doherty?"

Maureen asked for the drink for Jake and coffee for herself, and the two moved across the lobby to where a bamboo table, flanked by a couple of the ubiquitous white wicker chairs, served as a casual grouping that guests seemed to enjoy. Maureen had other plans for updating the lobby, but for now it served the purpose. "I need to stay close to the reception desk," she explained. "In case a prospective lodger calls or wanders in."

"Here's to wandering lodgers," he declared, lifting his glass in a toast-like gesture. "Business slowed down?"

"We've had a nice little flurry of spring breakers," she fibbed, knowing that the two kids from Charleston hardly constituted a "flurry." "We'll be fine. You say there's something you want to tell me about the . . . about Eddie?"

"It just struck me as an odd coincidence." He stirred his drink with the celery stick garnish. "It probably doesn't mean anything, but I did a little extra research on Edward Manuel. I had the time because the news business is slow too."

Get to the point already! Maureen leaned forward expectantly, thinking that Jake must believe that whatever it was meant something or he wouldn't have wasted time and gasoline driving across the bridge from Tampa to tell her about it.

"He'd graduated from St. Petersburg Junior College in 1992, back before it was a four-year school," he said. "Smart kid. He gave a little speech at his graduation. My paper covered it. In the speech he thanked his parents and his teachers—and here's the coincidence—he thanked an old friend of the family." Jake pulled a piece of paper from his inside jacket pocket. "Without her help," he read, "I could never have had the opportunity to become the first member of my family to graduate from college. That's what he said." He folded the sheet and put it back into his pocket.

"Without whose help?" Maureen prodded.

"Why, Penelope Josephine Gray's," he said. "Is that a coincidence or what?"

Chapter 8

Maureen put her coffee mug down on the bamboo table and stared at the reporter. "Penelope Josephine Gray," she repeated. "*My* Penelope Josephine Gray?" She knew as she spoke that it was a silly question. There couldn't be more than one. She remembered reading the woman's obituary online, just before she'd left Massachusetts for Florida. "Ms. Gray was known as an active and generous member of the community," the *Tampa Bay Times* had stated. Maureen herself had been a significant beneficiary of that generosity and there was no reason that a young Edward Manuel couldn't have been one also. It was, however, an interesting coincidence.

Jake answered the silly question. "Sure. I know she left you this place. Apparently she often helped Haven folks out with gifts of money here and there—at least until that crooked manager she had ran her out of dough. Eddie said she was a friend of the family, so it makes sense that she would have pitched in for his education."

"What did he study; do you know?"

"I asked his mother about that. He studied biology, specializing in marine sciences. He was working on a project for restoring Florida's shorelines."

"No wonder he was such a good fisherman," Maureen

said, thinking that Eddie would have been a great help in planning a tournament. Maybe he'd been making plans for restoring an eroding shoreline if he'd accidentally fallen from a Jet Ski. Or not. She took a thoughtful sip of coffee. *Maybe,* she thought, *just maybe, I should name the tournament after him.* She leaned back in the scratchy wicker chair. "Not for publication quite yet, Jake," she said, "but I'm working on an idea for a local fishing tournament. It'll be happening real soon."

She saw immediate interest in Jake's eyes and body language. "No kidding? That's a great idea. You'd be involving the charter fleet?"

She nodded. "Absolutely. I'll be meeting with some of the captains tomorrow morning."

"Can you keep me clued in about it? I'm a pretty good fisherman, if I do say so myself. It might make a good feature story. How long a tournament would it be?"

"A long weekend," she said. "Friday, Saturday, and Sunday." She watched for his reaction.

"Just about right," he agreed. "It would be good for the inn business, right?"

"That's kind of the point." She smiled. "I have some sample brochures coming today. I'll see that you get one and I'll email you information as it develops."

"I might have known you'd have something cooking." Jake finished his drink and stood. "Well, I'll be on my way. Thanks for the drink. I'm going to stop by the docks and try for some human interest stuff about Eddie. Maybe if his kid is there I'll grab a picture of her."

He'd just reached the front door and nearly bumped into Dr. Kimberly Salter. Lorna had described her outfit well. Rumpled khaki shirt and shorts and plain, industrial-looking boots. Somehow, the doctor wore it well. Her longish brown hair was swept up into a lopsided bun and her makeup-free face wore a broad smile. She said, "Excuse me," to Jake for the near collision, and approached Maureen with arms out-spread. "I've had such a wonderful day, Ms. Doherty. The guide you recommended was so informative. We climbed the mounds—the largest ones in this region—and he told me all about an early settler who lived there, and about the amazing Tocobaga tribe."

"I'm so glad you enjoyed it, Dr. Salter," Maureen said.

Jake had pushed the green door open, then turned and faced the women. "Dr. Salter? Dr. Kimberly Salter?" he said.

The woman turned the smile toward Jake. "Yes?"

He extended his hand. "Jake Aden. *Tampa Evening News.* You wrote *Mankiller.*

Maureen's eyes widened at that title. *That sounds like a mystery book*, she thought.

The doctor grasped Jake's hand and pumped it with en-thusiasm. "You've read it?"

Jake shrugged. "Not exactly. I read the review in one of our Sunday entertainment sections. The book editor likes it a lot."

Embarrassed, Maureen looked from one to the other. *I've been so busy with the inn, I hardly ever read past the front pages anymore.* "*Mankiller*," she said aloud. "I'll look for it at the bookshop."

"Yes. They have it there," the author said. "I saw it in the nonfiction section this morning."

Nonfiction? True crime?

Thankfully, the doctor clarified the situation. "I particu-larly enjoyed the research on that book. I was in North Car-olina visiting the Kituwah Cherokee mound when I got to meet Wilma Mankiller. She was the first principal chief of the Cherokee nation. A most remarkable woman. I couldn't re-sist putting the mound research aside for long enough to tell her story."

Things began to fall together. Probably the doctor's interest in Native American culture had led her to investigate Haven's Indian mounds. That was good news. Research for a book could take quite a while. Maybe the Joe DiMaggio Suite would be occupied for weeks instead of days. Another thing crossed Maureen's mind. If Aster Patterson had realized who her new customer was, she would have had those nonfiction books autographed in a hurry.

Dr. Salter excused herself and stepped into the elevator. Jake said a quick "So long. See you later" to Maureen, and she was once again alone in the lobby. Propping the office door open, she returned to the project at hand—the event she had already decided to call The Eddie Manuel Memorial Fishing Tournament—and wishing she hadn't already had those brochures printed with the "Haven June Fishing Tournament" heading.

Maureen glanced at the steamer trunk beside the desk, the curved cover still invitingly partially open. "I need to concentrate on all the stuff that's on my plate right now"—she scolded herself while at the same time pointing an accusing finger at the trunk—"and avoid getting involved in another one of Penelope Josephine's nutty hoards of miscellaneous junk."

Visions of old-time posters and advertising cards danced in her head. She'd already seen a couple of them in the trunk. She'd heard about others from the old-timers on the household staff—places with names like the Seaquarium and the London Wax Museum on St. Pete Beach, and a famous old department store called Webb's City. She reached for the latch. "This must be how Alice felt when she started down the rabbit hole," she muttered to herself, and raised the lid.

By the time she closed the trunk, some of the happy hour customers had begun to filter into the bar. Her desk now held a small stack of what might be called vintage memorabilia, and the tightly packed hoard had still barely been disturbed.

She stepped into the lobby, shutting the office door a little more firmly than necessary on the cluttered desk and the trunkful of someone else's memories.

A nice, ice-cold sweet tea would taste good about now.

Summoning Shelly back to the reception desk, she'd just started toward the dining room when George appeared with the completed brochures. "They look really good, Ms. D.," he said. "Even the guy at the Quick Print store said he'd sign up for a tournament like this." He waved one of the folded sheets in her direction. "Here. Take a look."

George was right. The hastily designed but professionally printed product looked even better than she'd expected it might. "Thanks, George." She picked a few of them from the box. "Would you ask Shelly to stash the rest of these under the reception desk? I think I'll show some to the folks at the bar and see what kind of reaction I get."

Maureen joined neighborhood happy hour regular customers Dick and Ethel Flannagan at one of the round tables. After the usual "How're you doing?" and "Good to see you," greetings, Maureen offered the couple a folded flyer. "This is just in the planning stages," she told them, "but what do you think about a fishing tournament this month for Haven?"

It turned out that both were avid fishermen. "We fish almost every day from our little motor boat. Fishing is why we moved here in the first place," Dick said. "Count us in."

"If we do it, I'm thinking of naming it after Eddie Manuel," she told them.

"Oh, he'd love that," Ethel said. "He was such a nice guy."

"Everybody says that. He was a friend of Ted's."

"I'm guessing he had a lot of friends," Dick put in. "I'll bet it will be a big funeral. Maybe you could put something about it on your Facebook page. I'm sure some of your guests must have chartered the *Tightline* before and they'd want to know about his passing."

"Thank you, Dick. I never thought of that." She paused, with a slight inward cringe, ashamed of herself because of the sudden realization that some guests coming for poor Eddie's funeral would be good for business. Ignoring the cringey thought, she posted Eddie's obituary on the Haven House Inn Facebook page before she went to sleep.

Chapter 9

It was barely light in the morning when Maureen dressed for the planned run on the beach with Ted. She'd put the blue-and-white brochures into a lightweight backpack, attached Finn's leash to his collar, and hurried down the stairs to where Ted waited for them at the inn's side entrance. Ted had already seen the finished products after dinner the previous evening and had enthusiastically approved the proposed name change. "All the boat skippers are going to like that it's named after Eddie." With Finn leashed and in the lead, they jogged along the quiet boulevard toward the white building at the edge of the beach. Pausing behind the Casino, Ted looked up and down the long expanse of sand. "Looks like we're all alone. It'll be okay to let Finn run free," he said.

"I think it's a perfect name," she agreed, unfastening the leash and stuffing it into the backpack. "As soon as we get their okay, we've got to start lining up sponsors. We'll need money to get this idea rolling."

"I'm sure some of the merchants will donate prizes and trophies, and there'll be an entry fee for everybody who wants to compete," Ted reasoned as the two, side by side, following the happily scampering golden, broke into a run. "Besides that," he added, "the local newspapers and TV and radio stations will help with the publicity."

It's difficult to carry on a conversation while running, and the two lapsed into a companionable silence as they increased their speed approaching the distant sign marking the beginning of the long pier, the town landing, and Haven's rugged, wooden-piling-lined sport-fishing docks. Finn, as usual when he was allowed to run free, reached the sign first and assumed his "I've been waiting here for you for hours" pose. Ted and Maureen, after each had given Finn a pat on the head and congratulatory "Good dog" or "Atta Boy," relaxed in a post-run cooldown, stretching calves, hamstrings, knees, and hips. They exchanged glances. Maureen thought about their first kiss, exchanged at this very spot, and wondered if Ted was thinking about the same thing. He held the look for what seemed like a long moment. "Shall we start with the big party boat fleet?" he asked.

Maureen shook away the intrusive—but happy—recollection. The party boats, large vessels that rented tackle and provided bait to paying passengers and took them for a whole or half day of fishing in the gulf, were popular with guests at the inn. "Yes," she agreed. "Let's start there."

The meeting with the fleet captains went well—better, actually, than Maureen had dared to dream it might. They were clearly enthusiastic about the tournament and wholeheartedly supported the idea of naming it for Eddie Manuel. Most of them offered some free trips and T-shirts as prizes. The two stopped next at the sport fishing docks and were greeted with the same interest and eagerness to help from the skippers of the smaller charter boats—including the *Tightline*.

Maureen, with her retail-trained eye for good promotion, was pleased with the smart appearance of the ticket and reservation booth. Colorful signs advertised T-shirts, caps, evening dolphin-watching cruises and Jet-Ski rentals. "It looks as though Eddie Manuel and his daughter had some clever side hustles going on," she whispered to Ted.

"That's Tommy on the deck." Ted waved to the young woman, who held a long-handled scrub brush in one hand and offered the other to Maureen and Ted as they approached. She recognized Ted, acknowledged the hurried introduction to Maureen, and graciously accepted the words of sympathy from both. "I'm scrubbing down the boat," she explained, "because that's what Dad taught me to do when things go bad. It helps get past the rough spots." Maureen understood. *Running is what does it for me.*

Tommy expressed immediate interest in the proposed tournament and brushed away tears when Maureen told her about the idea for naming it after her dad. "Count us in," she said. "Hey, Alan!" A young man stepped out of the cabin. "This is Alan Sanders, my galley guy," she said. "Alan, we're going to a fish tournament. They're naming it after my dad."

"Awesome," he said. "It'll be my first tournament, you know." He reached for Maureen's hand. "Hi, I'm Alan. *Tightline* galley specialist—bucking for first-mate status, then maybe captain."

"Maureen Doherty," she said, smiling and shaking his hand. "Haven House Inn proprietor, bucking for fishing tournament promoter status." She handed him a brochure. "It'll be my first fishing tournament too."

Maureen and Ted moved on to the next charter boat and again were warmly welcomed with fast acceptance of the idea and enthusiastic offers of "Let us know if we can help." Before long, they'd contacted all of the party boat captains and most of the smaller charter boat skippers too. They'd tacked a brochure to the bulletin board at the head of the dock, left copies on the windshields of unattended vessels, tugged Finn away from friendly head pats and interesting smells, and after sharing a silent victorious fist bump, began the run toward home.

In front of the Coliseum building once again, the pair stopped, shaking sand from their shoes and doing a few stretches. "I wonder what's going on this early in the morning." Ted pointed to a marked Haven police car parked at the edge of the beach. Maureen followed his gaze, then reluctantly looked toward the water—toward the spot where she'd so recently found the dead man.

The uniformed officer held a handled gray pail and a small scoop-shaped shovel. Trying to avoid softly lapping waves approaching his shiny black shoes, the man dug into the shell line bordering the shore, depositing shovelfuls of shells into the pail. "Frank Hubbard told me that Eddie Manuel had crushed shells in his pockets," Maureen said.

"There are shells—and there are shells," Ted said. "You find different ones on different beaches, different oceans, different lakes and rivers. Maybe Hubbard thinks Eddie drowned someplace else."

"Eddie didn't drown." Maureen spoke softly. "It's probably on the news by now. Hubbard thinks he might have had a heart attack and fallen into the water somehow."

"I guess that's possible. It's interesting that he's checking the shells, though, isn't it? Maybe Frank figures the body was moved from someplace else, where the shells are different."

"That's possible too," Maureen agreed. "I guess we'll find out eventually." She faced the boulevard. "I have to get to work. We've got two check-ins arriving today. One suite and one single room."

With Finn straining on the leash, they started along the quiet road. "It'll be good to see Trent and Pierre," Ted said. "Who's the single? Anyone we know?"

"His name is Ronald Treadwell. He sounded like he might be a travel writer. I hope so. We could use some good press right about now," she said. "He told me he'd been to Haven before, but it must have been before I arrived."

"The name's not familiar. Anyway, we'll be turning people away when word gets out about our tournament. That was a great response we got from the guys." Ted beamed.

"And the girl," Maureen corrected. "Young Tommy seems to know the charter boat business."

"She's taking the business seriously," Ted agreed. "She just lost her dad, but she's not going to take any time off working because of it. Eddie would be proud of her." They jogged the rest of the way to the inn and parted in the lobby. Ted headed for his first-floor room. Maureen and Finn started for the stairway, when the sound of the elevator purring to a stop surprised her. The light above the brass door shone and the cheerful chime sounded as the door slid open and Dr. Salter emerged. Maureen's trained eye for high-end sportswear, gained by her years as a buyer for a Boston department store, recognized the simple denim short-belted jumpsuit as a pricey Gabriella Hearst design, immediately picturing how it was going to look on Lorna.

"I'm off to see a wonderful archaeological site at Crystal River," the woman said, excitement evident in her voice and animated expression. "It's an enormous Indian mound that was used for more than sixteen hundred years. Don't worry about me if I'm late for dinner. I'll be having a marvelous day exploring." With a wave of her hand and a pat on the head for Finn, she left the inn.

Pleased that her guest was having a good experience, Maureen tugged on Finn's leash. "Maybe we'll have a marvelous day too, Finn." Maureen's tone wasn't confident, but she decided that Finn's "woof" surely was.

Chapter 10

It was late afternoon when Trent and Pierre arrived in front of the Haven House Inn via the TPA shuttle bus from the airport, and Maureen was sure the neighbors must have thought a couple of rock stars had come to town. Maureen, Finn, and all of the housekeeping staff including Gert, Molly, George, and Sam, along with Ted and almost all of the kitchen crew, had lined up on the sidewalk to greet the men. The two, in addition to devoting their time and talents into preparing a complete design portfolio to show Maureen how the Haven House Inn might look someday, had also been instrumental in ridding the place of a sorrowful ghost who for many years had made one of the best suites in the place completely unrentable.

Once inside, after Sam had taken the luggage up to the reserved suite and the rest of the welcoming committee had returned to their respective jobs, Maureen could hardly wait to show off what she'd accomplished so far. "I know there's a lot more to do." She pushed open the door to the dining room and stood aside while first Trent, and then Pierre, stepped into the refurbished area. "But what do you think of it now?"

The reaction from the pair was all that Maureen could have hoped for. Wreathed in smiles, Trent threw his arms around her shoulders. "Those draperies, perfection! And the bar! And the fish tank! It's all amazing."

Pierre ran to the bar. "Look at the carvings on the bar—fish and shells and even an octopus! And the angelfish in the tank! Exquisite. It's all even better than we could have hoped it would be. You've saved the round tables and the white linen tablecloths. Look, Trent. Fresh flowers on all the tables—and there's even a bouquet of day lilies on top of the piano."

The instrument in question, a vintage Haines Brothers player piano with matching bench, gleamed from a recent polishing. It was preprogramed to play piano roll versions of thirties and forties tunes while the keys moved up and down as "Ain't Misbehavin' " plinked in the background as though played by ghostly fingers. Maureen had come to realize that from time to time the ghostly fingers of long-gone barroom pianist Billy Bedoggoned Bailey actually *did* tickle those well-preserved ivories with song choices of his own—but she didn't share this with her two friends. She'd never actually *seen* Billy, but his occasional impromptu performance of 1980s hit song "Maureen" let her know when he was in the room.

"We're working on putting a little gift shop at the far end of the porch, as you'd suggested," Maureen reported as they returned to the lobby. "It's framed in, but it still needs quite a lot of work. We've given some of the suites special treatment with framed photos of guests who stayed in them. Little by little, we're getting there."

"The inn has its own charm," Trent said. "The decorating suggestions we've offered are just the frosting on the cake."

"Speaking of cake," Pierre said, "we're starving. Food on airplanes certainly isn't what it used to be. On the way here we talked about Chef Ted's amazing menus." His look was hopeful. "Are we between lunch and dinner? Do we have time to freshen up? Do you think Ted would prepare a bite for two old friends?"

"I know he will. You'll be in the Steve Lawrence and Eydie Gormé Suite on the second floor. Come down whenever you're ready." She gave the room keys to Trent and walked with them to the elevator, pausing as the brass doors slid open.

"Have you come across any more ghosts since we left?" Trent whispered.

She hesitated before answering. Trent and Pierre had good reason to understand that the inn had harbored at least one spirit, and she decided to trust them with information about a gentleman ghost friend of Lorna's she'd met fairly recently herself. "Don't tell anyone else, but if you ever smell pipe tobacco in the elevator, say hello to Reggie and remind him that this is a no-smoking hotel."

"Is he a nice ghost?" Trent wanted to know. "Other than the smoking?"

"He is, and if he's following my orders, you won't know he's there. He really likes the elevator."

"Who wouldn't?" Trent stepped inside, Pierre following. "This is one space that doesn't need a bit of improvement."

"Neither does our kitchen," Maureen promised. "I'll tell Ted you're hungry." Back at the reservation desk, she buzzed the kitchen on Penelope Josephine's vintage intercom system—the technology was old but as Sam had often reminded her, "If it ain't broke, don't fix it."

Ted answered on the first buzz. "Hi, Maureen."

"Hi, yourself. Trent and Pierre are hungry. I told them you'd take care of that right away."

"No problem. This evening's special is ready to go. How does a shrimp cocktail appetizer, tenderloin filet, baked potato, steamed mixed veggies, and Molly's famous Key lime pie sound?"

"It reminds me that I'm hungry too," she said. "Maybe I'll join the boys." Looking forward to the promised meal and the company of her talented friends, Maureen had almost forgotten about the second guest who'd been slated to arrive that afternoon. She looked again at the reservation list. "Ronald Treadwell," she murmured aloud. "He's arriving by plane from New York. He'll probably want food too."

"Who's Ronald Treadmill?" Ted asked.

"Sorry. I was talking to myself. Ronald Treadwell," she corrected. "He has a room reservation for tonight. I was thinking he might be hungry too."

"No problem at all. We have plenty of everything," he assured her.

"Sounds like Ronald might be a writer. I'm hoping it's for one of the travel magazines. That's the best kind of publicity."

"Yeah," Ted agreed. "The free kind! Hey, maybe it's a fishing magazine and he's coming to cover the tournament."

"He's a mind reader, then. We just thought it up."

Ted smiled. "Maybe he got a tip from the Quic Shop." They both laughed at the not-really-preposterous idea about Haven's local gossip mill.

"He'll be here pretty soon, and we'll know for sure," Maureen declared, "and we've still got a lot to do about publicity. Mainly the free or cheap kind. I'll start sending out press releases tonight."

Maureen was already scribbling notes for the press release on the back of a lunch menu when Sam appeared in the doorway, struggling to pull an oversized duffel bag through the door along with a suitcase and looking none too happy about it. He was followed by a tall man with a camera on a black leather strap slung around his neck. Sam, scowling, stood aside as the man approached the desk, and Ted gave a brief nod in the stranger's direction and headed back to the kitchen.

"Mr. Treadwell?" She pushed the guest register toward the front of the desk. "Welcome to the Haven House Inn."

He picked up the faux-quill pen, gave it a raised-eyebrow glance, and signed the book. "I'm glad to be here," he said. "You have much nicer weather than in New York."

She handed him his room key. "Your room is on this floor. Sam will show you the way. Dinner is at six o'clock."

"Can I get something before that? Plane fare was a bag of peanuts."

"The folks who checked in a little while ago said exactly the same thing." She handed him a dinner menu. "They've arranged for an early dinner. Tenderloin filet, baked potato, veggies, dessert. I'm sure you'll be welcome to join them. Come to the dining room as soon as you're ready." She pointed to the louvred door entrance.

"That sounds good." He followed Sam past the rack of brochures of local attractions toward the first-floor rooms. Maureen texted Ted. "There'll be a third for early dinner."

His reply was immediate. "No problem."

She returned to her press release scribblings. She'd just written "list categories" and pulled the original 2000 blue-and-white card from her file. Maybe she could cut the various fish categories down. It would make things much simpler. She made a side note. "See what fish are being caught the most in June."

The elevator whirred and gave the tiny clank announcing the arrival of someone from the upper floors. The door slid open, and Pierre and Trent, both smiling, almost tumbled into the lobby and hurried to her desk. "The suite is delightful," Trent said, "but best of all, we smelled the pipe tobacco."

"Reggie rode down with us. I'm sure of it," Pierre enthused. "We didn't actually see smoke, of course, but we both smelled it, didn't we?"

His partner agreed. "We did, but, Maureen, we remembered what you said, and I told him very sternly that this is a no-smoking inn."

"Reggie is very naughty." She tried to keep a straight face. "He probably overheard me telling you about him and he's just showing off for you." She thought for a moment about some of the other ghosts she'd encountered since she'd arrived in Haven less than a year ago. What if the others decided to "show off"? She'd have to be careful not to mention them to anyone—even trusted friends like the two designers. What if Billy Bedoggoned Bailey decided to appear to guests? Maureen was quite sure Lorna would know better than to appear uninvited, but what about Vice President Charlie Curtis, Herbert Hoover's veep? He was a seasonal visitor who spent his summers in Washington DC, but he might like a bit of long-overdue fame. Maureen knew that housekeeper Gert could see ghosts, but that Gert, like most of Haven, vigorously denied their very existence if anyone asked. "I'll never, ever tell anyone about Reggie again," she scolded herself, "or about any of the others."

She faced the two men. "I must ask you, as my good friends, not to tell anyone else here about Reggie. It's important. I know you are believers, because you helped free John Smith's spirit when you were here last year. But Haven likes to keep silent about her ghosts."

As one, the two made identical "lips are zipped" motions. She believed them absolutely. Reggie's secret was safe. Other guests might smell tobacco smoke in the elevator, and might even complain to her about it, but the blame would always rest on other inconsiderate humans. "Thank you, guys. Time for your dinner." She buzzed for waitress Jolene.

Alone again in the lobby, she stared for a moment at the silent vintage black telephone on the desk, almost willing it to ring. "We've got plenty of ghosts," she told it. "We need paying guests. Ring, darn you." Nothing. She returned to her back-of-the-menu list, but jumped anyway when the thing actually *did* ring. "Haven House Inn. Good afternoon," she said.

The caller was neither guest nor ghost. Frank Hubbard answered her courteous greeting with a gruff "Doherty? I'm coming over. Wait for me."

Chapter 11

Hubbard, still in uniform, came through the front door at the same time that Ronald Treadwell, now wearing khakis and a Buffalo Bills T-shirt and displaying a well-muscled upper body, arrived in the lobby. Maureen looked from one to the other, deciding that a paying inn customer trumps a visiting cop. She stood, nodding briefly to Hubbard, but moving toward the louvred door. "Just follow me to the dining room, Mr. Treadwell, and do enjoy your dinner."

The man frowned, facing the officer. "Is there a problem?"

"Not at all," Maureen told him. "Officer Hubbard, this is Mr. Treadwell. He's visiting us from New York."

Hubbard gave a curt nod. "How do. Here on business?"

"Yes, sir. I'm here on assignment from *Watching Birds* magazine."

"Birds, huh? Well, have a good evening." Hubbard tilted his head toward the office. "Ms. Doherty?"

"I'll be right with you, Officer." She escorted the guest into the dining room, hearing the familiar clink of china and glassware and the tinkling of the piano. "Enjoy your dinner," she said again. She closed the door, disappointed that Treadwell didn't represent a travel magazine after all, then hurried to where Haven's top cop stood, arms folded, clearly impatient. "What's going on?" she asked, opening her office door. "Come on in."

He remained standing. "So you and the bartender went down to the docks this morning."

"Yes," she said.

"You talked to Eddie's girl? Tommy?"

"Yes, we did."

"So you're interested in the case after all. Did you ask her about the Jet Skis?"

"The Jet Skis?" Maureen was confused. "No. We talked about the fishing tournament."

"What fishing tournament?" Hubbard's frown deepened. "I'm still talking about Tommy Manuel's blue Jet Skis with the white numbers on them. Like the one you saw when you found Eddie's body."

"Exactly what are we talking about?" she demanded. "And how do you know I even talked to Tommy this morning? Have you got somebody following me?" It was Maureen's turn to frown.

"Of course not. One of my guys saw you running in that direction. Another one was down there fishing off the pier and saw you two with the girl and the cook she takes with her on the boat. What is it with women and cooks anyway?"

Maureen recalled the cop she and Ted had seen digging at the shell line. He might have noticed them at the start of their run. There'd been at least a dozen individual fishermen on the pier. Ted had even handed brochures to a couple of them. *The Quic Shop isn't the only gossip mill in town*, she thought, ignoring the observation about the attraction to cooks. "I saw the sign advertising the Jet Skis," she said. "They have ones that can carry one to three people, but I didn't see any of the actual things there. Maybe they were all rented."

"She only had two of them to rent. They were on consignment from one of the big docks over in Clearwater. Eddie had one of them the day he died. Someone over in South Pasadena found it yesterday washed up on a sandbar."

"That's good."

"He returned it to the Clearwater store where it came from in the first place."

"That's good," she said again.

"Not good. One of their deck guys gave it a good wash down and waxed it before they sent it back over to Tommy."

Confused, Maureen asked, "What's wrong with that?"

Hubbard's tone was impatient. "If someone other than Eddie was driving the ski that day, any fingerprints, DNA, any identification was gone."

"You're thinking Eddie didn't fall from his ski. You think he was pushed?"

"I think he was dead. The ski *you* said you couldn't identify might have been driven by Eddie's killer, then abandoned. *You* probably witnessed the killer speeding away right after he'd dumped Eddie's body."

"Wait a minute. You're calling Eddie's death a murder?"

"So you're telling me you're not investigating Eddie's death on your own?" He sounded disappointed. "Eddie had one of the skis—the number on it checks out. Tommy is going to look up whoever rented the other one the day her dad died. It was returned to the *Tightline* on time. Whoever it was probably used a credit card, so it won't be hard to trace. She said she'd call the station as soon as she gets the name." He narrowed his eyes, still standing, looking down at Maureen. "You're sure you're not going rogue on me, right? You're not playing amateur detective? Using that thing—that thing you've got about murder?"

"Murder? Are you kidding? You're the one who's calling Eddie's death a murder, not me. Anyway, I keep telling you I don't have a 'thing.' And what makes you so sure the ski I saw was from the *Tightline*? They might be from the Clear-water place, for all you know."

He opened his mouth as if to answer, but stopped when his phone rang. He turned his back, his voice low. "Yeah. She called? What's the name?" Short pause. "Okay. Thanks." He returned the phone to his pocket and faced Maureen again. "Is that guy still here? That Treadwell guy?"

"Of course. He's in the dining room having dinner. Why?"

"One of the Jet Skis was rented on a company card. It belongs to a magazine called *Watching Birds*."

"Oh boy." She took a deep breath. "You're not going to go in there and interrupt my guests at dinner, are you? I mean, can you wait until he comes out? Or even better, can I just give him your number and have him call you later?"

That brought a cop-style eye-roll. "Oh, sure. Tell him to call me later and watch him run out the door. No. I won't spoil anybody's dinner. I'll wait right here." He crossed the lobby and sat in one of the wicker chairs beside the bamboo table. "Right here." He folded his arms, staring straight ahead.

This is just great, Maureen worried. *There's nothing like a grim-faced cop in uniform in the lobby to greet potential lodgers.* She pretended to be busy, shuffling papers on the reservation desk, while thoughts about negative cash flow, the unfinished gift shop, and the blank reservation list cascaded through her brain. What had made her believe she could manage a hotel business? She probably should have sold the darned place as soon as she'd arrived in Florida.

Hubbard's voice interrupted the brief poor-me session. "Hey, Doherty," he said as he stood. "There isn't a back door out of that dining room, is there?"

"Just through the kitchen," she told him. "If it will make you feel better, I'll peek in there and make sure everybody is where they belong. Okay?"

"Yeah. Thanks. You do that. Make sure that bird man is still in there."

She walked quickly and quietly to the louvred door and pushed it open a small crack—just enough to see the round table closest to the bar where all three men sat—Trent and Pierre together, facing her, and Ronald Treadwell across from them, his back to her, the tight T-shirt accenting broad shoulders. She closed the door. "All present and accounted for," she reported, returning to the desk. "The Key lime pie is just being served. Would you like a slice?" She barely resisted adding, "To go."

"No thanks," he said, straight-faced. Then, oddly off-topic, "I see you got the No Vacancy sign fixed."

"Yes," she agreed, glad for the change of subject. "Gaudette and Son to the rescue. It was barely minutes after they got it running correctly that a new guest saw it and walked in. A lady anthropologist."

"Oh, sure. Dr. Salter, right?"

Does everybody in Haven know things before I do? "Yes. You've met her?"

"She came into the station to find out about the laws here on removing artifacts from Native American protected sites."

"Haven has special laws about that?"

"There are some. The Florida Fish and Wildlife Conservation Commission tries to protect the sites the best they can, but there are so many sites, and the prices looters can get for the old tools and pottery and arrowheads and such makes it hard to enforce the rules. Just one Florida arrowhead can sell for over three hundred dollars."

"I didn't know that."

"Yeah." He spread his hand apart in a helpless gesture. "Some professor up at Florida State says that an Indian pot can sell for thousands."

"Wow. Thousands?" She looked up as the dining room door opened and Trent and Pierre returned to the lobby.

"A fabulous meal," Trent reported.

"As usual," Pierre added.

"Where is Treadwell?" Hubbard demanded, striding toward the dining room.

"He went out to the kitchen to ask Ted for the recipe for the pie," Trent told him. "Nice fellow. Quite a cook, apparently."

Chapter 12

Hubbard's dash for the front door was quite the fastest Maureen had ever seen him run. He'd left the door ajar and, curious, she followed him to the porch. She, as well as Sam, George, and the two women leaning forward in their rockers watched as he took the front stairs two at a time and rapidly disappeared around the corner of the inn. Maureen resumed her post at the reception desk, noting with the tiniest bit of satisfaction that the officer's hasty exit had caused him to miss Ronald Treadwell leave the dining room and join Pierre and Trent in the lobby, happily waving a piece of paper and exclaiming, "I got the recipe!"

It didn't take long for Hubbard, still slightly out of breath, to return to the empty lobby. "Did the three guys all go to their rooms, Doherty?" he asked in a conversational tone.

"I really don't know," she said. *If he wanted to pretend nothing unusual had just happened, she'd go along with it.* "Trent and Pierre took the elevator up, and Mr. Treadwell walked in the direction of the first-floor rooms."

"Thanks," he said. "What room number did you say Treadwell was in?"

"I don't believe I mentioned it."

The frown was back. "It's an official request, then."

"How about this? I'll ring his room and you can speak to him," she offered and reached for the desk phone.

"That'll work."

Hubbard didn't try to hide what he was saying to Maureen's newest guest, so she listened unashamedly. "Mr. Treadwell?" The tone was courteous. "Officer Hubbard speaking. We met briefly in the lobby. Could you come back here for a moment? There seems to be a problem with your credit card."

"What?" Maureen didn't try to suppress her outrage. *That's a dirty trick.* She reached for the telephone. Too late.

"Thank you." Hubbard replaced the black receiver in its cradle and faced her. "What?" he echoed her question. "So it's not exactly *his* credit card. It's the same company. I need to know who rented the Jet Ski."

Ronald Treadwell reappeared in the lobby almost instantly. "I'm sure my credit card is fine, sir," he said. "I'm a photographer for *Watching Birds*. It's a well-known publication, highly regarded in birding circles everywhere. Here. I brought the current copy for you, Ms. Doherty."

He's not a writer. He's a photographer.

The man handed Maureen a magazine with close-up cover photo of a long-billed, black-and-white bird with a tiny spot of red on its head. The caption under the photo read "Meet the Red-Cockaded Woodpecker." Treadwell faced Hubbard. "What's the problem, Officer?"

Hubbard moved toward the wicker chair and bamboo table grouping across the lobby. "Let's sit down, shall we? It will only take a moment to straighten this out, I'm sure." Silently, Treadwell sat in the indicated chair. "The problem, it seems, has to do with another *Watching Birds* cards, one that was used recently to rent a Jet Ski. Do you know anything about that card?" Hubbard leaned forward and pulled a notebook from his pocket, an intense expression on his face.

"Sure. That would have been my boss. Harvey Album." Treadwell smiled. "He always personally scouts out a location before he assigns a photographer. I just left Cooperstown, New York. I got some great shots of the red-shouldered hawk. Harvey is a real expert. He says that your Forest is an amazing find. Everything from common mockingbirds to roseate spoonbills and pelicans. I feel lucky to have the assignment."

"Harvey Album," Hubbard repeated, writing in his notebook. "What is his position with the magazine?"

"He pretty much owns it, as I understand it," Treadwell said. "He's listed as editor on the masthead."

"So, he was recently in Haven, checking out The Forest?" Hubbard put his pen in his breast pocket.

"That would be my guess," Treadwell agreed. "So, are we all clear on *my* card? No problem? Because I can't afford to stay here without it. And I can't stay long. My boss is— well—kind of cheap. He likes to trade stuff instead of paying cash for anything." A boyish grin. "I don't carry much cash. The last time I was in Haven, I stayed in a tent."

"A tent?" Hubbard's forehead creased. "When was that?"

Treadwell stood and walked toward the archway leading to the first-floor rooms. "Boy Scout camp," he said. "When I was twelve."

"You lived here in Haven?" Hubbard yanked the pen out again. "When you were twelve?"

"No. I never lived here. I spent a summer with my grandmother in Clearwater once. She thought the Boy Scout camp would be a good experience for me." He shrugged broad shoulders. "She thought I spent too much time reading books, that I should get outdoors more. She gave me a camera and signed me up."

"It must have been successful," Maureen said. "You work for an outdoors magazine."

"Exactly," Treadwell said. "I went to that camp, and the

first thing I learned was how much fun climbing trees is. I learned to use that little camera. I took pictures of birds and bees and butterflies and snakes and squirrels. When I finished school, I even became a licensed arborist and got all the proper equipment so I could keep climbing trees. The photography job came along later." His smile was broad. "It's all good." He turned and walked past the brochure rack and the guest laundry toward his room.

Frank Hubbard didn't linger after Treadwell's departure. Maureen gave him the current lunch and dinner menus, reminded him to post them at the local police station, tried to shake the idea that Eddie Manuel had been murdered, and returned to her so-far meager notes about a fishing tournament for Haven, slipping the *Watching Birds* magazine Treadwell had given her into the top desk drawer.

"I need to streamline the idea," she mumbled to herself as she ran a finger down the list of species that had been hunted in the earlier fishing competition. "Bass, trout, grouper, kingfish, grunt . . . wait a minute. What's a grunt? Never mind. I need to narrow it down to one kind of fish." Once again, she reached for her phone and texted Ted.

What's the most popular fish people want to catch this month?

Kingfish was the one-word answer.

"So be it," she said aloud, circling the word "kingfish" on the blue-and-white card, pleased that at least one decision had been made, then giving herself a thumbs-up when she remembered that Babe Ruth photo displaying "a nice kingfish." A happy coincidence. Was the new tenant's story about being in Haven when he was twelve a parallel to her own story about being here at the same age another coincidence? She shook the silly thought away and forced herself to concentrate on reworking the morning's hastily prepared brochure into something worth promoting.

Her concentration worked nicely, particularly since the phone didn't ring and no new guests opened the green front door. Within an hour the new headline—"The Eddie Manuel Memorial Kingfish Tournament" and a page of succinct body copy with blank spaces for information on fishing licenses and prizes to be offered and a few photos to complement the Babe Ruth one were ready. There must be rules for getting fishing licenses. She'd call the city hall about that, and then hit up some of Haven's leading merchants for appropriate prizes. Haven House Inn would have to come up with at least one of them. Bright idea: she remembered seeing several large silver-plated bowls in Penelope's hoard in the storage locker. Some polish and engraving and those would do wonderfully. If George was still in his chair, she'd send him to the locker right away. She pushed the door to the porch open and spied George, dozing in a rocker at his spot at the head of the stairs.

"Oh, Maureen, do you have a minute?" Trent and Pierre emerged from the elevator, wearing matching white shorts and colorful Hawaiian shirts. She paused.

"Of course. I always have time for you. Give me a sec to send George on an errand and I'll be right back." The men followed as she approached the four of her household staff. Gert had heard her comment and had already given George a tap on the arm.

"Wake up, Georgie Porgie." She laughed as the man sat up straight, looking from left to right, confused. "The boss has a job for you."

"What? Sure. Okay," he said, then slowly stood, facing Maureen and the two designers. "What's up?"

"I need you to go over to the storage locker. Remember you showed me a couple of those silver-plated Revere bowls once?" Maureen's department store background had made her familiar with the gracefully shaped reproduction bowls made famous by the early American silversmith. "I want to see if they're in good enough condition to be used for awards."

"Yes, ma'am. I know right where they are."

Trent joined her at the head of the stairs. "Oh, Maureen. Could we go along with George? I was just about to ask you for suggestions on what we might do this evening. I'd love to get a close look at Penelope Josephine's hoard. You never know what strange items Pierre and I can turn into treasures."

"That's right," Pierre declared. "You never know when or where you might find treasure."

George didn't wait for her to answer. "Sure. Come along, you guys. I'm glad for the company." He dropped his voice. "I'm not crazy about being in that locker all alone, and it'll be getting dark soon, if you know what I mean."

Pierre turned his head from side to side, as though being careful about who might be listening. "Ghosts?" he whispered.

George didn't reply, just gave a shrug of broad shoulders, followed with an affirmative nod of his head.

"You're sure it's okay with you if we ride along, Maureen?" Trent wanted to know.

"Absolutely. Why don't you take the big truck, George, in case our friends find something they can turn into treasures?"

George gave the two men an appraising look. "You might want to change out of those white shorts. The locker ain't the cleanest place in the world."

"Give us two minutes," Trent ordered. "We always pack coveralls for just such occasions!" Together, they dashed back to the lobby. Maureen followed, watching with a smile as they ran to the elevator and Pierre excitedly punched the UP button.

Pleased that her guests were having a good experience,

Maureen unlocked her office and went inside, leaving the door wide open, optimistically considering the chance that a paying customer might wander into the lobby. With the mock-up of the tournament brochure begun, and with the reminder of Penelope Josephine Gray's hoard brought about by the Revere bowls as likely prizes, she decided to spend some time with the old woman's trunk. As Pierre had recently pointed out, "You never know when or where you might find a treasure."

Dr. Salter believes that, Maureen thought. *She's gone to investigate Native American lore, and Ronald Treadwell is excited about taking amazing photos of birds.* With renewed visions of finding possible treasure, she lifted the curved top of the old trunk.

George poked his head in the door to tell her he was leaving and taking the designers—now dressed in identical coveralls similar to those the Goudreau father and son team wore—along with him. She heard the truck start up, revealing with a growl that it might soon need some costly engine work. Then she was suddenly aware of the silence of the place. "Not a creature is stirring," she mumbled. "Oh, well, it's almost time for the dinner crowd to start arriving. At least we have the food business—largely thanks to Ted."

At the top of the tightly packed trunk was another stack of flyers and posters for local and regional attractions. She rifled through the stack, surprised that several of them were still in business and that she'd visited a few of them herself. The amazing Weeki Wachee mermaids were still delighting audiences after sixty years. The newest brochure advertising the underwater show was prominently displayed at the front of the Haven House display rack. So was the one for Sunken Gardens, over a century old, and Cypress Gardens, which had opened its flowery gates in 1936. She put the three aside, planning to frame each one alongside its newest counterpart.

She moved the stack to one side in order to get a better look at a long brown envelope with the name "Trevaney" written on it in spidery cursive. That name had recently taken on meaning for Maureen. She had reason to believe that a woman named Charlotte Christine Trevaney had been the person who'd given Haven House to Penelope Josephine and that it had been given in exactly the same mysterious way that it had been passed on to her—in the last will and testament of a perfect stranger.

The envelope had once been sealed with a spot of green sealing wax—long since hardened and split, leaving the flap loose—revealing several sheets of paper inside. Maureen put the envelope on the top of the desk and stared at it for a long moment. Was there a treasure inside? Important answers? Or more confusion and secrets and annoying questions?

She'd seen a portrait of a woman at the Historical Museum with the name "C. Trevaney" written on the back of the canvas. Was the woman in old-fashioned clothing the subject—or the artist? The museum staff had been noncommittal. Maureen had come to believe the woman was the subject of the painting, largely due to Lorna's convincing story of having seen the same woman—or rather, her ghost— a number of times at the inn's bar. That ghostly Charlotte favored a green drink called absinthe, and the ghost had, in fact, chosen to use the name "Absinthe" for herself. Some of the few people in Haven who were brave enough to admit that there *was* such a thing as ghosts also claimed they'd seen a lady late at night at the bar, dressed in modern clothes— "Goth," Lorna insisted—sipping a green drink. Was the late night apparition indeed Charlotte Trevaney, Penelope Josephine's benefactor? And in some strange, time-spanning way, her own reason for being the current owner of Haven House Inn? The disturbing train of thought was interrupted by the appearance of several familiar faces and a burst of happy conversation as the first of the local dinner regulars made their way through the green door and into the lobby toward the dining room.

Almost glad for the interruption, Maureen slipped the Trevaney envelope into the top drawer of her desk to be dealt with later. She returned the brochures to the trunk, gently closing the curved top. She'd attend to each of those long-buried items eventually—she was, after all, not an anthropologist like her well-dressed Massachusetts tenant.

Chapter 13

It didn't take long for the round tables to fill up with diners. Maureen stood at the open door, welcoming local regulars and greeting newcomers. The menus distributed around Haven, along with the inn's growing reputation for good, home-cooked food and Ted's own excellent standing as a chef, were paying off. The dining room, if not the lodging rooms, was keeping the place financially afloat. One of the last of the locals to be seated was Frank Hubbard.

It wasn't unusual for Hubbard to stop there for dinner. A good many of Haven's single men did so. "Back again so soon?" Maureen said as she turned the officer over to Shelly, who was in charge of seating. He paused at the doorway and looked, cop-like, around the room. "Didn't you get a new guest this afternoon? After I left?"

"I wish," she said. "No. Not a soul. Why?"

"The *Watching Birds* credit card showed up again. That Harvey Album guy used it at the Quic Shop this afternoon. You know how fast word gets around when anybody new shows up in there." She knew, but was surprised that she hadn't heard about the new visitor yet. It must be because both Gert and Molly were on kitchen duty and hadn't caught up with the latest gossip. Hubbard looked puzzled. "I thought he must be staying here. A guy like that who owns a big fancy magazine isn't going to be staying in some little mom-and-pop cheap motel when he's in Haven. I figured he'd be here, chowing down with everybody else who has a few bucks to spend on food. I want to talk to him about that Jet Ski he rented. I called his office yesterday and they said he was out of town on business and he'd get back to me later."

"Remember, though, Mr. Treadwell said that his boss was—um—on the thrifty side. I'm sure a man like that is interested in the outdoors. Maybe he decided to come to Haven instead of just returning your call. He might be at one of the campgrounds in the area. Was he buying camping provisions at the Quic Shop?"

"He bought a few snacks, some beer, nothing major." Hubbard stepped back from the dining room entrance. "I'll be back later for that dinner," he said. "I need to start checking campsites." Maureen watched him leave, wondering about the man Hubbard was chasing, and at the same time hoping he'd be back. She didn't want to lose the income from even one dinner.

There were still quite a few lingering diners, and the evening bar customers had begun to trickle into the dining room when Maureen, still at the reception desk, heard the truck arrive outside with a growl and an ominous clank. Transmission? She hoped not.

Trent and Pierre burst through the green door, in an almost Laurel and Hardy–like entrance. "Maureen! You must come outside and see!" Trent exclaimed.

"Come outside," Pierre echoed. "You won't believe what we've found!"

"Are the Revere bowls in good enough shape to be prizes?" she asked, sure that they must be to cause such enthusiasm.

"Oh yeah. The bowls. Sure. There are three of them and a Revere water pitcher too. They just need a little silver polish and they'll be perfect."

She followed the two, who were fairly dancing with excitement as they crossed the porch, where several lingering dinner guests had already left their rocking chairs and gathered around the pickup truck. Even in the dim light from the porch and the soft red glow from the VACANCY sign, she could see that the huge, three-door armoire was indeed a treasure. "It was way in the back of the locker," Trent explained, "face to the wall, covered in dust and even spiderwebs."

Pierre winced, brushing away imaginary spiders. "Can you picture it, Maureen? We'll take the doors off, build shelves in it, and it will be your display piece in the gift shop."

"We'll hang the mirrored door in the fitting room and the other two doors—oh my God, the carved walnut—these could be the features in the new shop's décor."

She could almost see it. The mellow, carved wood body of the armoire would hold at least three tiers of shelves. She visualized plump glass jars of old-fashioned candies, rows of local shell craft, stacks of Haven T-shirts. Besides that, the fabulous doors were treasures all by themselves. And that mirror! Almost too gorgeous for a fitting room.

Between George, the two designers and a couple of the neighborhood after-dinner porch-sitters, they wrestled the enormous piece of furniture out of the bed of the truck, up the stairs, around the corner and—while Maureen held the door open—wiggled it into the empty, someday-gift-shop space. Almost as an afterthought, Pierre put a cardboard box containing the tarnished bowls and pitcher in there too.

"This calls for a drink," somebody said.

"On the house," Maureen agreed, leading the way back to the bar. Hilda, the night manager, had arrived and taken her place behind the desk. There were a few folks at one of the round tables lingering over coffee and pie, while Jolene and Shelly restored the remaining tables to their usual white-linen-clothed order, each with a vase of fresh wildflowers at its center. Bartender Lennie welcomed the group, placing the ordinary, but free, Miller Lite beer coasters at each place and taking beverage orders. Getting proper coasters with the Haven Inn name and maybe a special logo were items near the top of Maureen's to-do list. "Irish coffee, Ms. Doherty?" Lennie asked, remembering her favorite after-dinner choice.

Irish whiskey along with Baileys, poured with Lennie's heavy hand, would not sit well on her almost empty stomach. "Just coffee for me, please, Lennie," Maureen said. "I've barely eaten anything today and I still have some work to do."

"You're working too hard," Lennie advised. "Ted has a few of those filets left. Want some dinner?"

"Maybe later, she said, "after these guys finish celebrating." She raised her coffee mug and clinked it with Trent's raised champagne glass. After the men had emptied their glasses, she signed the tab, accepted Trent's offer to take care of the tip, and stood as the men left the bar, admiring once again the handsomely refinished woodwork and the tankful of angelfish swimming lazily among fanciful underwater pillars and shipwrecks and submerged treasure chests.

"Ready for some dinner now?" the bartender asked. "Steak, potato, vegetables, pie? Maybe a glass of wine?"

"I think so." She pointed. "I guess I'll sit at that table over in the far corner, out of everybody's way."

It felt good to sit, to relax, to be alone. After Shelly took her order, Maureen leaned back in the chair, glad she hadn't sold the rundown old place after all. When she'd first seen this dining room, it had featured dark walls, heavy draperies, and a random assortment of straight-backed dining-room chairs around the tables. Now, with the gorgeous bar, light colored walls and beachy accents, along with those mismatched chairs—each distinctive and one of them now refinished with harmonizing oak varnish—it was a room she could be proud of.

Her solitary reverie didn't last long. Shelly appeared, placing a glass of red wine on the coaster. "Do you feel like having company, Ms. Doherty? That new lady, Dr. Salter, just asked if she could get some dinner. I guess she's been away all day. I asked Ted, and he says there's enough steak and everything."

"Of course. Ask her to join me. No sense in using another table for one person," Maureen offered.

"I'll tell her." Shelly quickly prepared a second place setting, then hurried away toward the lobby. Within seconds she returned, Dr. Salter walking a few steps ahead of her. The doctor had changed clothes again, now wearing a softly draped, very simple periwinkle-blue crepe maxi dress. Maureen envisioned Lorna in this one, perhaps sparked up with some of the diamond jewelry the actress sometimes "borrowed" from Tiffany's show windows. Maureen stood to welcome her guest.

"How was your day?" she asked when the two were seated and Shelly had taken the doctor's order: "filet rare, skip the potatoes and pie and I'd like a glass of rosé."

"Was the site everything you'd expected, Doctor?"

"Even more," the woman said, "and please call me Kim. So far, this entire trip has been perfect—including this delightful inn. I understand that I missed a bit of excitement when your decorator friends found a piece of furniture they mean to convert into shelving in a new gift-shop area. I heard all about it as soon as I arrived on the front porch."

Maureen wasn't surprised. "Yes," she said. "Word gets around fast in Haven."

"So I've noticed." Kim smiled. "When I arrived here yesterday, I'd barely parked behind the building when I heard about a body being washed up on the beach just down the street from here."

Maureen nodded. "True. And unfortunately, I was the person who discovered the poor man."

"I heard that too."

"I'm not surprised." Maureen lifted her wineglass in a sort of salute to Haven's flourishing grapevine. Kim lifted hers, and the friendly clink of Penelope Josephine's better-than-average stemware broke the silence of the large, almost empty room. The silence was broken again—almost immediately.

"I told you I'd be back for dinner, Doherty. Good evening, Dr. Salter. Mind if I join you ladies?" Hubbard stood across the table from the two women. He glanced around the room, then echoed almost exactly what Maureen had said earlier. "No point in using another whole table for one person."

"Sure, Frank. Why not?" Maureen gave a slight lift of one shoulder. "Pull up a chair." *Maybe he'll pick up the tab*, she thought, then quickly dismissed that as pretty darned unlikely. Shelly, with an inquisitive look in Maureen's direction, arranged another place setting and took the third order. Hubbard declined wine, claiming that he was "on duty." *That must mean he can charge the meal to the city.*

"Dr. Salter was just telling me how she'd spent the day over at Crystal River," Maureen, always the good hostess, attempted to start a conversation that had nothing to do with police business, and certainly nothing about a possible murder.

"Nice little town," Hubbard offered. "Did you swim with the manatees?"

"I didn't," Kim replied, "although I'd certainly like to do that someday. They are such fascinating, gentle creatures. No. I visited the archaeological site and the museum."

"That's nice," he said politely, although clearly not particularly interested in the topic. He looked at Maureen. "I guess a couple of your other new guests did some digging down at the storage locker, right, Doherty?"

"They did," Maureen said, "and they came up with a wonderful old armoire that we'll be able to use when we build our gift shop."

"How wonderful," the doctor exclaimed. "That's the best kind of recycling—finding new uses for old items."

Shelly arrived tableside with the shrimp cocktail appetizers, each in its own rounded, mid-century-modern nested cup with a silver band overlay on the rim. "Speaking of old items," Maureen spoke proudly, "my predecessor bought dozens of these cups back in the nineteen sixties, and they continue to serve us well."

"These are fresh gulf shrimp." Hubbard dipped a large pink shrimp into spicy red sauce. "Undoubtedly from our local commercial fleet of fishing boats." He gestured with the plump crustacean toward Maureen. "Ms. Doherty knows a lot about fresh fish. Why, she was down at the docks chatting with the fishermen this very morning."

Kim Salter took a dainty bite of shrimp from a tiny oyster fork. "Absolutely delicious," she said. "I've been thinking about doing a bit of fishing while I'm here. Back home in Massachusetts, every summer I fish out of Gloucester at least once or twice. Perhaps you'd recommend a local charter boat, Maureen?"

What is Hubbard trying to do? Get me to talk about the Tightline? She decided to do exactly that. "I met a young woman this morning who captains her own boat. Her name is Tommy Manuel and the boat is the *Tightline.* It's a well-known, six-passenger boat. They do half-day or full-day trips. There's a galley aboard too. I'll give you her brochure after dinner. By the way, in a week or so there'll be a fishing tournament in Haven. I'll see that you get a brochure about that if you're still here by then."

Shelly arrived with their main courses, and the conversation turned once again to food. Maureen was delighted to accept compliments on the quality of the meal from both of her dinner companions, and was also happy to send some business Tommy Manuel's way if she could.

"The *Tightline* is a good boat," Hubbard agreed. "They rent Jet Skis too, if you want to do a little gulf exploring of your own. You can zip around and visit beaches and islands and maybe do some shelling."

Okay. I see where he's going. She didn't try to disguise a glare at Haven's top cop. "Officer Hubbard is particularly interested in shells because the poor fellow we were discussing earlier—the man who washed up on the beach who was Tommy Manuel's dad, by the way—that man had shells in his pockets and even in the cuffs of his pants," she reported. "As though maybe he'd been dragged across a shell line."

"Crushed shells," Hubbard said. "Messed-up crushed shells."

"Not a shell line, then," Kim corrected. "You'd be more likely to find crushed shells in an Indian mound—but of course it's against the law to disturb them." She raised a hand and signaled the waitress. "I believe I'll change my mind about that Key lime pie. Just a teensy slice."

Chapter 14

"Is that wild bird guy still in the house?" His meal finished, Hubbard put his napkin on the table and stood. "I found his boss—the editor of the magazine—parked in a converted van over on the old county road beside The Forest. He said he's 'gathering information about the shrinking habitat of the white pelican.' He seemed okay, legally parked, no litter in sight, all the right ID. But there's more than birds in that mess of a jungle. If I remember right, there's a small Indian mound in there, am I correct, Dr. Salter?"

"Yes indeed. Actually, there are two small ones, mostly composed of shells. The Tocabogas ate a lot of shellfish. They threw their broken dishes—pottery—in there too. It was a sort of a dump to them, you see, but to people like me, it offers a wealth of information on how the Native people lived all those years ago. Unfortunately, back when people began to move to this part of the state, somebody figured out that the remnants from Native civilizations made good road beds, so a lot of it was destroyed."

"Too bad." Hubbard actually looked sad. "Remember what I told you about that guy who died during that old fishing tournament, Doherty? Name of Sherman?" He didn't wait for an answer. "He got killed next to an Indian mound. Maybe Eddie Manuel got killed near one too. A different one, but it's made of crushed shells too, and it's in the middle of a doggoned bird sanctuary. I'll pass on that pie, Shelly. I'm going over to The Forest to have another talk with Harvey Album. Doherty, I'm going to need to talk to Treadwell again too. He said he wasn't going to be staying here long. When is he going to check out?"

"I don't know. I hope he'll stay for a while longer."

"I'll keep checking with you. Let me know if you get any feelings about—well, anything. Here. Dinner's on me." He handed Shelly a plastic card. "Put twenty percent on it for yourself." He leaned forward in what might have been a bow. "Nice talking with you, Doctor, and thanks for the tip about the shells."

"You're welcome. I've enjoyed talking with you too, and thank you for dinner," she said, then turned toward Maureen. "How exciting! My interest is usually in solving mysteries about people who died centuries ago. Now I'm suddenly in the position of helping the police figure out how someone died more recently. Haven is even more interesting than I thought it was going to be!"

"I'm sure what you told him about the crushed shells is truly helpful," Maureen told her. "I think it's going to establish where poor Eddie Manuel died. That's why Officer Hubbard is in a hurry to leave without his pie. He's going to check up on a man who may have been near the Indian mound when Eddie got killed."

"Fascinating. You have an interest in solving mysteries too, I take it?"

"What makes you say that?" Maureen was puzzled.

"Officer Hubbard asked about your 'feelings.' It sounds as though he trusts your instincts about such things."

Maureen's smile was wry. "Oh, that. He has some crazy idea that I have some special 'gift.' He says that people who have it don't know they have it, so he asks me impossible questions sometimes." She shrugged. "I've learned to humor him."

Kim finished the last bite of her pie. "This pie is absolutely decadent. I'm trying to watch my weight, but this was worth the risk. Please give my compliments to the handsome chef. I've had a busy day and I'm ready for bed." She stood. "I'll look forward to seeing you tomorrow. Perhaps I'll go over to the fishing dock and arrange for a ride on the *Tightline*."

"It's about time for me to take Finn for his evening walk," Maureen said, "and I'm ready for a good night's sleep too." She watched as Kim left the dining room. Her graceful walk was almost as perfect as Lorna Dubois's.

She checked with the night manager, asking if there'd been any calls for reservations. There hadn't been. She rode the elevator up to the third floor, sniffing for tobacco smoke all the way. There was none. When the brass door slid open, she heard Finn's soft welcoming "woof" from down the carpeted hall. "I'm coming," she called, then looked around, although she knew there was no one else on the third floor to hear her—at least no living beings. You never knew about the others, like Reggie and Lorna and Billy Bedoggoned and maybe even a late vice president.

Finn was all kisses and wiggles when she opened the door to her suite. "If everyone had a golden retriever like you, the world would be a better place," she told him, giving him a good head scratch. "Let's get your leash and we'll take a nice walk down to the beach." He followed her to the kitchen where she retrieved the leash from behind the door, clipped it to his collar, and led him through the living room. There were no cats on the cat tower or on the balcony outside the window. "Bogie and Bacall must be off on cat business of their own," she told the dog, who answered with a "who cares" kind of woof.

The two took the stairway down to the first floor and exited the building by the side door, avoiding visiting with whatever porch-sitters might still remain in their rocking chairs, and proceeded along the boulevard. Most of the shops were closed, but their lighted windows gave a cheery aspect to the scene. Erle Stanly was sound asleep on top of a stack of cozy mystery novels in the bookshop window, and music spilled from the open door of the L&M Lounge. Maureen wondered if Lorna would go there tonight for the after-closing gathering of convivial ghosts, and if she'd be wearing something from Kim's closet.

Maureen looked up and down the beach, and seeing a few people, decided to keep Finn leashed. They jogged together toward the hard-packed sand at the water's edge, crossing over the shell line, pale white in the fading light. This time they didn't head toward the fishing docks but faced the other way, toward the city lights of St. Petersburg. "There's a little different view this way, Finn," she told the dog, "and besides, there are more houses, more people this way."

"Woof," Finn said.

"Oh, I know I'm perfectly safe as long as you're with me," she assured him, "but it's dark out, and after all, there's a killer wandering around here somewhere."

"Woof woof." Finn slowed down and looked at her.

"Yeah, I know. You'd bite his face off. Come on. Let's run."

The two ran together for nearly a half mile, then turned and jogged at a comfortable pace back to the Casino. She sat on the back steps of the old building, removing her running shoes one at a time, shaking the sand from each one. She stopped, holding one shoe midair when she heard a whispered "Shhhh!" Finn gave a low growl.

"Who's there?" Maureen demanded.

"Shhhh!" came the whisper again, and a man stepped from the shadows.

Finn wagged his tail.

"Holy crap. You about scared me to death." Maureen stood, shoes in her hands, and faced Ronald Treadwell.

"Will you hush, for God's sake," the man whispered. "I'm trying to get a picture here." He held up his camera with one hand and pointed toward a small, brick-red bird perched in the overhang of the Casino porch. "It's a male Eastern screech owl."

As if to verify what the photographer had just said, the thing screeched—a trilling "hoot, hoot, hoot." Finn, remembering his long-ago guard-dog lessons and took a position between Maureen and the man. She backed away. Treadwell aimed his camera toward the narrow space where the owl's yellow eyes reflected light from the boulevard streetlamps. Maureen heard the slight click before the owl took flight and disappeared in a nearby stand of Australian pines.

Maureen had to make a quick decision. Should she take offense at being twice shushed, or was it up to her to apologize for interrupting the photographer at work? Silently, she sat on the steps and put on her shoes. Treadwell spoke first. "Sorry if I scared you."

"That's okay."

"They hunt at night."

"Excuse me?"

"They hunt at night. The screech owls." He rubbed Finn's ears. "You weren't scared, were you, boy?" Finn leaned happily into the rubbing.

"Did you get your picture all right?"

"I think so. Mind if I sit down and check it?" He didn't wait for her answer, but sat beside her on the wide step. He examined the back of the camera, then extended it toward her. "Yep. Got him. I got what I wanted and he got what he wanted."

The small owl was about the color of red mulch, and he'd been looking straight at the camera, his eyes and curved bill bright yellow. "He's so cute," she said. "What was he hunting for on the Casino porch?"

"A nice plump mouse. The Casino serves food, so there're always mice here. The owl hunts by dropping on his prey, talons first, from a height—maybe a tree branch, maybe a porch overhang. I was lucky to see him here since I don't have any of my tree-climbing gear with me. They're so well camouflaged—their coloring looks a lot like tree bark."

"Woof," Finn said.

"Not that kind of bark," Maureen explained.

Treadwell showed her another shot. "Look. I caught him when he started to fly away with his dinner. Nice wingspan for a little guy."

"I'm glad you got your pictures," she said, thinking of what he'd said about mice and food. *Does Haven House have mice?* Her next thought was of two plump and happy cats. Bogie and Bacall. Mouse problem solved.

"Me too," he said. "This trip is going well. It shouldn't take more than another day or two at The Forest, and I plan to wind up at the Suncoast Seabird Sanctuary to interview the bird rescue people."

"So you'll be around for a while." Maureen stood, and Finn strained at his leash. "That's good. Officer Hubbard told me this evening that he wants to talk with you again before you leave."

Treadwell returned the camera to a case on a strap around his neck and stood facing her. "No more credit card problems, I hope," he said. "I'll walk back to the inn with you, if that's okay."

"Okay," she said.

He fell into step beside her. "I wonder if Officer Hubbard straightened out the credit card thing with Harvey."

"I don't know. I believe he planned to speak with Mr. Album again tonight."

There was no further talk about Hubbard or credit cards on the short walk back to the inn. Maureen pointed out the bookshop and the thrift store and the Historical Society, and Treadwell said he hoped to have time to visit all of them. All four of the front-row rocking-chair brigade were in their accustomed spots when the two reached the inn. Maureen wondered how long it would take the word to reach the Quic Shop that Ms. Doherty and the magazine photographer had been on a moonlight walk together.

Chapter 15

In the morning Maureen was already at the side door before Ted joined her there for the morning run. She'd left Finn, still sound asleep, at the foot of her bed. It was already shaping up to be a busy day. Trent and Pierre would be excited to get started on the gift shop, she was sure, and they needed to make plans for Trent's birthday celebration too. The Eddie Manuel Memorial Kingfish Tournament was still in the planning stages and needed a whole lot of work to even get off the ground. She was going to have to involve the whole community somehow if this was going to be the success she envisioned.

Ted always knew how to make her feel better when she started to show signs of stress. "I got a good look at the new shelving for the gift shop," he told her as they began their warm-up stretches at the edge of the beach. "It's going to be perfect. What a find. Penelope's hoard turns out to be a gift that keeps on giving, doesn't it? Things seem to turn up exactly when you need them."

"You're right," she agreed. "The idea for the kingfish tournament came from her trunk, and the cabinet with the gorgeous doors and the magnificent mirror was just sitting there, face to the wall, in her storage locker."

"I wonder what surprise she has for you next." He smiled

his great smile. "Whatever it is, I know it'll be good for Haven House." He pointed. "Hey, look at all the birds. Seagulls and sandpipers and pelicans all over the place."

"Haven seems to be getting famous for our bird population. Last night I even saw a male Eastern screech owl." She looked at him expectantly, waiting for his surprised reaction, and she wasn't disappointed.

"No kidding? A screech owl? I haven't seen one around here since I was a kid."

"Well, they're hard to spot," she told him. "They're really well camouflaged by their color." She passed on her recently acquired knowledge but couldn't keep a straight face. "I never would have seen it by myself in a million years," she admitted, and told him about meeting Ronald Treadwell on the casino porch and getting shushed because she'd interrupted his bird-photography session. "He scared me out of my shoes," she said, "but I'm glad I got to see the cute little owl."

Ted's expression was serious. "Maureen, it might not be a good idea for you to be on the beach alone at night. There's a killer loose somewhere around here, you know."

"I know. I thought about that," she admitted. "Finn was with me."

"That's good," he said, "but a woman alone on a deserted beach at night is a vulnerable target."

Maureen didn't have a ready answer for such an obvious truth. Their warmups were almost complete anyway. *When in doubt, change the subject.* "Have you ever seen any mice in our kitchen?" she asked.

"Very rarely," he said. "Between Bogie and Bacall and the feral cats in the neighborhood, they keep the population down. Ready to run?"

"Ready," she said, glad the conversation about her safety was over and hoping they'd make good time this morning because she had so much to do. The wind had begun to pick up. It would be at their backs on the way to the dock sign, but they'd be running against it on the way back. She tried hard to think happy thoughts as she ran.

The run back to home base was, as she'd expected, a little harder, but the exertion, and her hair blowing back from her face instead of into her eyes, felt good. They arrived, simultaneously, at the Coliseum. Once they'd cooled down a bit and started for the boulevard, Ted asked a question. "What made you think about mice?"

She jerked a thumb toward the building they'd just left. "They serve food in there and they have mice. I figured Bogie and Bacall have always earned their keep, but I never thought about feral cats. Are there a lot of them around?"

"Yes. The woodlot out back is home to maybe fifty or so. We probably shouldn't feed them, but the girls—Molly and Gert—are softhearted, so I'm afraid we've spoiled a few of them."

"So the feral ones think they're pets now?"

"Not really. They'll never be truly tamed. But they've learned that we're good for the occasional handout. I'm worried about one of them, though. She's very pregnant, and I'm afraid she'll present us with kittens pretty soon."

"Will the kittens be feral too?" Maureen wondered.

Ted gave a short laugh. "Not if Molly has anything to say about it. She's determined to keep the kittens once they're big enough to leave the mama, if no predator animals get to them first."

"Oh, that's terrible. I hope they'll be safe." They'd reached the inn, and Maureen turned toward the side door.

"It's the circle of life, I guess." Ted headed for the opposite side of the inn. "But Molly and Gert have fixed up a little shelter with a soft bed in it," he said. "The mother cat seems to be more comfortable around people than most of the ferals. Molly thinks she might have been a housecat at some point. Anyway, it's in that alcove between the outside door and the back entrance to the kitchen. It's where the milkman from the old Florida Dairy in Tampa used to leave the bottles of milk. Gaudreau and Son volunteered to install a cat door on the outside entrance, so hopefully the mama cat will choose to have the babies in there."

Maureen hoped so too, but she had more on her mind than mice and kittens, and she still had a dog to walk. She hurried up the stairs, down the corridor, and into the suite and a welcoming and clearly anxious-to-go-out golden. After a super-quick shower she dressed in jeans, white shirt, and high-top Converse sneakers, grabbed the leash, hooked up Finn, noticed that the cats were safely snoozing in the tower, and hoped that Molly and/or Gert wouldn't try to give her a kitten, however cute it was.

Finn led the way down the stairs, out the side door, and onto the sidewalk in a hurry. He made it as far as the first lamppost to lift his leg, then proceeded at a more decorous pace toward the beach. Maureen felt guilty just walking the dog when she had so much else that needed doing, but at least dog walking provided some good solitary thinking space. She thought about the gift-shop décor, and about the retail vendor names she'd been saving for when it became time to stock the place. She could almost see the way it would look—and with Trent and Pierre on the job, the grand opening would be soon—maybe in time for Trent's birthday.

Finn was in for a short walk, just enough time for him to take care of business, and then she'd be back behind her desk working out the details of the Eddie Manuel Memorial Kingfish Tournament. She began to see light at the end of the tunnel and remembered Ted's comforting words: "*Things seem to turn up exactly when you need them.*" There was a new energy in her step when she cleaned up after Finn and began the walk home—right up until she spotted the police car parked in front of the inn, Frank Hubbard leaning against it. Another visit from Haven's top cop was exactly what she *didn't* need just then.

"Good morning, Ms. Doherty," was his more polite than usual greeting.

"Good morning, Officer," she answered. "What brings you here so early? One of Ted's breakfasts?"

"No. Maybe later. He's making those giant blueberry muffins." He lowered his voice. "I wanted to talk to you about last night. Did you get anything?"

"Get anything?" Maureen was sincerely puzzled. "What do you mean?"

"You know. From Treadwell. I didn't get much of anything out of talking to him, but I figure last night you must have had plenty of time to dig out whatever he knows about what went on over in the Forest the day that Eddie died."

Things clicked into place. Maureen couldn't suppress an eye-roll. "Been over to the Quic Shop already, have you?"

"No. I got it from Molly. You were out with the bird man, Doherty. Did you get some information? At least some feelings about the case?"

"How many times do I have to tell you, Frank?" She spoke slowly and distinctly, as one would talk to a child. "I'm not a detective. I don't have 'feelings,' as you call it. I happened to meet Mr. Treadwell on the beach. He was photographing a nocturnal owl."

"Sure. What did he say about Album, his boss?"

Maureen was silent for a moment, then put one forefinger under her chin in a thoughtful pose. "Let's see. He said he wondered if you had straightened out the credit card problem with Harvey." She switched hands, posed again. "Then *I* said that you planned to talk with Mr. Album again." She folded her arms. "Anything else?"

He made a grouchy face. "That's all you got?"

"Frank, I wasn't trying to *get* anything."

His eyes squinted up tight. "You going rogue on me, Doherty? Trying to do this all by yourself? Hanging around with fishermen? Let alone being dumb enough to wander around alone on the beach at night. You could be a target. There's a killer loose, you know."

The implied message, except about going rogue, was very similar to the warning Ted had recently given her, and Maureen knew for sure that they were both right. "Frank, really, I'm not the least bit interested in playing detective. I don't have time for it, but I promise you that if I overhear or discover some piece of information that might be helpful to you, I'll call you immediately." She reached over and touched his arm. "I'll be more careful about where I go at night too."

His facial features relaxed slightly. "Not everything bad happens at night, Doherty. You be careful, hear?" He bent and gave Finn a neck scratch. "Keep this guy around too."

"I will," she promised. "Ready for that breakfast yet? I'm buying."

Chapter 16

When Ted's giant muffins are on the menu, breakfast at Haven House Inn is served buffet style and included bacon and scrambled eggs, lots of hot coffee, all kinds of juices—including honest-to-goodness fresh-squeezed Florida orange juice. As usual, the event was well attended, and Maureen was pleased to see both Dr. Kim and Ronald Treadwell, as well as Trent and Pierre, among the guests. The two decorators took their muffins and coffee to go because they were anxious to get to work on the gift shop. Sam and George had been pressed into carpenter and painting duty too. Molly passed out butter and assorted jams and jellies at the buffet table. Gert, who admitted to already having eaten two muffins, manned the reservation desk while Maureen took a breakfast break.

Maureen and Hubbard sat together at a round table beside the one where Treadwell and the doctor faced each other across a loose arrangement of wildflowers. Several local folks completed that setting, while two of Haven's junior police officers, both in uniform, along with Aster Patterson and the Historical Museum director Claire Davis made lively conversation at Maureen's table. The topic was mostly about Eddie Manuel.

"Are you still feeding uniformed cops free coffee and muffins and doughnuts?" Hubbard whispered. The custom had started with the previous manager of the inn—whose aim had been to run the place out of business and sell it—and even though it cost money, Maureen had kept the tradition going because it was, well, tradition. She nodded. "Yes."

"Next time I'll wear my uniform," he declared, pulling his chair back so he'd be closer to the next table—actually back-to-back with Ronald Treadwell. Maureen began to make a retort, but Hubbard quickly put a finger to his lips. He was clearly listening to the conversation behind him. She saw him put a hand into his jacket pocket. *Was he possibly recording it?*

She wasn't about to sit idly by while one of her guests was recorded without his knowledge. She ignored his shushing motion. She'd been shushed enough at the previous night's involuntary bird-watching session. "Frank," she said, loudly enough for others at the table to hear, "I'm thinking about going to a lecture over at the Historical Museum about early Haven settlers. Can I just record it to listen to later, or do I need permission from the speaker? What's the law about that?"

"If it's a public speech, they don't expect privacy. You can record it. No problem." He spoke hurriedly, clearly still leaning back, listening to the conversations going on behind him.

Museum director Claire nodded agreement. "That's right," she said.

Maureen pressed further. "What if I called the lecturer on the phone later to ask a question. Can I record that?"

"Third-degree felony unless you get permission. Florida is a two-party state." He removed his hand from his pocket and tore the top from a pink envelope of sugar substitute, still looking grouchy. "You know I don't use the pink stuff in my coffee. When are you going to stock my brand?"

Properly chagrined for doubting his integrity, she promised to order the blue-enveloped sweetener immediately and made a silent vow to actually make time to attend the lecture she'd mentioned. Maybe the speaker would know something about the mysterious Charlotte Christine Trevaney, who might possibly have been the one who gave the inn to Penelope Josephine in the first place—and also might be the Goth-garbed, absinthe-drinking, after-midnight ghost haunting the nicely restored Haven House Inn bar. She concentrated on staying quiet and eating her blueberry muffin.

Aster Patterson was the first to leave the table, pleading that she had to open the shop and feed Erle Stanley. This gave Maureen the needed excuse to leave also. She wished everyone a good day, reminded them that the inn would be serving lunch, left a tip for Shelly, and headed for the comparative solitude of her office.

Maureen thanked Gert and left the office door ajar so that she could keep an eye on the lobby. She expected that when Hubbard finished his breakfast and/or finished eavesdropping on the next table, he'd probably want to talk to her some more about Eddie's murder. She assembled the various pieces of information—photos and art clips she'd prepared for the tournament brochure—determined to get it finished and ready for the printer before five o'clock.

Once the prints and papers were spread out on top of her desk, she began to realize that not all of the prizes were lined up. The bowls were ready and waiting to be polished and engraved, and although she had verbal commitment for a few other items, she wanted to have them actually in hand ahead of time. It would be bad form to promise a winner a three-hundred-dollar Penn Spinfisher VI spinning reel and then find that the donor had sold his last one and they were back ordered.

Maureen began to make the necessary phone calls. While she waited on hold for some or left voice messages for others, she couldn't resist opening the trunk once more, and with her free hand, moving some of the papers around. She'd just confirmed with Jimmy the jeweler that he'd drop off the promised gold-plated bracelet with "Love" spelled out in enameled signal flags for one of the women's prizes and arranged for Jimmy to pick up the three silver-plated bowls and the pitcher for engraving at the same time. She hung up the phone when she spotted a small blue card partially covered by a long-out-of-date Maas Brothers department-store catalog.

She reached for the card, then drew her hand back. It looked very much like two similar cards she had locked in a bureau drawer in her room. One had come from a Zoltar fortune-telling machine at an arcade at South of the Border, where she and Finn had stopped on their way to Florida. The second one, which also stated "Zoltar knows all," she'd found among some of Penelope Josephine's old Christmas cards. Each of them had carried cryptic, rhymed messages that had somehow proven to be accurate. Was she about to receive another message from a bearded, animated amusement-park mannequin, wearing a turban and waving his hand over a plastic crystal ball?

This one was different. The heading didn't say "Zoltar." It said "Grandmother's Prophecies." She read the verse at the top of the card aloud.

> *Do your bills get you down?*
> *Do they make you fret and frown?*
> *Despair not, my own fair one*
> *Your battle against them will soon be won.*

Looking around to be sure nobody had heard her, she read the rest of the card silently. "You'll soon find a change for the better in your financial affairs. This'll make you very happy indeed. You have a strong driving power within you, that may sometimes exhaust those about you. You are very easy tempered, slow to get angry, but also slow to forgive. Someone close to you has caused you some worry, but I see no cause to worry about that person in the future. You will be invited to take a short trip which will bring you happiness."

The message was followed by a series of numbers: "2-15-27-37-52-53"

Maybe I should play those in the next Lotto game.

This looks as if it came from an old-fashioned penny arcade fortune-telling machine, she decided, and googled "Grandmother's Prophecies." Sure enough, the site showed a 1930s coin-operated version with a gray-haired grandma wearing a shawl and pearls dispensing advice instead of the bearded, turbaned Zoltar. The site also contained a picture showing several of the cards—including the one she'd just found in Penelope Josephine's trunk. *So this isn't some weird message meant for me. There must have been thousands of them printed. But maybe I'll play those Lotto numbers, just in case.*

Relieved that the blue card didn't deserve being locked up with the Zoltar messages, she tossed it into her top desk drawer, closed the trunk, and returned her full attention to gathering prizes for the upcoming tournament. A few calls later, satisfied that the offered gifts were guaranteed to be secure, she returned to the lobby desk in time to see Hubbard emerging from the dining room with Ronald Treadwell at his side.

An odd couple for sure.

"Hello there, Doherty." Hubbard's tone was unusually friendly. "Ron here is going to take a ride over to the Forest with me to meet up with his boss. We're going to get this credit card thing straightened out."

Maureen knew that, as far as Haven House Inn was concerned, there was no "credit card thing" to straighten out. Ronald Treadwell's company card was perfectly valid. Assuming that Hubbard knew what he was doing, and regretting her earlier momentary doubt in his professionalism, she didn't say so. She offered the usual "Have a good day," and wondered for a fleeting second if Hubbard was the "someone close who'd caused her some worry."

The photographer touched the camera slung around his neck. "I'd never pass up a chance to visit a bird sanctuary for any reason!"

She nodded and smiled and watched them leave.

Chapter 17

It was shortly after noon when Ronald Treadwell arrived in the lobby again. Frank Hubbard wasn't with him, but a gray-haired, well-tanned man, with a neatly trimmed beard and horn-rimmed glasses Maureen hadn't seen before, was. "Ms. Doherty," Treadwell said, "I'd like you to meet my editor, Harvey Album. I got involved in taking pictures and Officer Hubbard had to leave, so Mr. Album kindly offered to drive me back here."

Album held out his hand and Maureen shook it. He had a good grip. She figured that Album might be a still-buff sixty. "How do you do, Ms. Doherty. My top photog here has been telling me great things about your inn. Do you have a room available for tonight?"

"I do," she said. "Would you like a room or a second-floor suite? I have either one available."

"Oh, a room something like the one Ronnie has will do me fine," he said. Maureen wasn't surprised at the choice of the lower-priced accommodation, remembering Treadwell's observation that his boss was "thrifty." She quoted him a price and accepted the *Watching Birds* credit card. "Is it okay if I park my van in your parking lot out back?" he asked.

"Yes. Of course. Shall I send a houseman to help with your luggage?"

"No luggage, hon," he said." I travel pretty light."

Maureen cringed inwardly at the "hon," but smiled and handed him the room key. "Lunch is being served in the dining room now, if you're hungry." She offered him a menu. "Here are today's specials."

Album studied the menu for a long moment, then turned to his companion. "What do you say, Ron? Shall we go dutch on some lunch after I check out my room?" The two disappeared into the hallway beyond the brochure rack while Maureen considered that renting a first-floor room for one night on a credit card she knew was good was certainly better than nothing. The regular lunch crowd had begun to arrive, so Maureen remained at the reception desk greeting patrons and answering questions, pleased by the number of people who'd made lunch at the inn a regular habit. *Ted's cooking is the main reason we're staying afloat during the slow times*, she told herself.

Trent and Pierre had been at work on the gift-shop-to-be with George's help for most of the morning, and Maureen had been told not to peek until they were ready to show her the result. Gert emerged from the kitchen and carried lunch out to them, explaining that the boys didn't want to take the time to change into "proper" clothes for the dining room. Gert, not known for her ability to keep a secret, returned and gave Maureen a whispered report on the progress of the new space.

"They've taken that big bureau thing apart," she said, heavily mascaraed eyes wide. "You could never tell what it was in the first place. They've made shelves in the biggest boxy part of it, and then they hung some bureau drawers with their bottoms on the wall to put more things in. And you're going to love the paint colors they've picked, and—"

"Don't tell me anymore," Maureen interrupted. "I'm supposed to be surprised!"

"Oh, okay, but it's going to be so cute. Have you ordered things to go out there yet?"

"Not yet," she admitted. "I guess I'd better start getting some merchandise. How many shelves do you think are in the boxy part?"

"Three, I think," Gert said, "and wait 'til you see the front of the counter where the cash register will be. They made it out of a beautiful carved door hung up sideways. It's going to be prettier than any of the shops I remember from when I worked in Vegas."

"Shhh." Maureen put a finger to her lips. "Don't tell me any more. Maybe I'll start an order for some beachy merchandise today. And maybe I'll have lunch to go too, if you don't mind, Gert. Could you bring me a BLT and a sweet tea?" The sweet tea was a habit she'd picked up in Florida, along with an unexpected fondness for cheddar cheese grits.

Harvey Album and Ronald Treadwell returned and headed for the dining room just as the elevator stopped and Dr. Kim, elegant in an off-the-shoulder white silk blouse and colorful flowered palazzo pants, stepped into the lobby, spoke a pleasant "good afternoon" to the two men as they passed, and approached the desk. "Who is that fellow with Ronald?" she asked. "I know him from somewhere, but I can't place it."

"He's Ron's boss, the editor of *Watching Birds* magazine. His name is Harvey Album."

"Hmmm." Dr. Kim looked thoughtful. "That doesn't ring any bells," she murmured. "Oh well, it'll come to me. I'm bad with names but good at faces."

Maureen returned to her office, the door to the lobby still ajar. With the prizes to be awarded for the various winning categories of kingfish nailed down and photos of the actual articles themselves received from the donors via email, writing the copy and selecting photos and art for the advertising brochure and newspaper advertising moved ahead nicely. She spread her notes and photos and write-ups of other tournaments on her desktop.

Gert, bearing a tray, gave a dainty knock at the office door. "Here's your lunch, Ms. Doherty. It looks like you don't have room on your desk and the top of that old trunk is too curvy to balance it on. Where do you want me to put it?"

"Wait a sec, Gert." Maureen stood, gathered the materials, and put them into one of the hundreds of manila folders Penelope Josephine had provided for the inn. "I'll just stash this stuff into the trunk so it'll be right here beside me when I finish." She lifted the curved lid, and placing the folder on top of the trunk's crowded contents, closed it.

Looking at the tray—the perfectly plated, carefully garnished sandwich with ripe red tomato slices, crisp lettuce, and crunchy bacon all visible between the slices of her favorite toasted Italian bread, beside the frosty glass of iced tea, displayed on the absolutely clear desktop—brought an unexpected, audible, sigh of relief.

Everything is going to be all right. The kingfish tournament brochure is almost ready to go. The gift shop is nearly complete, and there's surely enough money in the inn's account to begin modestly, carefully, thriftily stocking it.

Was she beginning to believe that 1930 "Grandmother's Prophecy"? She took a bite of the BLT, a sip of sweet tea, leaned back in her chair, and recited to herself the cheerful ditty she'd already memorized.

> *Do your bills get you down?*
> *Do they make you fret and frown?*
> *Despair not, my own fair one*
> *Your battle against them will soon be won.*

Why not believe it? she asked herself. *As soon as I finish this lovely lunch and finish getting the tournament brochure ready for the printer, I'll begin ordering merchandise for my new shop.* Putting the tray, plate, and empty glass on the floor under her desk, she retrieved the folder from the trunk, and resisting the temptation to delve further into Penelope Josephine's paper hoard, closed the lid firmly.

Time passed quite pleasantly as she worked. Creating advertising for her inn, designing menus, and putting together the celebrity-themed guest rooms had been a fun part of inn ownership for Maureen, and she'd found that she was good at it. As the layout for the Eddie Manuel Memorial Kingfish Tournament came together, she became more confident about the event itself—not just because it could be beneficial to the inn's bottom line, but perhaps, even more important, it would provide a fitting memorial for Eddie Manuel, one that he surely would have liked, one that his daughter would appreciate, and one that she hoped would become an annual Haven celebration.

When the job was finished, read, reread, and reread again, she decided she wanted another pair of eyes to look it over. She buzzed Ted's kitchen phone. "I have the tournament brochure ready—I think. If I bring it out there, will you take a look at it before I send it to the printer?"

"Sure. Come on out and take a break with me. I just made a fresh pot of coffee, and Aster dropped off a big plate of cookies."

Maureen picked up the tray of dishes from under the desk, slipped the new layout into a fresh folder, put the dog-eared BACK IN FIVE MINUTES sign on the reception desk, and cut through the dining room to the kitchen. She joined Ted in his tiny so-called office in the corner. He'd already pulled an extra chair up to his desk, poured her coffee, and positioned the plate of shortbread cookies in the center of his desk. She put the tray beside the dishwasher and sat beside him. "I hope you'll like it." She picked up her coffee mug and one cookie and handed him the folder. He smiled his great smile and opened it.

Chapter 18

Ted took his time. Her coffee was nearly finished and the cookie was gone when he looked up. "I wouldn't change a thing," he said. She knew he meant it.

"It's going to work, isn't it? I mean people are going to come to Haven and actually pay to fish for the kingfish and to stay at Haven House and eat in our dining room." Even as she spoke, she believed her own words. "Thanks so much, Ted," she said. "I needed your encouragement—and thanks for the coffee and cookie too." She stood, turned to leave, and had to fight an urge to kiss him. "Gotta go. I left the five-minute sign on the desk." She hurried away before she was tempted to do something dumb.

Back in the lobby, she pushed the green door open and stepped onto the porch to see if Sam was available to make a quick trip to the printer's. He wasn't at his usual post, but Molly was. "Sam's still around the corner there, working on your new shop. You're gonna love it," Molly declared. "Why not go take a peek at it? Say you have to tell Sam something."

Why not indeed? She *did* need Sam to get the layout to the printer ASAP. *Maybe*, she rationalized inwardly, *I could stand outside the door and call for Sam, and only take the tiniest peek at the inside—just an instant to get an impres-*

sion. She thought for a second about Lorna. *Just to get the essence of the place.*

She did it. Maureen stood about a foot away from the partially open door of the gift-shop-to-be. A show window had been framed in, but brown paper covered the glass. She smelled fresh sawdust and paint and heard the sound of an electric drill and the click of what might be one of those pneumatic nail guns. "Sam," she called. "It's Maureen Doherty. Could you come out here for a minute? I need you to do an errand. It won't take long."

The door swung open. Wide. "Yes, ma'am. What do you need?" She looked past Sam. It was only a glimpse—the tiny peek she'd promised herself. She couldn't help thinking of Howard Carter's exclamation on getting his first sight of Tutankhamun's tomb. "Wonderful things!"

"Do you have time to deliver something to the print shop for me?" she asked, scanning the scene behind him, noting the amazing carved door turned sideways on the front of a counter. She saw Trent attaching antique brass hinges to a matching door, with a narrow space above and below it, providing an entrance to a dressing room. There were three broad shelves within the "big box" Gert had described, and the bureau drawer shelves on the wall were lined with photos of vintage bathing beauties. There were hooks on one wall, fashioned from elegant drawer pulls, for hanging dresses or shirts. The paint colors Gert had said she was going to love were the beachy tones of tans and blues and grays.

"Sure. Give me a minute to wash my hands and I'll see you in your office," Sam said, and pulled the door shut.

She'd only had a peek, but it was enough. "Wonderful things," she whispered to herself as she retraced her steps across the porch and into the lobby. Feeling only the smallest pang of guilt, she was pleased to have at least an idea of how much display space she'd need to fill with merchandise in order to get the new shop started. She'd retained the phone numbers of many of the wholesalers she'd done business with back in Boston. She'd order some Haven T-shirts first. She knew they were available from a St. Petersburg firm. She'd get some Haven Inn shirts later, maybe with a picture of the inn on them. Shirts would go on one of the shelves in the main cabinet. There'd be room there for beach towels too. She already had names and numbers of local candy wholesalers who specialized in the old-fashioned penny-candy sorts of confections. She'd been planning for those for quite a while. Penelope Josephine's hoard had boasted several large glass candy jars that Ted used sometimes for small individual packages of nuts or boxes of raisins. She'd liberate those from the kitchen, sure he wouldn't mind. She was still on friendly personal terms with wholesalers of the best sportswear lines and knew she could get good buys and fast shipment from them. Besides all that, there were some local craftspeople who'd be happy to have their goods on display in such a beautiful venue.

Back in her office, door ajar, she picked up the phone and began the ordering process. She'd have thirty days to pay for most of it, and with all the confidence in the world, she used the Haven House Inn credit card.

When Sam appeared, obviously freshly showered, dressed in jeans and Tampa Bay Rays T-shirt, she handed over the folder, complete with written instructions regarding dimensions, paper stock specs, and ink-color preference. "Please tell him I'd like them as soon as he can manage, like maybe this afternoon, and to call me with any questions."

"This is for the fishing tournament, right?" he asked. "Everybody's talking about it already. The guys down at the L&M Lounge say they'll be chartering a couple of boats just for the regular customers."

"No kidding? That's great," she said. "That means the town is already getting excited about it. This afternoon I'll get press releases into the area newspapers and travel sites and maybe we'll get some action in the reservations department."

"Sounds good. Been a little too quiet around here lately." He held up the folder. "I'll take good care of this!" She assured him that she was sure that he would, hastily prepared the press release, and blasted it to all the likely outlets she could think of. It was with a sense of a day's work well done that she resumed her place at the reservation desk.

She was just in time to see Ronald Treadwell and Harvey Album enter the lobby. Treadwell carried the large duffel bag that Sam had complained about earlier and his camera was slung over his chest. Album carried a briefcase. "We're heading for the Forest. Just grabbing a few pictures when the afternoon light is pretty, and taking some notes about bird species."

"Would you like to come with us?" the photographer asked. "It'll just be a short trip." Maureen paused before answering. Was this invitation for a short trip the one the mechanical grandmother had prophesied would make her happy? "It's one of the best places around to see lots of peacocks."

The promise of seeing close up the colorfully plumed birds with their iridescent feathers magnificently fanned made the decision for her. "It sounds like fun," she said. "Could you gentlemen wait just a moment so I can try to find someone to fill in for me here?" It didn't take long to find a reservation desk stand-in. Shelly volunteered immediately and happily. The young woman put in all the hours she could at the inn to help pay off her student loan. Maureen looked down at her own jeans, cotton shirt, and high-tops, found the outfit adequate for a short trip, arranged with Gert to walk Finn if she wasn't back by four o'clock, and followed the birdwatching team out to the rear parking lot.

Album's converted van was a study in efficiency. It was long, black, and sturdy looking. It reminded Maureen of the one the medical examiner used. Harvey slid into the driver's seat while Ron held the rear door open for Maureen, then climbed into the front passenger side. There were two rear seats, and the rest of the space had been converted into a small but neat and tidy camper. Treadwell's duffel bag was on the floor. There was a narrow air mattress with pillow and quilt, a Yeti cooler, an alcohol stove, and two folded beach chairs. A wooden box held folded clothes and another held pans and plastic dishes. *No wonder he claims to travel light*, Maureen thought. *He has everything he needs right here.* It made her wonder why he'd chosen to pay for a room at Haven House.

Maureen recognized the winding county road leading to the Forest. Harvey swung the van into a space close to the edge of the dense tree line, got out of the front seat, and quickly released a rolled-up awning on the side of the van while Ron opened her door. Harvey pulled an old-fashioned, green-handled garden rake from a long container on the roof rack and proceeded to clear away fallen leaves on the ground beside the van, then bent close to the ground, peering carefully at the grass. "Damned peacocks poop everywhere," he grumbled. She stepped out and Ron pulled the beach chairs from beside the rear seats, flipped them open, and put them under the awning, commenting quietly, "Harvey likes everything just so. He carries a rake and a hoe and everything to keep things neat around him." She remembered Hubbard saying that the converted van had been legally parked there earlier and the area was litter free, so none of the activity was surprising. What was surprising was the Audi with Massachusetts plates parked nearby.

"That's Kim Salter's car," Maureen said.

"Is she a birdwatcher too?" Ronald wondered. "I could tell she's really smart."

"She sure is. I suppose she has a lot of interests," Maureen told him. "But I think she's here to see the Haven Indian mounds. She took the guided tour earlier, and she must want another look."

"Not much to see," Harvey offered. "Couple of bumps on the forest floor is all. Contractors dug it all up back in the twenties, I heard."

"I heard that too. They must have not known what they were digging up. Just shells, I understand."

"Yeah. Those tours are just something to amuse the tourists who don't know any better." His tone was defiant. "Anything to make a buck. Oh, you must know that. Your business depends on those suckers, doesn't it?"

Maureen could only gasp at the rudeness of his remark. She realized right away that the man, however insufferable, had been her transportation on this "short trip," and that she faced a long walk back to the inn if she wanted to get away immediately. *If this had been a dinner date, I would have climbed out the ladies' room window to get away from this jerk*, she thought. She was encouraged by the sight of the Audi. *If I can locate Kim in the Forest, I'll just hitch a ride home with her.*

Refusing to dignify the "suckers" remark with an answer, she addressed Ron. "Are you expecting to get pictures of any particular birds today besides peacocks?"

"Oh, I have more than enough peacock pictures. But one of my spotters says there's a nest of newly hatched baby ospreys in a tree over near the beach side." There was excitement in his voice. "It won't be easy to get close enough to them, but it's worth a try. If it's too difficult for me, Harvey can do it with his drone."

"Forget about that idea, Ronnie. This could be a cover shot," Harvey said. "You put your tree-climbing gear in the van already, so climb the damned tree and get it."

The photographer didn't reply, but pulled the bag from the van and opened it.

Since moving to Florida, Maureen had often seen osprey

nests at the tops of very tall telephone poles or streetlamps and even special platforms designed for the birds to build on. Climbing a tree of that height could be dangerous to life and limb, she realized, to say nothing of how the very large mother osprey—with her hooked beak, sharp claws, and two-yard wingspan—might feel about it. "It's a good thing Ron is a licensed arborist," she said. "He'll know how to do it safely."

Harvey shrugged. "Safely shmafely. Just so he gets the damned shot before the stupid birds grow up. Like right now. I have a publication deadline."

By then Treadwell had donned a helmet, a harness around his chest, and tall boots and shin protectors that reminded Maureen of the ones hockey players wear, except that these had short, pointed blades on them that flashed silvery in the sunlight. Without comment, he took a smaller, bright-yellow bag from the duffel and removed a neatly coiled rope, which he slung over one arm. "Ready," he said, and moved toward the gate.

Maureen tried to lighten the mood. "June must be time for all kinds of hatchings," she said. "Molly is watching and waiting for new kittens from one of the feral cats who live near the inn."

"All cats are pests," Harvey observed, who, having ex-changed his loafers for tall, sturdy-looking boots, opened a small gate bearing a sign saying PARK CLOSES AT SUNSET and led the way into the Forest. Ron and Maureen followed him onto a dirt path between the trees. Observing the change in footwear, she whispered to Ron, "Is it wet in there? It hasn't rained lately."

"Dry as a bone," he whispered back with a hint of a smile. "Those are his snake boots."

"Snakes?" She'd never thought about snakes in the Forest. "What kind of snakes?"

"Rattlers, I guess," he said. "He doesn't like snakes. I've

tramped through there plenty of times and I've never seen or heard a rattler. There may be some harmless black snakes, but nothing poisonous that I've ever seen there. Don't worry about it."

Trying not to worry about snakes and glad at least of her own high-tops, she followed the two men, now firmly convinced that this wasn't the happy trip the grandmother had promised and determined to make the fastest, most graceful exit she could manage.

"I'd been planning to take that Indian mound tour the Historical Museum offers," Maureen said, loudly enough so that both of her companions could hear her, "but as long as we're already here, can you show it to me?"

Harvey answered. "Sure. We go right by it on the way to the beach. If I didn't point it out to you, you'd walk straight past it without noticing that it was there. Like I said, it's a couple of bumps on the forest floor. No big deal."

"Thanks." She decided to go along with his story. "Then I won't have to take time away from running my inn to take a tour."

Harvey indicated a narrow path to the left of the one they were on. "It's right down this way, if I remember correctly. There's a sign somewhere around here that says some explorer landed here back in the fifteen hundreds."

"Panfilo de Narvaez," Ron offered.

"How'd you know that?" Harvey demanded.

"I read the sign," was the simple answer.

"Yeah. Well, anyway, here we are. There's one of your mounds." Harvey pointed. Maureen would have described it as more than a bump. It was covered with green grasses and native wildflowers and stood around twelve feet high, but it covered a broad area so it didn't look very tall. "The other one is just beyond this one." He pointed again. "It's a little taller. Go ahead and look if you want to. Just stay on this road to catch up with us. We have to grab a shot of that osprey tree while the sun is still high."

Once again aware of the possibility of snakes, walking carefully and resisting the urge to whistle a tune, Maureen moved along a path that seemed to have been made by many feet tramping through the grass. She paused more than once to admire a boy peacock showing off his fine feathers. Ron had been right about the peacocks. They strolled around as though they owned the place—and maybe, in a way, they did. The second mound was much taller than the first one—probably over a hundred feet tall and spread out in a wide circle. She'd begun to walk around it when a voice called her name. "Maureen! I'm up here."

"Kim! Is that you?" She shielded her eyes. Dr. Kim was halfway up the side of the mound.

Chapter 19

The archaeologist began to descend the sloped, grassy hill. "What are you doing wandering around out here all alone?" she called, and slid down the gradual incline upright, landing on her feet. Always mindful of Lorna's interest in the doctor's wardrobe, she decided that she could describe today's carefully tailored khaki outfit as Indiana Jones meets Balenciaga, with knee-length shorts, snug-fitting jacket, with a tasteful hint of cleavage, and boots not unlike Album's, but ever so much sleeker.

Maureen hurried to her side, explaining how she happened to be there—and that she'd arrived in Harvey Album's van. "I'm so glad to see you, Kim," she said, meaning it sincerely. "I saw your car, and I've been hoping I'd find you and be able to hitch a ride home."

"Of course you can. I've been taking measurements. The ground has shifted some since the last dimensions were posted by a colleague," the woman explained. "I'm just about finished here."

"I'll have to catch up with Harvey and Ron and tell them what I'm doing," Maureen told her, "so they won't think I'm lost in the woods. They've gone over to the beach side so Ron can get pictures of some baby osprey chicks."

"Osprey chicks? How wonderful." Dr. Kim tucked a tape

measure and notebook into a low-slung leather waist-pack. "I'll come with you." She fell into step beside Maureen. "Have you seen the mounds before?"

"I never have," Maureen admitted, "and if I hadn't been told what they were, I'd have walked right past them."

"Most people would, and it's probably a good thing." Kim frowned. "Mounds all over America have been robbed of their contents. We're lucky that these are so close to a road on one side and a beach on the other, besides being a bird sanctuary and a county park that closes at sunset. This place is visited fairly regularly, so robbers would have to be both bold and lucky to get away with disturbing either mound without being seen."

Maureen could tell that they were close to the beach because she heard the sound of Jet Skis. *I wonder if they're blue with white letters?* "It might be fun to get here by boat or Jet Ski too. Have you tried it?"

"Not yet. Maybe we should rent one of those two-person skis and try it together someday," she said. "Want to?"

"I'd try to make time for that. I have the fishing tournament to run this month, though. How long do you plan to stay in Haven?"

"This trip is actually pretty open-ended," she said. "I'm scheduled to do several speaking engagements in southwest Florida, and Haven is within easy driving range of all of them."

"So you'll stay with us for a while longer?" Maureen was hopeful.

"If my suite will still be available," Kim said. "The fishing tournament will bring lots of guests, won't it?"

"That's kind of the point of it," Maureen admitted. "Yes, of course the suite is yours for as long as you want to stay."

"I'm glad I don't have to move. I'd miss the Joe DiMaggio photos. Do you think Marilyn might have stayed here with him?"

"It's possible. We know she was here in the area at the same time he stayed here in 1961."

Kim lowered her voice and looked around, even though they were quite alone. "I'm asking because sometimes I swear I can smell Chanel Number Five in the bedroom."

"Marilyn's favorite."

"Right. If I believed in ghosts, I might think your inn is, well, a little bit haunted."

A little bit?

"Even so, it makes a really good story," Maureen faked a laugh. "It's still a popular scent. Maybe one of the cleaning girls wears it."

"I suppose so." She looked wistful. "I like to think it's Marilyn, though."

So do I!

They'd reached the beach. Maureen was surprised by the number of people gathered there. A long narrow pier extended into the water at one end of the sandy expanse. There were a few small boats tied to the pier, and a pair of kayaks and one of the blue-and-white Jet Skis were pulled up onto the sand. She saw intermittent patches of sea grapes, a healthy-looking row of sea oats, and several palm trees. She spotted Harvey and Ron along with a small crowd of people all looking up into the branches of a tall slash pine at the edge of the forest. Maureen pointed. "They must have found the osprey nest."

The doctor shaded her eyes, squinting against the sudden brightness, then suddenly stopped walking. "I remember," she said. "CSU. Chico, California. 2004. He was there."

"Who was there? Ron Treadwell?"

"No. The other one. Harvey Album. I gave a talk there at the Museum of Anthropology on the Mechoopda Indian culture. I was fresh out of graduate school. He was there. He asked a lot of questions. That's why I remember him."

"Do you think he knows who you are?"

"I wouldn't be surprised. My hairstyle was different back then, but I'm sure he'd recognize my name anyway." She brushed her hair back from her face in a nervous gesture. "I'm sort of, maybe, a little bit famous in my field. I'm a licensed archaeologist in several states."

"Officer Hubbard is interested in him," Maureen said. "I'm not sure exactly why, but I think it has something to do with the Indian mounds."

They'd resumed walking toward the pine tree. "I think it does too," Kim said. "His questions back then were about the Mechoopda mounds—like what might have been in them, and had they ever been disturbed by robbers. But if there had ever even been any Mechoopda mounds, and if they'd been robbed, they were all long gone by then anyway. But his questions back then have stayed in my mind. I remember thinking that he might have been trying to find out how to contact the robbers—or the buyers."

"Now he's here and he seems to know an awful lot about Haven's Tocobaga mounds," Maureen offered.

"He was at least twenty years younger then. Now his main interest is birds, of course." She spoke firmly. "I mean, he edits a bird magazine and it seems that he's maintained a casual interest in Native American culture. Let's join them and look at the osprey nest." Kim stepped out ahead of Maureen. "Then we should get going for home if you're going to make it back in time for Finn's four o'clock walk."

"He'll like that," Maureen said. "And I have a feeling that Trent and Pierre may be ready to let me have an official look at the new gift shop."

"They're certainly excited about it. Trent says that with the wonderful armoire in it, it looks even better than the original sketch he made for you."

"I can hardly wait to see it full of merchandise. I've already begun ordering," Maureen admitted.

"I have some connections to the Seminole Tribe," Kim

said. "They make some wonderful Native American crafts. Had you thought of stocking a collection of them?"

"I hadn't, but I should have. Do you have phone numbers?"

"Sure do." They moved toward the people gathered beneath the many-branched pine. Maureen spoke to a woman at the edge of the group. "Can you see the nest at all from here?"

"No," came the answer. "But the mother bird flew away a few minutes ago, so we know it's up there."

"She's gone hunting for food for the babies," Kim said, sounding confident that she was right.

I doubt that Ron will even get a look at the bottom of the nest through all those branches, let alone a peek at the chicks, Maureen thought as they moved closer. "I see Harvey," she murmured, "but where is Ron?"

Kim tugged at her elbow and pointed. Ron, helmeted, harnessed, and camouflage suited, with his camera in hand, had shimmied halfway up a nearby palm tree, the slim trunk bending with his weight as skinny tall palm trees do. He'd apparently taken his boss's order seriously. A picture of the chicks was definitely a possibility. "I hope he gets the shot before mother osprey gets home," she said.

Chapter 20

The osprey tree had gathered quite a crowd. The people who'd been sunbathing had left their beach towels and folding chairs, the Jet Skier, kayakers, and boaters had secured their crafts, and most everybody had phones at the ready for pictures of the daring photographer who by then had nearly reached the fronds of the palm tree. Another foot and he'd almost surely be able to see into the nest. *Young Ronald is brave but not foolhardy. The multibranched pine tree would have been impossible, but he's found another way,* Maureen thought, just as the man leaned away from the palm, one arm around the skinny trunk, and lifted the camera with the other hand, arm outstretched at an impossible angle. There was a collective gasp from the crowd.

It seemed as if a long moment was frozen in time—then, as the photographer brought the camera back to his chest and the palm swayed back to its upright position, it seemed as though everyone exhaled at once—with relief. Ronald began to shimmy down the tree, carefully, inch by inch. "I hope he got good pictures of the babies," Maureen said.

"I'm sure he did." Kim clapped her hands. "Look at that smile!" The two women made their way to the foot of the palm tree, joining the others anxious to learn whether or not the semi-aerial shoot had been successful.

Ron happily shared the saved photos from his camera screen. Three little birds, eyes and beaks open, feathers in soft shades of pink and blue, sat among pieces of brown-and-white-speckled eggshells. "Those look like magazine cover shots to me," Maureen said. "I hope *Watching Birds* appreciates what a wonderful photographer they have."

Kim glanced at her watch. "This day has been even more fun than I'd expected it to be, but perhaps we'd better head for home if you're going to keep your date with Finn."

"Yes, I'm ready whenever you are," Maureen agreed. "I'll just let Harvey know I'm leaving."

"Here he comes," Kim said. The two watched as the editor of *Watching Birds* approached his tree-climbing photographer who was still sharing his photos with excited onlookers.

Album waved his hands at the crowd. "No free looks at the birds. You can buy the magazine if you want to see pictures! Scram. Treadwell, put that camera away and let's get going. You coming with me, Ms. Doherty?"

"No thanks, Mr. Album," Maureen said. "Dr. Salter will give me a ride."

"Okay. Good." He turned his back.

Maureen shook her head and Kim barely suppressed a giggle. "Real charmer, isn't he?" They stepped back into the cooling shade of the Forest. Maureen pushed her sunglasses up onto the top of her head, adjusting her eyes to the changing light. "It must be absolutely pitch-black in here at night."

"It must be," Kim agreed. "No wonder they close the gate at sundown. It's a nice quiet place for Mother Osprey to raise her babies." The two made their way along the cool, green, woodsy path, admiring the occasional passing peacock and commenting on the variety of trees and bushes they passed. The path circled the largest of the mounds, and Kim paused. "Hold on a sec, will you, Maureen? I need to check on something." The woman scaled the gradual slope with a few easy strides. "Odd," she said. "Quite odd." She moved gracefully down the incline and rejoined Maureen at the base. "I noticed a weed on the east side of the mound that I hadn't noticed before. White clover. There's a patch of it about a foot square. It has a shallow root system. It makes me wonder if the mound has been disturbed somehow in that spot."

"An animal burrowing?" Maureen wondered aloud.

"Could be. But many of the plants around the mound are rare, and yet they still survive after all this time, like marlberry and snowberry." She pointed to a tall, gnarled tree. "That live oak is over three hundred years old." They continued walking toward the parking area. "I picked a bit of the clover." She showed Maureen a plastic bag with bits of green in it. "I'll check with the county extension service about the weed. It's probably nothing."

"But the mound might have been disturbed somehow?" Maureen recalled Hubbard's recounting of the death of the Yankee named Sherman. He'd told her a mound had been disturbed back then.

"You know something?" Kim asked. "I've been thinking about Harvey Album. He was awfully interested in Indian mounds. I'd be really interested in just what old Harvey has been doing for the last twenty years—besides wearing glasses, getting gray, and growing a beard." The doctor's tone was thoughtful.

Maureen couldn't help thinking about those twenty years. *If Harvey was interested in Indian mounds in California in 2004*, she thought, *maybe he was interested in the mounds in Florida a few years earlier—like in June of 2000. I'm definitely going to tell Frank about this. If that counts as a "feeling," so be it!*

They emerged from the gate to the Forest path right behind Harvey Album's long black van, passed it, and headed for Kim's sweet Audi. "He keeps his area nice and neat,"

Kim observed, then laughed. "My mother always told me if you can't say something nice about somebody—"

"—don't say anything at all," Maureen finished the sentence. "I know. My mother taught me the same thing. You're right, though. Ron says he carries a rake and a hoe and everything he needs to keep his surroundings tidy. He seems like a very orderly type. His van is neatly organized. A place for everything and everything in its place."

Chapter 21

They reached the inn with time to spare before four o'clock. Maureen thanked Kim for the ride home, meaning the thanks most sincerely, considering the alternative transportation. Shelly agreed to stay at the desk until the night clerk arrived at five. *Okay. That's settled. Now, first things first,* Maureen told herself. *Take Finn for a walk, then call Frank Hubbard and tell him about the "feelings," even if they don't mean a darned thing. After that I'll definitely do a little more ordering for the new shop.*

The golden's happy doggy dance of greeting told her that he'd missed her and that it was surely time for a walk. She picked up his leash from behind the kitchen door. They took the stairs down to the lobby, passed the brochure rack and the guest laundry, then ducked out the side door. A peek onto the back parking lot told her that Harvey's van hadn't returned from the Forest yet. She and the dog hurried along the narrow path to the boulevard and headed, as usual, for the beach at the end of the street.

Finn gave a brief "woof" of acknowledgment to Erle Stanley, who was dozing on Aster's chair. Maureen thought she detected the scent of cookies baking from inside, and hurried on toward the Coliseum. The pleasant view of sand and water and the historic building was marred by the presence of a by now familiar vehicle. Frank Hubbard stepped from the Ford, almost as though he was expecting her.

Finn did his little prancing thing that he did when he saw someone he liked. "Hello, Frank," she said. "I was just about to call you."

He nodded, not changing his expression. "You went for a ride with Album but you came back with the doctor. Are you okay? What happened?"

It sounds as though he was worried about me!

"I'm fine. No problems. I simply don't like the man. I was really relieved to see Kim Salter there so I could bum a ride home."

"What's the doctor's connection to Album?"

"That's what I was going to call you about. She remembered where she'd seen him before—a long time ago in California." By this time Finn's prance had changed to an insistent pull on the leash. "Can you walk with me while I tell you about it? Finn needs his exercise."

Hubbard paused for barely a second before removing his shoes, carefully tucking a black sock into each one, and depositing them into the front seat of the Ford and locking it. "Let's go," he said, falling into step beside her. "You got a feeling?"

"The photographer you met at the inn, Ron Treadwell, was there to try to get pictures of some baby ospreys in a tree for the *Watching Birds* magazine," she began. "Kim told me that she remembered Album from somewhere—they met near an ancient Native American settlement in California back in 2004."

"Good job, Doherty," he said, limping a bit on the hot sand. "Indians again, right?"

"That's right. I thought you might want to know about it."

"If you're thinking what I'm thinking," he said. "Maybe Album's even been here in Haven before."

"I'm thinking that. He seems to be all about birds right

now, but he's camped awfully close to our mounds in the Forest."

"Anything else I should know?"

Maureen bit her lip, hesitant to mention details that Hubbard might find silly or irrelevant. "Well," she offered, "it might not mean anything, but according to Ron, Harvey is an absolute neat freak when it comes to the area around his van at the edge of the Forest. He keeps brooms, shovels, and rakes handy to police the area."

Hubbard didn't dismiss the idea. "I noticed that right away when I went there the first time. Not a blade of grass or a petal out of place. Thanks for the information, Doherty. Anything I can help you with?"

"I have a lot to do and a short time to do it," she said. "I need to know all about fishing licenses and local rules about bait and tackle and all that."

"All of your charter boat skippers are aware of the rules," he said. "Just ask one of them to fill you in."

"Good idea. Thanks, Frank. Maybe I'll ask Tommy Manuel."

"She's a good kid," he said. "Chip off the old block, like they say. Did I tell you they've made funeral plans for Eddie?"

"No. When and where?"

"Not a traditional funeral. Eddie wouldn't like that. The family and friends will scatter his ashes from the *Tightline*, then there'll be a 'celebration of his life.' That's what they call it. They've booked the Coliseum for next Wednesday afternoon."

That's two days before the tournament.

"A lot of his old customers who stayed at the inn have been asking about it. Is it okay if I let them know what's going on?"

"I'm sure it is. It'll probably be in tomorrow's newspaper anyway." He stopped walking, gave Finn a pat on the head, and jerked a thumb over his shoulder. "If that's all you've got, Doherty, I'll get back to work now. But remember, even something you don't think is important might be—well, important." He limped a few steps toward the white building in the distance, then turned back, facing her. "And, Doherty, be careful. We don't know exactly who we're dealing with here. But somebody, maybe somebody right here in Haven, is a killer."

Finn sat, ears alert, eyes bright, watched Hubbard's slow trudge back to the boulevard, then tugged on the leash, propelling Maureen toward the worn, familiar fishing sign. "Maybe if Tommy Manuel is around at the charter-boat dock, we'll talk to her about those fishing rules," she told him, "and I'll ask her if the restaurant can help out with some food for Eddie's celebration of life."

Tommy Manuel waved to Maureen from the deck of the *Tightline.* "Hi, Maureen. Hi, Finn. Glad to see you again. Come aboard."

Galley guy Alan stepped forward, opening the gate at the stern of the vessel, speaking an encouraging "C'mon, boy, you can do it," to a hesitant Finn while at the same time extending a helping hand to Maureen. *He's working toward that promotion to first mate,* she thought, thanking him and approaching Tommy.

"How are you doing, Tommy?" Maureen asked, concerned, knowing that the young woman was in mourning for her dad yet showed brave determination to keep his business moving forward.

"Keeping busy, thankfully." Tommy's smile was forced. "We had a half-day group this morning, and now we're getting ready for a last-minute night charter. I'd already sent the mate home, but these guys just want to go to the Forest. One of them is going ashore to take nighttime pictures of owls, and the other one just wants to cruise around the area and maybe drop a hook and try his luck at fishing. All they want from the galley is coffee."

"Owls?" Maureen asked, already guessing who'd booked the nighttime trip. "Are they magazine people?"

"Yes. Do you know them? The man I talked to said that there are several different species of owls in the Forest and they're looking to photograph and record a great horned owl and a screech owl and maybe, if they're lucky, a critter they call a burrowing owl."

"Interesting," Maureen said. "I asked because there's a photographer staying at the inn who's interested in owls and his boss is the editor of *Watching Birds* magazine. Their names are Ron and Harvey."

"Yes. Same guys. This will be an easy trip. We'll take the camera guy ashore, then just poke around fishing for a couple of hours." She looked at her watch. "They've chartered us from eight p.m. to eleven p.m. That means we leave the dock at eight and get back at eleven. So I hope they can get the owls to screech or hoot, or whatever owls do, in two hours or so."

"I've heard that the Forest closes at sunset," Maureen said.

"It does, from the county road side. There's a little gate there. But there's no way to block access from the water side, so sometimes people take their boats over there to have beach parties and such. The only rule is no fires and they have to leave it clean. The parks department people do regular monthly checks, and my dad kept an eye on it whenever he had a chance."

"Tommy, I don't want to interrupt your preparations for the nighttime trip. Just a couple of things. I'm trying hard to get the tournament set up properly and I'm trying to find a list of the rules I need to know—like about fishing licenses and the kind of bait and tackle that can be used. Frank Hubbard said charter boats have them. Do you?"

"That's an easy one. Dad was a stickler for following those

rules. He had them printed out for the passengers. I'll give you a copy."

"That'll be great. Also, I understand that you'll be having a celebration of life for Eddie at the Coliseum. Our restaurant would love to provide some refreshments for your guests—maybe some charcuterie boards and cookies—if you'd like us to do that."

"Oh, that's so generous of you. It would be appreciated." She motioned to the man. "Alan, would you get one of Dad's rule sheets for Maureen?"

"Glad to," he said, ducking back into the galley, "although I can recite them all from memory, you know."

Tommy laughed. "Alan is working hard toward that first-mate job," she said, "but it's hard to replace a man who can cook."

"Tell me about it." Maureen tucked the folded sheet into her back pocket as she and Finn started back toward home.

Chapter 22

Maureen and Finn hadn't quite reached the inn when she saw Trent and Pierre waving to her from the front steps. "There you are!" Trent called. "What took you so long? We're ready!"

"The shop is ready!" Pierre ran toward her. "We can hardly wait to show it to you! Come on!"

Her housekeeping staff had left their rockers and stood at the head of the stairs. Molly gave a sweeping one-armed "come on up" gesture.

"And there's a pile of boxes here waiting to be opened," George called. "Hurry up!" Kim Salter was there too, now in crisp all-white linen, displaying her newly acquired tan to advantage. Her handbag and shoes were black.

Lorna won't even have to adjust the colors this time.

Maureen dropped Finn's leash, following close behind the golden as he raced up the stairs and around the corner of the porch toward the open door of her new shop. That corner, with its neat wooden railing and strong pine floorboards, had not so long ago held for Maureen the terrible memory of a murdered man in a rocking chair. She approached the open door, where the lights of a new, small but brilliant chandelier illuminated the entrance, grateful that of all the ghosts haunting her adopted town, the spirit of that man had not lingered on her porch.

The tiny glimpse she'd taken earlier had not prepared her for the full impact of her new shop. Teary-eyed, she ran careful fingers over the carved doors that now formed the front of the sales counter and the door to the dressing room. A vintage brass cash register stood atop the counter, which had somehow been given a covering of real poured terrazzo—and a push on the dressing room door revealed the handsome bevel-edged mirror was now surrounded by a hand-painted trellis of pink hibiscus with a minute hummingbird hovering in one corner. The shelving in the cabinet and the artfully arranged bureau drawers on the walls awaited the contents of the stack of boxes stashed in the stockroom behind the dressing room. She could hardly wait to begin filling the shelves and hangers.

Jolene appeared with a silver tray of filled champagne flutes, followed by Ted, offering tiny finger sandwiches from one of Penelope Josephine's oblong cut-glass platters. Maureen, tears unabashedly flowing, raised her champagne flute in a salute to Trent and Pierre. "Thank you, my dear friends. This couldn't be any more perfect."

"Yes, it could," Trent said, meeting her glass with his. "Let's start filling it up with whatever's in those boxes."

"Good idea. I had to help the FedEx guy lug all these up the durn stairs," George grumbled. "We might as well empty this bunch before another pile arrives."

" 'Many hands make light the work,' " Molly quoted. "That's what my mother always said. Let's all help Maureen open them."

"Molly's mother was right," Maureen decided, when within an hour, Florida-themed T-shirts, flip-flops, and beach towels were neatly stacked on shelves, while dresses, caps, cover-ups, and handbags hung on the walls from a variety of brass and wrought-iron hooks, knobs, and pulls—most of the hardware cannibalized from pieces of Penelope Josephine's cast-off furniture. An assortment of costume jewelry yet to be arranged on seashells in a small glass aquarium—minus water—and the wall-hung bureau drawers awaited merchandise that hadn't yet arrived. To Maureen, the show window already looked like a colorful painting, full of textures and patterns with a sunshiny island vibe. The gift shop definitely looked ready for business—business that Maureen hoped would be forthcoming before much longer.

The evening dinner crowd had begun to arrive—mostly Haven local customers and one or two regulars from St. Petersburg or Clearwater. The open door to the almost-ready gift shop drew immediate attention. Ted and Jolene scooted back to the kitchen, but the prospective diners lingered, peeking into the door of the shop where Gert had taken a defensive position in the doorway, announcing to everyone, "We're not ready yet. Watch for the grand opening real soon, right, Ms. Doherty?"

"Right," Maureen agreed. "We're not fully stocked yet, and I need to learn how to operate that cash register, but we'll be open soon. Maybe," she added hopefully, "even by tomorrow. But right now"—like the Pied Piper, she moved around the corner to the front of the porch and pulled open the green door to the lobby—"it's time for dinner."

The sound of the player piano plinking out "The River Kwai March" in double-time sped the line along nicely, making Maureen wonder if the selection was in the normal rotation of tunes or if Billy Bedoggoned Bailey was being especially helpful. Kim Salter paused to tell Maureen that Marilyn's Chanel fragrance was definitely lingering in her suite and that it made her happy. Regular dinner guests Dick and Ethel stopped at the door, and Dick pointed to where the sun was low in the western sky. "Looks like it's going to be a pretty sunset," he observed.

The Forest gate closes at sunset, Maureen recalled. *Ron*

and Harvey what's-his-name will be getting ready to start on their nighttime owl-hunting cruise. She wasn't surprised that the two weren't among the evening's diners. Knowing of Harvey's thriftiness, she figured they'd found a less expensive place for their evening meal. She decided to skip the meal herself in favor of taking care of that jewelry display. Maybe she'd have a cheeseburger and a nice glass of wine at the bar later—maybe after Ted had finished in the kitchen and might have time to join her there. The thought brought a smile.

"Thanks for guarding the door, Gert," she said. "I think I'll go inside for a while and try to get acquainted with how things work."

"Like the cash register?" Gert asked. "I can show you that. There was one just like it at a bar where I worked in Vegas. I'll show you, if you want."

"Come on in." The two stood behind the counter. The machine was, Maureen thought, a thing of beauty; the entire brassy surface was embossed with garnishes and florals and border designs with the word "National" spelled out on the cash drawer. George had volunteered that he thought it must have been used in the inn back when it first opened almost a century ago. Gert was a good teacher and the mechanical workings were simple, once memorized. "The cash drawer is different from modern ones," Gert explained. "More sections. See, there're places for the bills, but there's room for more coins than we use now. She pointed to the separate compartments. "Pennies, nickels, dimes, quarters, half dollars, and silver dollars." Her eyes took on a faraway look. "Silver dollars," she said again. "Those were the days."

"Maybe tomorrow I'll get cash from the safe in my office and get it ready to work," Maureen said, "and we can figure out later how to use the extra coin spaces. Thanks for all your help, Gert."

"You're welcome. I'd better get back to the dining room

and help out." She patted the register. "Thanks for the memories."

Arranging the jewelry on seashells in the aquarium went quickly and Maureen was pleased with the result. With another admiring look around her new space, she turned out the interior lights, including the dainty chandelier, closed and locked the door, putting the key carefully into her back pocket beside the fishing rule sheet Tommy had given her. Rounding the corner to the front part of the porch, she realized that she was alone there, among the vari-styled rocking chairs. She sat in the nearest one, leaning back and enjoying the soothing motion.

I should take the time to do this more often. But I have so much to do. I should be in at my desk right now organizing those fishing rules for the tournament information packages. She looked toward the beach at the end of the boulevard where the sky, streaked with improbable shades of orange and purple and pink, promised a perfect Florida sunset. Her thoughts returned once again to her newest first-floor tenants and their expressed shared interest in observing and documenting the Forest's significant bird population. Her other new tenant, though, whose interest in the Forest was devoted to Haven's historic Tocobaga population, had brought up some conflicting views of the man called Harvey Album's reasons for being in Haven.

What my tenants do while they're here is none of my business, she told herself. *I'm an innkeeper . . . their host, not their parents. As far as I know, none of them are breaking any laws. I have no "feelings" about them, one way or the other—no matter what Frank Hubbard chooses to think.* She gave the floor a hard push with sneakered feet—rocking faster—and a lot less peacefully.

Hubbard's recent words of admonition replayed in her head. *"Even something you don't think is important might be important,"* he'd said. *"Be careful. Maybe somebody right here in Haven is a killer."*

She reached for her phone. "Frank? Harvey and Ron have charted Tommy's boat to take them to the Forest tonight to look for owls." Her conversation with Hubbard was brief. He asked for details, time, and place for the planned owl hunt and thanked her for the information, closing the call with "Anytime you get feelings like this about something, you call me, Doherty. Day or night. Good job."

"This has nothing to do with 'feelings,'" she mumbled into the phone, but he'd already ended the call. It was still too early for that cheeseburger at the bar and too late for a sit-down meal in the dining room. She returned to her original slow and easy rocking, enjoying once again the unexpected pleasure it brought. *Maybe I'll get a rocker for my bedroom.*

Glad that she'd shared the information about Harvey Album with Hubbard, she thought of Kim Salter's observation that Harvey had shown an interest in Native American culture back in 2004. That wasn't far removed from that unexplained death that had happened during the first Haven fishing tournament. Had that tournament filled the inn with visitors? She could check the guest registers easily enough and find out.

The chair was still rocking by itself when she raced into the lobby and dashed into the elevator. "I've got a feeling . . ." she whispered to herself as the door slid closed and she pushed the button for the second floor. The pipe smoke smell began immediately. "Reggie?" she questioned aloud. "You know the rules."

She watched, fascinated, as the ghost shimmered into sight. This time he wore the unmistakable uniform of the Royal Palace Guards, with a shaker hat so tall it touched the ceiling of the elevator. Her face must have conveyed astonishment. He removed the hat, his expression sheepish. "I was just trying it on. I want to tell you something. Those two blokes who have rooms on the first floor were talking in here this afternoon. I couldn't help overhearing. I told Lorna about it, and she said I needed to tell you."

"Harvey and Ron?"

"Yes, ma'am. They were arguing. The older fellow wants the younger one to help him get something out of Florida. 'It's not like you'd be doing anything illegal,' the one they call Harvey told the Ronnie bloke. 'You're just the bag man.' Ronnie doesn't want to do it, but he's risking his job if he doesn't cooperate."

"What are they planning to steal?"

"Sorry. I don't know. But whatever it is that Harvey's planning to nick, sounds to me like it's going to happen after dark tonight."

The elevator slowed, then bumped to a stop on the second floor. At the same time, the ghost dimmed to a misty glow, then disappeared completely as the brass door slid open, while the faintest hint of tobacco smoke lingered. Fortunately, there was no one in the second-floor corridor to observe either the odor or the glow.

Maureen was pleased that she'd already shared the information about the after-dark owl rendezvous planned aboard the *Tightline* with Hubbard. She hoped, though, that he'd be able to figure out for himself that the birdwatchers—at least one of them—planned to steal something. Relaying a hot tip about it from a dead Brit would have been awkward. She hurried down the corridor to the upstairs office and the old guest registers. She already knew that the unfortunate Everett Sherman had been a guest during the first annual Haven fishing tournament. Now she was interested in a couple of other names.

There were fresh vacuum cleaner marks on the room's Oriental rug, and the broad desktop showed evidence of a recent polishing. Having a dedicated housekeeping staff was one of the best parts of owning the inn. She made a silent vow to thank them more often as she pulled open the closet door. The neat red-and-black-leather-covered guest registers stood in an orderly row, identified by dates. She reached for the one marked 2000. The heavy book easily fell open to the page where she'd left a recent lunch menu as a marker.

Maureen began reading slowly and carefully through the pages dated from a week before the June 16 start of the tournament. Sherman had arrived on the fifteenth of the month. She already knew that he'd checked out—permanently—on the last day of the tournament, June 18. Unlike Sherman's bold signature, most of the guests had hurriedly scrawled names and addresses, automobile license numbers, and states they'd come from. A certain Harvey Album had checked into a single room on June 17, and checked out on the morning of June 19. A weird coincidence? Maybe. It was time to call Hubbard again. This was more than a feeling.

Her call went to his voicemail.

Chapter 23

"Frank?" She strained to keep any hint of anxiety from showing in her voice. "I checked the old guest register for names of people who stayed at the inn during that first fishing tournament—the one in 2000. The man who you said was murdered, Everett Sherman, was there, but so was a Harvey Album. . . ." She looked down again at the open register. "He registered with a Massachusetts license number and the home address he gave was unreadable. He checked in on the day before Sherman died and checked out the next day." She paused. "Frank, Harvey will be on Tommy's boat tonight."

Maureen closed the register leaving the old menu in place as a bookmark, then ran a finger over the number "2000" on the cover. Penelope Josephine had been the owner of the inn when the book was new. She'd been there when Haven's first fishing tournament happened. She'd put the blue-and-white card in her trunk. Had she planned to write about it in the book but never found the time to actually write? Had she known the two men—Sherman and Album—or had they just been nameless, faceless, short-term tenants to her? With a quick, impatient motion, Maureen shoved the register back into its place on the shelf.

That was then. This is now. She'd done what she could to

alert the proper authorities about Harvey's connection to both the year 2000 and the present, even though she hadn't passed on the ghost-gleaned information that a planned theft might be involved. Even without that bit of ghostly gossip, she knew that Frank Hubbard would make the same connection she'd already made. A decades-old cold-case murder might be close to being solved—but that several innocent people, at this very moment, stood in the killer's way. She thought about Kim Salter's observations about Harvey's interest in Native American artifacts. Tonight the same man who'd been in Haven when Everett Sherman's lifeless body had been found close to the Indian mounds was once again planning to visit the Forest where those same mounds were located and he'd be aboard the *Tightline*—whose owner's body Maureen had found on the beach. Tommy Manuel would be hosting a possible thief—and, she almost shuddered at the thought—a man who might be involved in her father's death.

Maybe Kim had some more information about Harvey that might be helpful to Frank—information that Kim didn't know could be important. Maureen adjusted her position behind the desk so that she faced the dining room door where she'd be sure to see Kim as soon as she stepped into the lobby. She had an unusually strong feeling of urgency about it, and wondered if this was one of those "feelings" Frank was forever talking about—and that she'd forever denied.

Maureen raised a hand and waved as Kim—white-linen suited, black accessorized, and stunning as always—left the dining room and approached the reception desk. "Good evening, Maureen," she said. "Did you work through dinner? It was delicious."

"I plan to grab a quick bite later, but if you have a moment, I need to talk to you about Harvey Album." Maureen leaned across the counter and lowered her voice. "I'm afraid he might be up to something—well, something really bad."

"That doesn't surprise me," Kim said. "Where can we talk?"

"Let's go into my office." Maureen indicated the open door behind her. "I can watch the desk from there." The two moved into the crowded space. "Have a seat"—she indicated the white wicker chair—"and forgive the décor. This room is pretty far down on the list for redecorating."

"I like the old trunk," Kim said.

Maureen smiled, remembering their earlier conversation about things their respective mothers had taught them. " 'If you can't say something nice,' " she began the old saying.

Kim finished it, laughing. " 'Don't say anything at all.' Now tell me about Harvey. I'm sure it isn't anything nice, is it?"

"Far from it," Maureen agreed, and phrasing things as concisely as she was able, she related what she'd learned about Harvey's whereabouts at the time of two separate unsolved murders. She added the information about the two men chartering Tommy Manuel's boat for a nighttime trip to the Forest—supposedly to look for owls. "I have some information from a confidential source—someone I trust—that Harvey and Ron are going there to steal something."

"Native American artifacts," Kim said. It was a statement, not a question.

"Exactly," Maureen agreed. "How do they do it?"

"It occurred to me that *somebody* might be trying to dig into the mound when I began to notice some grasses, weeds, even wildflowers, that don't belong there."

"You didn't tell anybody?"

"No proof. It was just a feeling. Those plants and grasses could well have grown there naturally. The place is full of birds. Sometimes they drop seeds onto the ground, sometimes the seeds are in their poop." She smiled. "I had a puppy when I was a kid who ate the whole insides of my Halloween pumpkin and the next year we had a crop of pumpkins growing in our backyard."

It was just a feeling. "Sometimes feelings are very important," Maureen told her. "How would somebody dig into the mound?" she asked again, "and what are they looking for?"

"It's not difficult to dig into comparatively small mounds like these. They contain mainly shells. Our indigenous forebears ate a lot of shellfish, and these mounds were largely made of the discarded oyster, clam, or other crustacean shells. But a digger might also find animal fossils, arrowheads, pieces of broken crockery, sometimes even bits of jewelry. It's illegal to take these things from the mounds, but they bring surprisingly high prices from some collectors." Kim gave a small, sad shake of her head. "Both of our mounds are big enough, high enough, to contain quite a lot of interesting finds. Some Florida mounds have turned up teeth from giant sharks and bones and teeth from giant panthers who once roamed the state. I've read that there were once armadillos living here that were as big as a Volkswagen."

"But it's absolutely against the law to dig here, right?"

"Absolutely. I understand that the county park department does regular checks from the road and that Eddie Manuel kept a watchful eye on it from the waterside," Kim reported. "Yet, when I keep seeing the grasses disturbed, I have to wonder if that's enough. So you believe that the unpleasant Harvey person is guilty of digging there, and that he's possibly guilty of—of something much worse? Have you told Officer Hubbard?"

"I've told him about my suspicions. I left him a message about Harvey being in Haven at the same time as *both* of the murder victims."

"And you say young Tommy will be taking the two men to the beach side of the Forest after dark tonight?"

"They'd chartered her from eight to eleven. Tommy says they hired her because they want to take pictures of owls. It makes sense, you know. They do represent a major wildlife publication," Maureen said. "The owls are nocturnal, for sure. They *could* be telling the truth."

"If Officer Hubbard shows up, though, obviously they won't attempt anything illegal, they'll actually come away with pictures of owls," Kim reasoned. "So they'll just postpone the robbing until another day—or night."

"Would they have tools with them, though? Things a policeman would recognize as—well, as burglar tools?" Maureen wondered aloud.

"Probably not," Kim said. "It's not like safecracking or housebreaking. Just plain old garden tools like trowels and claw rakes and shovels. Maybe a sifter of some kind."

"Harvey has a lot of tools in his van," Maureen remembered. "He's very fussy about his parking area. He sweeps and rakes up every tiny bit of sand or rocks or any kind of litter around his area."

Kim glanced through the open door to the lobby where a few of the departing dinner guests stood in small groups. She leaned closer to Maureen and whispered, "If they do manage to steal something, they won't carry it back to the charter boat, will they? They'll probably stash it in Harvey's van sometime before they get back to the dock at eleven, won't they?"

"I guess so. Wouldn't you like to be a fly on the wall—or an owl in the tree—when they actually do it?" Maureen giggled at the idea.

"I know. It would be crazy—but fun." With an elbow on Maureen's desk, and a fist under her chin, Kim struck a pensive pose. "Wouldn't it?"

"Being an owl?"

"No. Being there when they do it."

Chapter 24

It was, of course, a crazy idea. Maureen knew it. They both knew it. But there they were, a few minutes before nine o'clock, parked under a tall stand of bamboo in Maureen's green Subaru—which would surely attract less attention than Kim's sweet wheels—on the old county road a hundred or so yards beyond the Forest parking lot where they'd already passed Harvey's van in its usual spot.

Kim peeked at her watch. "Shall we start walking now?"

"I think the time is just about right," Maureen said. "They've had just enough time to nick—I mean steal—whatever it is they came for and stash it in the van. Then they'll just run back to the beach and get on the boat with nothing but a camera full of owl pictures. After that, they'll have to walk on the beach from the boat docks back to the boulevard—and we'll be home, innocently sitting on the porch, having a glass of wine when they get there."

"If Hubbard hasn't grabbed them first."

"Right. Let's go." Both women had changed into dark clothing—Maureen in jeans and a black turtleneck sweater, an unspoken nod to Sue Grafton's sleuth Kinsey Milhone's favorite outfit, while Kim's all-black wide-leg pants with matching hoodie jacket practically screamed Bergdorf Goodman. Sticking close to the side of the road, even though not a single vehicle passed them, the two made their way to the parking lot. Light from one lone streetlamp cast its pale beam onto the pavement.

"It looks like nothing's going on yet," Maureen whispered.

"I hope we haven't missed them." Kim took Maureen's elbow, moving them both into the shadows at the far end of the paved area. "We'll be able to see them and hear them from here, I think."

"Shhh. I think I hear an owl," Maureen whispered.

"Yes. I hear it too." Kim squeezed Maureen's arm. "Look. Is that a flashlight?" The two shrank farther back into the foliage and watched as the men came through the gate at the edge of the Forest. One stayed beside the gate. The other one, with a yellow bag over his arm and a flashlight in one hand, approached the van. Kim pointed, whispering, "That's Harvey."

"And that's the yellow rope bag from Ron's tree-climbing gear," Maureen breathed.

The sound of one of the van doors opening broke the stillness. The swish-swish sound of a broom on pavement followed, then the door slammed shut. The man, holding the flashlight, moved once again toward the gate. He stopped suddenly, turned, and swept the beam across the lot, barely missing the spot where the women, now terrified, stood in frozen silence.

"What's wrong?" It was Ronald Treadwell's voice.

"Nothing. I thought I heard something. Let's get out of here," Harvey answered. The men's shadows merged as they opened the gate and moved into the Forest, the light beam bobbing away from the parking lot, deeper into the trees.

Wordlessly, the women moved—slowly at first, then faster, then at a near run, onto the lonely county road. They stayed close to the trees, ducking back into the shadows whenever headlights appeared. What if they'd been seen? What if someone was following them? There still wasn't much traffic. They watched from the darkness as a red Jeep full of teenagers

going too fast whizzed by. When they were close enough to
Maureen's car to run along the pavement, a giant eighteen-
wheeler passed and gave a friendly blast of his horn just as
they reached the Subaru. They each waved an acknowledgment. A dark-colored Chevy passed at a normal rate of speed
as Maureen climbed into the driver's seat. "Let's get out of
here," she echoed Harvey's pronouncement. "Heading for
home, a rocking chair, and that glass of wine."

"Are you going to call Hubbard and tell him what we discovered?" Kim asked as they pulled onto the road.

"I'll call him as soon as we get to the inn," Maureen
promised. "I'll get a stern lecture, of course, but I think he'll
be secretly proud of us."

"Really?"

"Maybe."

They rode the rest of the way back to the inn in silence.
Maureen had just pulled the Subaru into her regular space
behind the inn when her phone vibrated. Hubbard's name
flashed on caller ID. "Oops. Speak of the devil." She smoth-
ered a laugh. "Hello, Frank."

"Okay, Doherty. What the hell do you think you're doing?"

"What do you mean?"

"Nine-one-one got a call from a trucker on the old county
road." His voice was gruff. "Two girls running. He thought
they might be in trouble. Who've you got with you?"

"What makes you think it was me?" Maureen asked.

"The trucker got you on his dashcam but I already knew it
was you."

"How could you possibly know it was me?" Maureen demanded.

"Never mind that now. You're home safely at the inn.
Who's the other girl?"

Was she being watched? How did Frank know where she
was anyway? Maureen stepped outside the car and looked

around. There was no one else in sight. "Where are *you?*" she demanded. "And how do you know where *I* am?"

"I tracked your phone." The answer was indistinct. She wasn't sure she'd heard it correctly.

"You did what?"

Louder this time. "I tracked your phone."

"Why?"

"Because I can. Because I was worried about you, okay? Now, who is that with you?"

"Dr. Kim is with me, not that it's any of your business." Maureen didn't try to disguise her outrage.

"The doctor? No kidding. That's a surprise."

Curiosity surpassed outrage. "A surprise? Why so?"

"I figured she had more sense than you do." He sounded amused. "So, what were you two trying to achieve out there in the dark?"

She didn't want to lie to him. She motioned for Kim to get out of the car and, holding her phone, she led the way to the front porch. They needed to be rocking, eating burgers and drinking wine, before the two first-floor tenants arrived. "We were checking up on a couple of wandering guests," she admitted.

"Thought so," Frank said. "Album and Treadwell, right? Well, that was a waste of time, wasn't it?" Maureen and Kim exchanged glances. She had no ready answer to the question. He continued. "It's not that I don't think those two could be up to something, but whatever it is, it didn't happen tonight."

"It didn't?" the two women answered in chorus.

"I sent one of my plainclothes guys aboard the charter boat. He pretended to be a mate. He actually worked on the party boats when he was in high school, so they didn't catch on. Tommy knows what's going on, though." Maureen could tell that Hubbard was pleased with himself. "My man watched them every minute. They let the camera guy off at the dock with all his gear and the other one stayed on the boat. He brought his own tackle box. Did a little fishing. Chatted it up with Tommy and the mate. He'd brought along one of those fancy lighted lures that are illegal in Florida. Tommy doesn't allow them. He didn't catch much of anything, but he seemed to be having a good time. Then he went into the Forest for a while to check on the other one to be sure he was all right. They didn't take anything with them into the Forest except a camera and tree-climbing gear, and all they came back with was pictures of owls."

"Frank," Maureen interrupted. "Listen. Harvey came out of the Forest on the road side. He had a yellow bag like the one Ron keeps his rope in. He put it in his van."

"You're sure?"

"Yes. Kim is afraid he's been taking things from the mounds somehow and trading them. You'd better get that bag before he has a chance to get rid of it. You can't miss it. It's bright yellow. We have to be at the inn before they get here. I'll talk to you later. Bye."

The women used the side door, hurried past the ice machine, the guest laundry, and the brochure rack and emerged into the lobby. The night manager greeted them. "Hilda," Maureen said, "we're going to have a snack and some wine on the porch. Would you order two cheeseburgers, some fries, and a couple of white zinfandels for us?" She didn't wait for an answer but hurried out the green door. There were only a half dozen people on the porch, and none of them even looked up. The housekeeping staff wasn't present at the head of the stairs either. It was still cleanup time in the kitchen and dining room. That would keep the four busy for another hour or so.

"What about our clothes?" Kim whispered as soon as they'd each selected a rocking chair. "The all-black look isn't casual enough."

"T-shirts. Come on." Maureen pulled the key chain from her purse and ran for the gift shop. She opened the door, without turning on the light, grabbed two shirts from the shelf, tossed one to Kim. "Change!" Maureen commanded, pulling the black turtleneck over her head, then dropping it on the floor. Kim shed the hoodie, and they donned the T-shirts. Maureen locked the door, and they dashed back to their respective rockers just as the ordered burgers, sweet potato fries, and drinks arrived. "Perfect timing. Thank you." Maureen signed the tab.

When the two men appeared under the boulevard street-lamps, making their way past the closed shops, there were two women on the porch—one wearing a bright yellow shirt proclaiming "Spring Break is Better in Haven, Florida" and the other in purple with a pink flamingo on it and bold lettering spelling out "I'd Rather Be in Haven, Florida"—chatting happily together and clearly enjoying their late evening repast and wine, judging by their nearly empty wineglasses.

Harvey and Ron climbed the front steps to the porch, perhaps a little more slowly than usual. *They've had a fairly long walk on the beach. Ron's carrying that big gear bag, plus he's been climbing trees*, Maureen reasoned. *Harvey just has his tackle box, but even so, he must have been hustling to dig up whatever he hid in the van and still make it back to the boat on time.* She gave a casual wave in their direction. "Hello there. It's a pretty evening, isn't it?"

"Sure is," Ron responded. Harvey gave a wave back, and the two crossed the porch to the green door and disappeared into the lobby.

"I wonder," Kim whispered, "if now that they've done whatever it is that they've done, they'll check out of the inn. I hope Officer Hubbard can figure it all out before they leave town."

"If they've been stealing artifacts, how will they get rid of them?" Maureen asked Kim.

"If they're experienced at it, and I have a feeling they are," she said, "they probably have a regular market for everything they find. Someone who doesn't ask questions about how they got them, where they came from. I think they may buy stolen goods too and mark them up to sell to unscrupulous collectors. Do you think you ought to let Hubbard know they're here?"

"I think you're right." Maureen reached for her phone. "If he's been able to get a search warrant for the van, I think he'll have to come here to serve the paperwork to Harvey."

Hubbard answered his phone on the first ring. "You okay, Doherty?"

"I'm fine. Those two men just arrived at the inn."

"I know. I'm right around the corner. I finally got a judge away from his dinner long enough to get a warrant to search that van." He sighed. "Can you and your doctor friend please just mind your own business and let me handle this from here on?"

"Of course we will." Maureen smiled in the darkness, then added, "Do you think you should search their rooms here too? Or does that mean the inn gets the warrant?"

"MYOB," he commanded. "And no, we just need to see what's in the van for now." The call ended at the same moment Hubbard's cruiser, with lights flashing, pulled up in front of the inn.

At least he isn't using the siren this time.

"I wonder if they'll see those lights and try to run out the back way." Maureen stood, moving to a spot just above the side door exit from the first floor. Kim was beside her. The other guests on the porch watched from the front railing as Hubbard dashed up the stairs. There was no activity at the side door. Instead, as Hubbard pulled the green door to the lobby open, he nearly collided with the two men in question.

"What's going on?" queried Harvey.

"Is everything okay, Ms. Doherty?" Ron, frowning, hurried to where Maureen stood. "Do you ladies need help?"

Too surprised to form an appropriate answer, she mumbled, "Thank you. No," and watched the open doorway where Frank Hubbard and Harvey Album faced each other—the officer, eyes narrowed with one hand on his weapon, and the suspected artifact thief, with right hand extended in greeting and a smile on his face.

Chapter 25

Without changing his expression and ignoring the other man's outstretched hand, Hubbard moved his hand from the weapon to his breast pocket, removing a folded paper. "Are you Harvey Album?" he asked.

"Yes, sir," came the answer.

"Are you the owner of a 2015 Hyundai cargo van . . ." He paused, consulted the paper, then read aloud the Florida registration number.

Once again, Harvey answered with a respectful "Yes, sir."

"I have here a search warrant, allowing me to inspect the contents of the vehicle I just described. Someone may have entered your vehicle without your knowledge."

"No kidding. A trespasser? Yeah, sure," Harvey said. "You didn't need to go to all that trouble, though. You're welcome to look around in it as much as you want." He raised an eyebrow. "You'll have to excuse the mess, though. I don't think I rolled up my sleeping bag, and there may be some fast-food wrappers laying around. I guess you know where it is. Do you need for me to come with you to unlock it?"

This time Hubbard's expression revealed surprise. This time Hubbard replied with a "Yes sir."

"All right, then," Harvey said. "Let me change into clean clothes. I'm all sweaty. It'll only take a minute. My room is just down the hall." He turned back toward where Ron still stood. "Ron, while I'm gone, make a few prints of that great horned owl in flight. It might be a double-truck center spread for the new issue."

"I'll come with you." Hubbard followed the man from the room. Kim and Maureen exchanged glances.

"What was that all about?" Kim whispered.

Maureen shrugged. "Beats me."

Kim moved closer to the photographer. "So you got some good pictures tonight? Can you show us that flying owl?"

Ron's camera was, as usual, suspended from the leather strap around his neck. He lifted it with both hands and held it forward so that Maureen and Kim could see the screen. "I got him both still and video," he said proudly. "Here. Watch."

He was right. Even in low light and from among high tree branches, he'd captured the image of the owl in flight, its large yellow eyes looking into the camera, wings spread wide showing bars of black and brown feathers.

"Look," Maureen said. "He has pointy ears, almost like a cat."

"Those aren't really ears," Ron corrected. "Just tufts of hair. Here's the video. You can hear him hoot." At the first shrill "hoo-hoo-hoo" emitting from the camera, the other guests on the porch joined the three; the police car, with its engine still running, was momentarily forgotten.

"You must travel around the country a lot," Kim said. "I guess there are different birds for you to photograph in different parts of America. Do you have a favorite town or city?"

"Not really," he said. "As you said, they're all different." He adjusted the camera's screen. "For instance, we were in Mississippi a while back. We stayed at a campground at McKaskey Creek and I got great shots for a feature about migratory birds." He sounded excited as he displayed a shot of a small gray bird. "This is a blue-gray gnatcatcher. Mississippi is literally the first and last stop for hundreds of migratory birds every season. It was an amazing trip."

Maureen and Kim and the others were still hovering over Ron's camera when Hubbard and Harvey returned, Harvey in a similar outfit to the one he'd just shed—blue shirt, navy jeans, and white boat shoes—spoke in a low tone to his photographer, then without further comment, Hubbard and his companion climbed into the cruiser and sped away. Ron secured his camera and headed indoors.

"What's going on, Ms. Doherty?" asked a female guest from Louisiana. "Is Mr. Album in some kind of trouble? I hope not. Such an interesting man."

He sure isn't acting as if he's in trouble. I wonder why. "I'm sure there's an explanation," Maureen said. *I'd love to know what it is.*

Those remaining on the porch returned to their rockers. So did Maureen and Kim. "Now that Harvey and Ron are out of the way, maybe we should retrieve our clothes from the floor of the gift shop," Kim suggested. "I wish we could figure out why those two aren't worried about Frank finding the yellow bag in the van."

"They must know it's in there," Maureen agreed. Pulling the keys from her purse she opened the door to the shop without turning on the lights. Scooping up the sweater and jacket, shoved them into one of the brand-new shopping bags, handing it to Kim. They scooted outside, and she closed the door quickly behind them. Not quickly enough.

"Oh, is the new shop open?" asked the Louisiana lady. "I've been dying to see inside."

"Sorry," Maureen said. "We're planning a sort of soft opening soon. Maybe even tomorrow. We're not quite ready for sales yet."

"Really?" Louisiana lady raised a well-bred eyebrow and stared pointedly at the pink shopping bag Kim held—the purple script lettering proclaiming "Haven House Gifts, Haven, Florida."

Maureen was about to tell the truth—to explain that she and her friend had been dressed for cooler weather, so she'd grabbed a couple of T-shirts in a hurry and put their sweater and jacket into the bag and that they'd settle payment for the merchandise later. But Ron Treadwell had returned, sans camera, and was now sitting in a rocker facing them and sipping what looked like a Bloody Mary. She couldn't very well admit to the quick change of clothes in front of the photographer after setting up the "we've been here for hours" scenario so carefully, could she?

She did what seemed like the next best thing. "Okay. You caught us. I'm not set up for cash or credit cards yet, though. You can come in and take a peek. If you're a guest of the inn, you can charge your purchase to your room; if not, I'll put your purchase aside and you can pick it up later."

"Fabulous!" The woman clapped her hands together, then turned to face the others on the porch. "Come on, everybody. We're going to get a sneak peek at the new gift shop." It was a wonder, Maureen thought, that the rocking chairs didn't get knocked over as everyone raced for the shop. She reached once again for her keys and, with a sigh, unlocked the door, turned on the lights. And stepped to one side to admit the shop's first customers.

Considering the impromptu circumstances, it seemed to Maureen that the unplanned opening went off pretty well. As diners continued to leave the restaurant, the crowd on the porch grew. The shop itself drew raves. Everyone loved the décor. The merchandise selection, even though it was far from complete, resulted in several hundred dollars' worth of sales to those who were current guests, and nearly as much again in the layaway category. Kim proved to be a helpful assistant, bagging purchases and pointing out the merits of items the customer may have overlooked.

When Maureen glanced up from the counter after Kim had bagged the last purchase, she noticed Hubbard standing just outside the doorway, arms folded. He did not appear happy. *How long has he been standing there?* she wondered, motioning for him to come inside while several guests, most of them holding new pink-and-purple shopping bags, looked on. *Oh boy. This isn't the kind of soft opening I'd pictured,* she thought.

"We had a surprise shop opening," she said.

Frank Hubbard apparently wasn't in the mood for small talk. He pulled the shop door closed, shutting out the onlookers, moved close to the counter leaning forward, arms braced against the terrazzo surface. "What in merry hell gave you two the idea that Album put a bag full of stolen goods into his van?"

Maureen and Kim answered in unison. "We saw him."

Hubbard pointed a finger at Kim, then at Maureen. "You personally saw Harvey Album put a large yellow bag into his van this evening."

"Yes." Maureen didn't flinch under his withering gaze. "I saw him put a large yellow bag into his van. It was around nine o'clock."

"I saw him too," Kim offered.

"You told me that you witnessed him coming out of the Forest gate, putting this bag into the van, and leaving by the gate. The photographer was with him."

"Yes."

"Ms. Doherty," Hubbard spoke slowly and distinctly, as though speaking to a child, or someone not quite bright. "I have just humiliated myself by thoroughly searching said van and the immediate area in which it was parked in the company of a deputy, with Mr. Album looking on, and found no yellow bag. No sign of contraband of any type whatsoever. Shortly after nine o'clock, when you two claim to have seen what you described, Mr. Album and Mr. Treadwell boarded a charter boat and traveled to the Haven fishing boat dock area. He and Mr. Treadwell then proceeded on foot along the beach to this inn. Several witnesses saw them on their way, Mr. Treadwell carrying a large duffel bag and Album with a tackle box. Where now, do you suppose that mysterious yellow bag has gone?"

"I know what I saw." Maureen felt anger rising. "Do you think I would make something like this up?"

"I was there too," Kim said. "I saw Harvey put the bag into his van. I believe it contained valuable artifacts stolen from the Indian mounds in the Forest."

"How valuable?" Hubbard growled.

"I don't know. Maybe thousands of dollars. There are plenty of collectors for artifacts. Some of them are completely unscrupulous. These mounds are quite likely not the only ones Harvey has robbed."

"Hello. What's going on?" The door swung open. Ted stood at the doorway, his tall frame filling the space, his voice level, his eyes fixed on Maureen, the shoppers still on the porch behind him.

Hubbard remained close to the counter. "I'm discussing a police matter with these ladies."

"Have you called Larry Jackson, Maureen?" Ted moved closer to the counter.

"No need for an attorney," Hubbard growled.

"It's late," Ted told him. "Maybe you could discuss it with them sometime tomorrow." The "after they've consulted a lawyer" remained unspoken—but clearly understood.

Hubbard gave a brief nod in Maureen's direction. "I'll give you a call in the morning, Ms. Doherty."

Ted moved aside, giving Hubbard access to the doorway.

The policeman moved quickly onto the porch, leaving the onlookers scattering back to their rocking chairs or to the nearby entrance to the lobby.

"Thank you, Ted." Maureen breathed a long sigh. "That was getting very uncomfortable. Hubbard's in bulldog mode for sure."

"Pressuring you two is uncalled for. What's he after?"

"We reported something we thought the police should know about," Kim offered. "It didn't turn out the way he thought it should."

"The way we thought it would too," Maureen said. "I can see why he's upset."

"Is it something you want to talk about?" Ted held up both hands and added, "If it's none of my business, just say so."

The women looked at each other. Kim spoke first. "It started because we did something we probably shouldn't have done."

"You'll think it was foolish," Maureen said. "And maybe dangerous too."

"Is that why the officer is angry about whatever it is?"

"Partly," Maureen agreed.

"He worries about us," Kim said.

"A lot." Maureen looked down at her shoes. "Things didn't turn out the way we expected them to at all."

"Do you want to close the shop, grab a table in the bar, and tell me about it?"

Maureen hesitated, then looked up at him. "I don't think you're going to like it—but yes. First I need to take Finn for a short walk; then I'll meet you two in the bar and we'll talk."

Chapter 26

Kim said that she needed to change her clothes—the T-shirt and pants didn't match very well—and headed for her suite. Maureen took the stairs up to the third floor where the golden greeted her with such a loving welcome that she didn't at first notice Lorna reclining on the couch, stunning in a black bodysuit with deeply fringed long sleeves. "Nice outfit, Lorna," she said.

"Like it?" She stood and did a quick model walk and turn, then sat in the aqua lounge chair. "When I was in Nashville, I borrowed it from Miranda Lambert. Reggie came by earlier and he said he ran into you in the elevator and told you about some guys planning to heist something. What's going on?"

"It's a long story," Maureen said, "and I'll tell you about it later. Right now I need to change my clothes—the old-fashioned way—not the way you do it. If you see Reggie, tell him his information has sent me down quite a rabbit hole."

"I'll tell him tonight. We're going over to St. Augustine. It's waltz night at the Casa Monica Hotel. I'll be out late."

"Have fun." Maureen shed the hastily selected T-shirt and dark jeans, opened her closet, and chose a pink denim pants-and-jacket set. She gave her hair a quick brushing, dabbed on fresh lip gloss, and clipped Finn's leash to his collar. With the golden fairly prancing in the lead, they hurried back down to the side door and out onto the boulevard.

It was, as she'd promised, a short walk. Kim and Ted greeted her in the bar and welcomed Finn with pats and scratches and loving words.

The three sat at one of the small cocktail tables in a corner of the bar area of the dining room with the golden resting quietly beside Maureen. There were a few other people, mostly couples, at similar tables, and almost all of the barstools at the newly renovated bar were occupied. There were still some diners at the round tables across the long room enjoying desserts and after-dinner drinks. At a signal from Ted, Gert appeared with a thermal coffee carafe, three mugs, and a plate of Aster's cookies.

Maureen began. "It was my fault, really," she said. "I mean, I started the fly-on-the-wall conversation."

"I agreed right away," Kim said. "We both wanted to do it."

Ted interrupted. "Slow down and start at the beginning, please. Before the fly on the wall part."

"Okay. I guess it all began when Harvey Album and Ron Treadwell arrived in Haven," Maureen said.

"The bird magazine guys?" Ted wondered.

"Right." Maureen told him what she'd learned about Harvey—about how he'd stayed at the inn back when the first death had occurred—at the time of the first fishing tournament.

Kim chimed in with details about Harvey's interest in Indian mounds dating back to her first encounter with him in California. "I admit it. I believe the man is a thief. We thought we had proof of it."

Slowly, with Ted interrupting to clarify points only a few times, the women—together—related the reasons for their suspicions and the details of their clandestine, after-dark trip to the Forest.

"But, according to Hubbard," Maureen finished, "there was no yellow rope bag in the van. It *was* there, though. We both saw him put it inside, close the door on it, and even sweep up the parking lot around the van."

"It was there a few hours ago," Kim agreed. "For sure. But how did it disappear?"

"What do you think, Ted?" Maureen asked.

"First of all," he said, "I agree with Hubbard. It was a dangerous, foolish thing to do."

"I know," Maureen told him. "And I'm sorry. Sort of sorry anyway."

Ted tried to hide a smile. "Just sort of?"

"Me too." Kim put her mug down so hard that some coffee splashed onto the table. "The man is a thief. At least I'm pretty sure he is, and the Indian mounds need to be protected—even small ones like the ones here in Haven. Someone had to do something right away. So we did it."

"I understand," Ted said. "I don't approve of what you did, but I think I understand why you did it. So the question now is, if you saw what you say you saw—and I believe you did see it—then what became of the rope bag? Right?"

"Right." Maureen covered the spilled coffee with a plain white paper cocktail napkin with a passing thought to order some with a Haven Inn logo on them as soon as the budget allowed. "We were sure there was nobody else around who could have seen us there—but what if there was someone? What if they got into the van after we left and took it?"

"That makes a certain amount of sense, you know," Ted said. "If there was a rope bag in Harvey's van when you girls left, but it wasn't there a short time later when Hubbard investigated, it didn't disappear by some kind of magic."

"By the time Hubbard decided to search the van, Harvey already knew the bag wasn't in it," Maureen pointed out. "Otherwise, why was he all glad-hand-y and happy to unlock the van for the police?"

Ted took a bite of a shortbread cookie. "I think the only explanation has to be that shortly after Harvey stashed the bag in his van, someone else came and removed it. Someone he'd made an arrangement with."

"The buyer!" Kim exclaimed. "I'll bet the buyer left money somewhere in the van and grabbed the bag."

"That makes perfect sense," Maureen said. "Someone came along after we left and picked it up."

"I'm sure Hubbard searched thoroughly," Ted said, "but he would have been looking for something big and bulky and yellow, not for an envelope or a wad of bills. Do you two have any idea of who the buyer might be?"

Kim sighed. "Not a clue. Could be an artifact collector, could be a middleman who sells to private parties or even to museums."

"Maybe we should call Hubbard and tell him about somebody else being involved. Somebody who bought and paid for the rope bag," Maureen reached for her phone.

Ted put a restraining hand over hers. "Hubbard said he'd call you in the morning. It might be a good idea to talk to your lawyer about all this first."

"You're right," she said. "I'm too impatient to get this thing solved and behind us. It all started with me finding Eddie Manuel's body, then poor Tommy had to be in the same boat with an actual suspect, now Kim and I are witnesses to the same suspect hiding what might be stolen Indian treasure, and somehow I seem to be in the middle of all of it." Ted hadn't moved his hand and Maureen found the gentle pressure comforting. "Larry's office is closed by now, but when we get back from our run in the morning, I'll call him."

"You have an awful lot on your plate right now." Kim's tone was sympathetic. "You have an inn to operate and a fishing tournament to organize and a grand opening of the shop to handle—let alone dealing with the cops. You know you don't have to do all this alone. I can help with the shop, and you said that Gert can run the gorgeous register. Ted knows about fishing, and your household staff clearly adores you and will do anything you ask of them. Your lawyer may be able to simplify at least the police involvement in the mix."

"That would be a relief," Maureen admitted. "Hubbard is in total bulldog mode."

Finn lifted his head. "Woof," he said. "Woof woof."

"Not that kind of bulldog, Finn." She gave the dog a calming pat on the head. "Maybe Larry will see something in all this that we're missing."

"Eddie's memorial service isn't far off," Ted reminded her. "We'll be sending over a big charcuterie board and some pastries. I've heard from some of the folks that stayed here at the inn and have fished aboard the *Tightline* are coming to Haven for it."

"Yes. The reservations have started to trickle in." Maureen had begun to relax. "Eddie had so many friends. It seemed as though everyone who knew him liked him. Yet someone killed him. Tommy Manuel is having a hard time dealing with the sad way he died."

"So am I," Ted said. "I've known Eddie for years, and I can't remember ever hearing a bad word about him."

"That sounds as though he wasn't killed in anger, then, or because he wronged somebody," Kim offered.

"Frank Hubbard told me once that there are only three reasons for murder," Maureen said. "Money, love, and revenge. I'm thinking this one was for money."

"Money from selling artifacts from an Indian mound?" Ted asked.

"Yes," Kim said. "There's one more thing I guess Officer Hubbard might like to know about. Remember what Ron told us about that Mississippi trip where he photographed all those migratory birds?"

"He was so excited about it," Maureen said. "Even though they stayed at a campground instead of a hotel there too. Probably because Harvey is so 'thrifty.' "

"I think they had a better reason for staying there. I've stayed at the McKaskey campground myself," Kim said, "because it's a hop, skip, and a jump away from the famous Etowah Indian Mounds."

"That's something that should definitely be shared with Officer Hubbard," Ted said. "I wonder how many of the birds featured in *Watching Birds* were photographed near a Native American historical site. Hubbard may want to vet Harvey Album more thoroughly."

"Woof," Finn put his head on Maureen's lap. "Woof?"

"Not that kind of vet, Finn," she said. "But seriously, Ted. We can research that ourselves. I'm sure Aster can order some recent back issues of the magazine for us."

"Right," Kim said. "Haven's police department is small. They won't have time to pore through a bunch of bird magazines, but I have time."

"I can *make* some time," Maureen offered.

"I know where the most famous mounds are," Kim said. "If you can pinpoint the state Album is writing about by the birds he features, Maureen, I can tell which local sites he could have visited. Then I'll contact the curators and see if anything there has been disturbed. We can get the information we need within a few hours, once we get those magazines."

"Actually, we can start now," Maureen spoke excitedly. "I have the current issue in my office. Ron gave it to me when he checked in. I'll get it. Here. Hold my dog."

Chapter 27

Handing Finn's leash to Ted, Maureen hurried past the bar and the grouping of cocktail tables, acknowledging the greetings of patrons with a smile here, a nod there, a fluttering wave to the room in general, exiting the dining room doors and dashing into the lobby.

Night manager Hilda looked up from the reservation desk. "Calls for the weekend of the tournament are starting to come in, Maureen. I've already booked three suites in the short time I've been on duty tonight."

"Wonderful news, Hilda," she said. "I've been a little bit worried lately."

"I know you have, and according to the guests who've seen the new shop, that's going to be a big success too." The woman beamed. "The player piano was just playing 'Happy Days Are Here Again.' Timely, heh?"

Good timing, piano man, Maureen thought as she unlocked the door to the office. She pulled open the top desk drawer. Carefully, she picked up the magazine with the little black-and-white bird on the cover and had started to push the drawer closed when she noticed the small blue card marked "Grandmother's Prophecies."

Do your bills get you down?
Do they make you fret and frown?
Despair not, my fair one
Your battle against them will soon be won.

She turned the thing face down, closed the drawer, slipped the magazine under her arm, and headed back to the bar. *One mystery at a time, please.*

Finn gave a soft, welcoming "woof" as she approached the table where Ted and Kim waited. She held the magazine up with both hands as she slid into her chair. "Here we go. More than we probably ever wanted to know about"—she glanced at the cover caption—"about the red-cockaded woodpecker."

Ted moved the cookie plate aside, making room in the center of the table for the open copy of *Watching Birds*. "If we move our chairs closer together, we can all read at once." He pulled his own chair closer to Maureen's while Kim did the same.

" 'Once fairly common in the southeastern United States, this bird is now rare, local, and considered an endangered species,' " Kim read aloud. She touched the picture of the bird. "He's endangered. The poor little guy."

"Wow. Look at this," Ted said. "No wonder they're endangered. It takes up to three years just to build a nest. They have to dig out a cavity in a live pine tree that has some kind of heart-rot disease that makes the wood softer."

"Interesting. But where were the pictures taken? Does it say? That's what we need to know." Maureen leaned closer. "Ronald Treadwell has the photo credit, but where were they taken?"

"Here it is." Kim pointed to the page. " 'Photographed at the Piedmont National Wildlife Refuge in Georgia.' " She leaned back in her chair. "I've been there. It's about twenty-five miles out of Macon."

"Any mounds nearby?" Maureen's voice dropped to a near whisper.

Kim nodded. "Yep. The Ocmulgee Mounds. I've been there too."

"That just about settles it, doesn't it?" Ted asked. "What do you bet when we get the back issues, we'll find similar pairings—birds and mounds, mounds and birds?"

"I'll call Aster first thing in the morning and order those back issues," Maureen said. "And what do you say one of us talks to Ron? Tell him you've read the article, ask some innocent questions about what else was going on when he took the pictures."

It was quickly decided that since Ron had given the copy now on the table before them to Maureen in the first place, she should be the one to discuss it with him.

"That makes sense, I guess," she agreed. "I'll be in my office for a little longer tonight finalizing the fishing tournament plans, so if he's still out I'll be able to watch for him in the lobby."

Kim muffled a yawn. "It's past my bedtime. I'll see you two tomorrow." She stood, gave a little bow, and headed for the exit.

"I've still got some breakfast prep to do in the kitchen." Ted handed her Finn's leash. "Maybe I'll catch up with you later for a nightcap, Maureen."

"Sounds good." With the magazine once again tucked under her arm, she stood. "Come on, Finn. Up to the third floor for you." The golden seemed to be ready for bed, and strained at the leash as they left the bar and climbed the stairs. Once inside the suite, he headed straight for the bedroom and was asleep in his spot beside the bed by the time Maureen had hung the leash behind the kitchen door. She paused in the living room for a long moment, enjoying the silence. Neither of the cats were on the tower, and there was no shimmering apparition lounging on the furniture. Bogie and

Bacall often stayed out late on pleasant nights and let themselves in via the downstairs cat door, and Lorna, dressed in something borrowed and fabulous, was surely having a ghostly good time waltzing with Reggie in St. Augustine. "So much for dogs and cats and spirits," she said aloud, locked the door behind her, walked down the corridor, and punched the down button on the elevator. "Back to work for me."

With a reminder to Hilda to let her know if Ron Treadwell came in, she once again sat at her office desk. Winding up the details of the Eddie Manuel Memorial Kingfish Tournament didn't take as long as she'd expected it might. A few updated press releases to the local media, follow-up emails to the prize sponsors, a sincere thank-you to the participating charter boat captains along with a copy of the rules Eddie had written and Tommy had shared. She allowed herself a mental pat on the back and an unspoken "well done."

There were, of course, other things that needed attention, but checking off one box felt pretty good. The enthusiastic approval of the gift shop had given her enough confidence to order some more merchandise. The evening's soft opening had already made a dent in the candy jars. She filled out an online order form for some more Necco Wafers, Sky Bars and Mary Janes. She'd made a note of the Seminole crafts Kim had told her about, and ordered a sampling of baskets woven from pine needles, handmade beaded jewelry, and a dozen wonderful 1950s vintage souvenir dolls, made from palmetto fiber and dressed in colorful patchwork costumes.

The evening's earlier foray into the top desk drawer had revealed the long brown envelope she'd found days earlier in Penelope Josephine's trunk with the handwritten word "Trevaney" on it. She'd put it aside "to read later." Hesitantly, she lifted it from the drawer, aware of the dried and brittle green sealing wax, the folded papers—still unread—inside. Maureen realized that she'd been avoiding the thing. But why?

Attorney Larry Jackson had told her some months ago that he'd come across some documents in his firm's old paper files indicating that the person who'd left the inn to Penelope Josephine was named Charlotte Christine Trevaney. Oddly, though, he'd found no birth, death, or census records of anyone by that name. The history museum had a portrait they called "the woman in green." The back of the canvas was marked "C. Trevaney." Lorna had seen the painting and was convinced that one of the inn's more elusive apparitions, a Goth-garbed wraith who called herself Absinthe, was the same person.

Maybe the envelope contained the formula—the reasoning—the instructions for how each owner knew how to determine who the next heir should be. She slid several folded, slightly yellowed papers from the envelope and began to read.

To *whom it may concern:*
My name is Charlotte Christine Trevaney. I am twenty-one years old and I live in Haven, Florida, in the Haven House Inn, which my father, Horatio Davenport Trevaney, built especially for me so that I would always have a pleasant place to live. I have never lived anywhere else. In fact, I have never even visited anywhere else. I like talking to the guests who come to stay at the inn. They tell me about the wonderful places they have seen. Boston. New York City. Even places like London, Athens, Paris, Rome, the islands of Hawaii. Father buys books for me about these places so that I can learn about them. Sometimes I watch the children who live in the city of Haven as they pass my window on their way to school. I do not go to public school. Father teaches me all the things I need to know about. I can do algebra and business mathematics. I keep the books for the inn. I used to help Mother with the cooking and cleaning

here, but she has gone to Heaven so now we hire people to do those things.

Father says that I can live here all my life and leave the inn to my children. I have a secret. I do not want to live here all my life, and if I ever have children, I don't want them to live here either. We have plenty of money, so as soon as Father dies, I will hire a manager to run the inn while I travel to all of the faraway places I've read about—especially Paris. I plan to give the inn to a little girl whose photograph I saw in the Clearwater Sun newspaper. It was a picture of a child named Penelope Josephine Gray. She is twelve years old. Her picture was in the paper because she won a prize for horseback riding. It must be fun to ride a horse. They have such kind eyes. Someday I'll be able to pat one and even ride one if I want to. It must be fun to have a photograph of yourself in the paper too. I have never seen a photograph of myself. We have a painting of a girl who looks just me but she is wearing an old-fashioned dress. I don't like the dress at all, but don't tell Father that. Someday I'll buy my own dresses and have my picture taken whenever I want to. Now I shall learn all I can about the child, Penelope Josephine Gray—who goes to school and rides horses and wears pretty dresses. As soon as Daddy goes to Heaven. I will hire a manager to run the inn and a lawyer to find Penelope Josephine Gray when she grows up and to give her the inn and plenty of money to maintain it. She will be so surprised. I wish I could be there to see her face but I will be far away from Haven. Maybe even in Paris.

It was signed "Charlotte Christine Trevaney," and was dated October of 1945.

Maureen thought once again of what Lorna had said about the ghost who called herself Absinthe after the strong green liquor. According to Lorna and others who'd seen the apparition late at night in the bar, she favored green cocktails, short skirts, lots of black leather, fishnet hose, black boots, and traveled in the company of several good-looking Goth guys. All kind of steampunk.

If Absinthe is really Charlotte, I hope she had a wonderful life. It seems that she's enjoying the afterlife anyway. Good for her.

Maureen lifted the cover of Penelope's trunk and carefully, almost reverently, placed the envelope inside. She'd learned a surprising truth about the original owner of the inn, including how Penelope had become the second owner, but there'd been no secret formula in Charlotte's letter telling how the subsequent heirs should be chosen. She sat for a long moment, staring at the untidy assortment of letters and posters, pamphlets and pictures—a true hoarder's collection of total miscellany—and began to lower the top of the trunk.

"But wait a minute." Maureen snapped her fingers. "Penelope was chosen because of a newspaper picture of her when she was twelve. Then Penelope picked me because of a picture taken when *I* was twelve. Does this mean that I need to find a picture of a twelve-year-old kid and somehow stalk her—or him—until I get old?" She reached once again for the calculator. "I don't think so." With some simple addition and subtraction involving Penelope's age when she died and her own age when the picture was taken next to the weather-beaten sport-fishing dock sign, she realized that Penelope hadn't actually chosen Maureen Doherty as heir to the inn until she'd reached almost seventy.

"That means I have a lot of years before I have to deal with it," she told herself. "Maybe someday I'll have kids and they can worry about what to do with it." She closed the lid with a satisfying clunk. "Meanwhile, right now I have a date for a nightcap with a handsome chef." Smiling, she buzzed Ted's number.

Chapter 28

The bar area of Haven House Inn's dining room was especially attractive late at night. A lot of regular customers said so. Maureen sat on a recently reupholstered barstool, watching angelfish lazily swimming among backlit greenery, a pastel-colored castle, a partially sunken treasure chest, and assorted perfect specimens of shells and coral in their decorator-designed underwater world. The player piano tinkled a subdued selection of oldies. There were a few couples at the small tables—no one else at the bar.

"Penny for your thoughts?" Ted took the seat beside hers.

"I was thinking about our contented fishes." She pointed to the tank above the bar. "I wonder if they ever sleep."

"I don't think so. I've been in this room at every possible time of day or night and they always look the same—gliding around just like that." He signaled for bartender Lennie. "What would you like to drink?"

"I think I'll try a Fairy Godmother," she said, naming the fruity, elderberry-based cocktail mixed with a few potent drops of green, anise-flavored absinthe. "I was thinking about the lady-in-green ghost tonight. Gert claims that she's seen her in here."

"Gert's not the only one. I've heard other people talk

about her too. To tell you the truth, whenever I'm in here by myself, I can't resist looking at that last stool over there." He pointed to the seat at the very end of the bar. "That's where they say she sits, but I've never seen her." He ordered Maureen's drink along with a rum and Coke for himself.

Lennie put a generic cork coaster in front of each of them and delivered the beverages with a flourish. "You two were talking about *la fée verte*. The green fairy." He glanced around and dropped his voice to a whisper. "I saw her once." He pointed to the same barstool Ted had indicated. "Right there. Plain as day. Long straight hair. All dressed in black. She was laughing and holding a drink just like that one you're having, Ms. Doherty." Smiling, he poured beer from a tap into two vintage Pilsner glasses, each with a perfect head of foam, placed them on a 1965 Rheingold Beer tray, and handed it to late-shift cocktail waitress Dolores.

Maureen lifted her glass in a toast. "Here's to happy angelfish and happy ghosts."

Ted touched her glass with his own. "While we're at it—here's to happy endangered woodpeckers."

"I know," she said. "I keep thinking about the birds and the Indian mounds too. I'm going to call Aster first thing in the morning about getting those back issues."

"If she's at the shop when we get back from our run, we can talk to her then," he said. "We'll be able to smell the cookies baking if she's up and around."

"Peter Patterson's favorite cookies. Almost every building in Haven has a ghost or two except for the bookshop—where one is really wanted."

"We don't need any more ghosts here," Ted said. "We need live, paying guests. How're the tournament bookings coming along?"

"Not bad," she said. "Some of our regular visitors are

coming early so that they can attend Eddie's memorial service before the fishing starts. Besides that, it looks as though the gift shop is going to turn a profit quickly. I ordered some more merchandise today." She tapped the cork coaster. "I may even spring for some Haven House coasters and cocktail napkins."

"I've upped the orders for the kitchen too," he said. "Between the regular breakfasts, lunches and dinners, the trays for Eddie's service, Trent's birthday party, and the box lunches the fishermen might want, we'll be working overtime. Besides all that, our mother cat is about due to present us with kittens." Big grin. "Gert and Molly are acting like expectant grandmothers. I wouldn't be surprised if they threw Momcat a baby shower."

Maureen sipped her cocktail. "Momcat. That's cute. When the kittens arrive, maybe we should ask Aster to put kitty faces on the daily cookies to celebrate."

"I'll bet she'd love to do it. Maybe she'll take one of the kittens too."

"Maybe. Although Erle Stanley might not think much at his age about having a baby sibling. I'm sure Bogie and Bacall will opt out on that idea too, in case I'm next on the prospective cat-parent list."

"You are," he admitted. "Would you like another Fairy Godmother?"

"No thanks. Are you plying me with a strong drink to talk me into adopting a kitten?"

"It was worth a try," he said. "What got you thinking about the ghost—about Absinthe—tonight?"

Should she tell him about the letter from Charlotte? He'd already expressed interest in the ghost. He'd even admitted looking for her, a mysterious woman in black sitting in the dark on that special barstool.

"I have a secret," Charlotte had written. "Don't tell Father," she'd warned.

Am I nuts? Maureen asked herself. *Am I supposed to keep a secret for a woman who wrote a letter long before I was born?*

It's okay. The letter says "to whom it may concern."

It concerns me, she thought, and began to tell Ted everything she'd learned about Charlotte Christine Trevaney. It occurred to her, during the telling, that one of the things she admired—even loved—about Ted was his ability to truly listen. His eyes were fixed on hers. His occasional nod of understanding encouraged her to relate small details of her thoughts, not just about the letter, but about her ongoing search for the past means of passing the property to others. The cocktail lounge area was nearly empty when she stopped speaking, looked away from Ted, and focused once again on the fish tank. There was no one else at the bar. Dolores cleared the tables while Lennie began counting his till, preparing for the next day's business.

"It's still quite a mystery, isn't it?" Ted said. "The letter has answered some questions. We knew that Penelope Josephine had somehow selected you as her heir because of a picture she found when you were twelve. Now we know that Charlotte used a similar method to select Penelope. You're wondering now if there's some sort of formula involved in passing the property on to your own future heirs. Is that right?"

"In a nutshell, yes."

"You want to know what I think?"

"Of course I do."

He reached for her hand. "There is no magic formula. The picture thing is coincidental. You can sell the place if you want to and never worry about it again. You could get married and pass it on to your own kids. Who knows? It could get wiped out by a hurricane and be replaced by a ten-story condo."

"There is no magic formula," she repeated.

"You could get married," he said again. The eye contact was back.

The moment was interrupted by a voice from the dining room entrance. "Is the bar still open?"

Ronald Treadwell had finally arrived.

Chapter 29

Lennie gave a welcoming wave. "Come on in. We're open until two o'clock."

Ronald ambled up the bar and selected a stool just one seat way from Ted. "I'll have a light beer, Lennie. It's been a long day." He smiled at the couple. "Hi, Ted. Hi, Ms. Doherty. You're up late too. Hilda said you'd been looking for me."

Maureen made a fast—and reluctant—attitude adjustment. She'd already thought about some questions she'd ask the photographer, encouraging him to talk about what else might have been going on during the photo shoots. "Yes, hello, Ron. I read the article about your visit to that wildlife refuge in Georgia in the *Watching Birds* magazine you gave me. The one where you photographed the red-cockaded woodpeckers. The photos are amazing, and Mr. Album's article is so well researched. Absolutely fascinating. You two certainly get to visit some interesting areas. Do you mostly choose wildlife refuges for your stories?"

"No, although that would suit me just fine." Ron took a long drink of his beer. "In the refuges, they keep the underbrush cleared and the birds are always healthy and no hunters are apt to be shooting at me."

"I'd never thought about that," Ted put in. "Some of the birds you photograph are game birds."

"Sure. Some of the ducks, the quail, and the wild turkeys are mighty tasty. I tell Harvey sometimes I ought to be getting 'hazardous duty' pay."

"Well, at least nobody can shoot the red-cockaded wood-peckers. According to the article, they're an endangered species," Maureen said. "You surely weren't in any danger on that assignment."

"Not from hunters," he agreed. "The damned woodpeckers caused plenty of trouble by themselves."

Maureen was surprised. "Are they aggressive?"

"No." He shook his head. "They're just tiny little guys. Shy too. No. It's the way they build their nests. They pick live pine trees. The bark is full of sap. They like it because it keeps snakes from climbing into their nests. It also messes up a couple of hundreds of dollars' worth of camo gear so bad you can never wash the gooey gunk out of it."

"Did Harvey buy you a new set?"

"No. He didn't even see what happened. He writes those articles ahead of time. He mostly just tells me what kinds of pictures he wants, and then he goes off trading stuff online or whatever he does while I'm on site, working my butt off climbing trees or wading through mucky water, dodging alli-gators."

Trading stuff online?

Maureen and Ted again made eye contact. This was the kind of information Kim needed. If Harvey wasn't usually on site where the birds were, that meant he had plenty of free time for investigating Indian mounds. For making contact with buyers or sellers of stolen archaeological treasure.

Or for stealing it and selling it himself.

"He's been with you in the Forest on this trip, though, hasn't he?" Maureen asked. "He was right there directing the whole process when you got those amazing pictures of the baby ospreys, and Tommy Manuel said that he stayed nearby while you photographed owls last night. Is Haven special to him?"

"It seems to be," Ron agreed. "We've been planning this trip for a long time. I've never been sure why the Forest was so special, but he's been talking about coming here ever since I met him. Not that it isn't a wonderful place," he apologized quickly, "and Haven is a cute little town, but frankly I've taken pictures of hundreds of the same species of owls and peacocks and pelicans and ospreys in other places in Florida." He glanced around the nearly empty room. "And most of them are a lot more lively than this place." Again the apologetic tone. "Not that your inn isn't charming and all that, but Miami and Key West have the same birds—and a lot more going on—if you know what I mean. No offense intended, Ms. Doherty."

"None taken, Ron," she said. "I'm sure Harvey has his reasons. Maybe he's been here before and has special memories of the place."

I know darn well he's been here before. Like back in 2000.

"That could be." Ron signaled Lennie for a refill. "He seems to know his way around here without a map. I was here when I was a kid in Boy Scout camp, and all I remember about it is seeing my first alligator up close. I was too scared to get the picture. Say, can I buy you two a drink? I guess I interrupted your conversation."

"Not at all," Ted told him. "We're just talking business. We've got a fishing tournament coming up, you know. We're tying up loose ends."

"Still, I'd like to buy you guys a drink. Not on the credit card either. I got a little bonus from the boss. How about another one of those green things, Ms. Doherty? What about you, Ted?"

Did he get a little bonus for being a bag man? Let's hear more.

"Thanks, Ron." Ted pushed his glass toward the bartender. "I'll have another Coke."

"Okay," Maureen said. "You twisted my arm. Something lemon and lime, Lennie."

"Sure, Ms. Doherty. Will a 7UP work for you?"

"Sure. That'll be fine. My grandmother used to make 7UP cake," Maureen said, keeping the conversation light.

"I think my grandmother did too," Ron said. "The grandmother in Clearwater. The one who gave me my first camera." He lifted his glass. "Here's to grandmothers."

Lennie poured the two nonalcoholic drinks, embellishing Maureen's soda with a parasol and Ted's with a slice of lemon. They raised their glasses to meet Ron's. "To grandmothers," they echoed the sentiment. Maureen mentally added the long-ago grandmother who made prophecies to the verbal salutation.

"That Clearwater grandmother had a great impact on your life, Ron. Without her influence you might never have become a famous photographer," Maureen said. "Thanks to her, and thanks of course to Harvey, your name is in a national magazine every month."

"I know." Ron smiled. "Guess what? Harvey and I are planning to do a big coffee-table book someday soon about the birds with my pictures and his articles. My name will be on the cover of that one."

Another bonus? What will he have to do for that?

"You deserve the recognition. You've surely been a big help to Harvey." She tried hard to make it sound as if she wasn't prying.

Ron laughed—a short, unfunny laugh. "Yeah. Sure. He's even got me doing his laundry."

"What? You're kidding."

"Nope. You were there when he left with Officer Hubbard. He came up to me and whispered for me to wash his dirty clothes. 'Immediately,' he said. 'Right now.' Didn't even give me the quarters for the laundry room either." He took a long swig of the beer. "The man is a hell of a good writer, but he sure is cheap."

"I'm sure he must help you out sometimes," Ted said. "We heard that Harvey was really enjoying fishing, but he stopped and went into the Forest to check on you—just to be sure you were okay."

Ron looked down at the counter, played around with the coaster, and didn't say a word. Maureen thought about Kim's admonition: *"If you can't say something nice about somebody—don't say anything at all."*

It was one of those weird, long moments that happen once in a while—when it seems like everybody in the room stops talking at once. There was no clink of bar glasses. The player piano was strangely silent. Maureen imagined that she could almost hear the angelfish swimming.

Ron broke the silence. "Well, it's late. I'd better go get Harvey's stuff out of the dryer. See you guys tomorrow."

Chapter 30

Why had washing Harvey's dirty clothes been such a matter of urgency?

Maureen was sure that she needed to get a look at the man's laundry. What was in there that needed to get washed away in such a hurry? Maybe it meant something. Maybe nothing. Maybe this was one of those "feelings" Frank Hubbard obsessed over. She blurted out the first word that popped into her head: "Quarters." She said it softly at first, then again, a little bit louder. "Quarters!"

Both men wore quizzical looks. Ted frowned. "What about quarters?"

"Thank you, Ron, for the reminder!" She clasped her hands together, pasting on a big fake smile. "I had it on my to-do list this morning," she lied. "I'd been so busy I'd almost forgotten about it. I have to empty the coins from the washers and dryers and restock the change machine. Want to help me, Ted?"

"Sure," he said. "Wait up, Ron. We'll come with you."

Single file, with Ron Treadwell in the lead, Maureen and Ted left the bar, proceeded through the lobby, where they greeted a surprised Hilda, then paused long enough for Maureen to pick up the round key ring from the office. Long enough too, to whisper an idea about Harvey's laundry to

Ted. They passed the brochure rack and entered the guest laundry.

"This is an area that needs updating for sure," Maureen said, observing the faded blue walls and a vintage NORGE sign over the change machine. "There are only half a dozen mismatched machines, but I guess they still work. I don't think many of the guests use the place. It's not very inviting, is it? Fixing it up simply hasn't been a priority for me so far."

"Some of these have been here since the old woman had the place." Ted touched a stainless-steel washing machine marked SPEED QUEEN. "This one has been here at least since the late 1990s."

"I've used that one myself," she said. "I had no idea it was an antique."

"The newest Speed Queens we have here are at least thirty years old. George knows how to work on them. I guess he's responsible for keeping them alive all this time."

Maureen unlocked one of the largest washing machines. "They were all here when I inherited the place. I didn't even think about how old any of them were." She watched Ron as he lifted garments from one of the small dryers, shaking each item out before folding it carefully and placing it into one of the plastic laundry baskets she'd provided for each room or suite. She tapped Ted's shoulder and pointed to the dryer Ron had used. He'd washed a blue shirt, navy jeans, a white T-shirt, white boxer shorts, and white socks and sneakers. *He must have used cold water because none of the colors ran*, she thought. *Somebody brought him up well.*

"Did everything come out all right?" Ted moved close to Ron and peered at the neatly folded garments.

"Perfect." Ron picked up the basket, then reached for the dryer's lint filter.

Ted waved him aside, stood in front of the dryer, and made a motion to reach for the lint screen beneath the drum. "You have your hands full. I've got it. Have a good night."

"Thanks." Ron picked up the basket and headed for the hallway leading to the single rooms. "You're right, Ms. Doherty. They're good enough machines and this is a good place to stay. Someday I hope I'll be able to come here for a real vacation. For now, I think maybe I can afford at least one more night."

"You'll always be welcome here," she said. "Good night."

Maureen watched as he walked away, then, without comment but with ears alert, she emptied another machine of its coins, then another. Ted continued refilling the money changer, and after a couple of minutes had passed, he put a finger to his lips and approached the entrance to the hallway. "I don't hear anything. He's in his room for sure. Let's check out that dryer filter."

"Wait a minute," she said. "I think we have to wake Kim up. If there's anything in this puff of fluff to tie Harvey to the Indian mounds, she'll spot it." Without waiting for an answer, she called Kim's suite. "Are you still up?" she asked. "Listen to this." She gave a speedy rundown on what they'd discovered. "Come on down here to the guest laundry. If there's anything to interest the police in there, they'll expect a clean container. There are some clear plastic bags in the vending machine beside the ice maker. While we're waiting for you, I'll get one. Hurry up."

She faced Ted with a mischievous grin. "Got a quarter?" Deftly catching the coin he tossed, she hurried toward the cubicle housing the soda machine and the ice maker.

Satisfied that the plastic bag was large enough to accommodate anything they might find inside, she scampered back to the laundry room. Maureen held the bag open while Ted slowly and carefully pulled the filter up and out. "Maybe we should wait for Kim," she said.

"Good idea. Look. Not too much lint," he said. "I was afraid maybe somebody else might have used this dryer and not cleaned the filter."

"There's not much chance of that—Molly and Gert do a walk-through every day and clean them all. Anyway, we don't have many guests now."

She heard footsteps and moved to the doorway. What if a guest had decided to wash clothes at this late hour? Kim appeared, wearing a terry-cloth bathrobe and bunny slippers. Relieved, Maureen drew her into the room and asked, "What do you think?"

"Don't touch the stuff with your hands, Ted," Kim warned. "Do you have a clean piece of cardboard or something like that?" The women watched as Ted, using the edge of a Haven House Inn business card, scraped the contents of the fine mesh screen, inch by inch, into the clear bag.

Maureen leaned closer to the bag. "Can you tell if we've got anything aside from the usual fuzz?"

"I could feel something sort of crunchy when I was scraping," he said. "What do you think, Kim?"

"It might just be beach sand," she said. "I'm sure we all have it in our clothes around here. I can't be sure, though. I wish we'd brought a magnifying glass."

"I have one in the junk drawer in my kitchen," she said. "Let's go get it."

Carefully, gingerly, Ted tucked the plastic bag inside his jacket. The three raced past the surprised night manager, past the elevator, and onto the staircase. When they reached the third floor, Maureen slowed her steps, hoping that Lorna's promise to stay out late proved to be accurate and they wouldn't walk in on a shimmering spirit. Maybe Ted and Kim weren't people who could see ghosts, but in Haven, one never knew for sure. "Finn usually woofs when I get this close to the door," she said. "He was sound asleep when I left."

"I guess he's had a busy day. We all have."

"It isn't over yet." She turned the key in the lock and pushed the door open. "Look. Both cats are home." Bogie and Bacall each looked up from the couch briefly, then simultaneously closed their eyes as the two humans tiptoed past on their way to the kitchen. Maureen pulled open the drawer she'd designated as the junk drawer, cringing as it made a squealing sound. "Everything's old and creaky," she complained. "It can't be helped." Moving aside a package of rubber bands, a roll of cellophane tape, and a pair of scissors, she pulled out a large magnifying glass. "Ta-da!" she said in a stage whisper.

A sleepy "woof" issued from the bedroom doorway.

"Come on, Finn. You can help too," Ted invited the golden. "Let's spread the bag out on the kitchen table under the overhead light and see what we can find without opening it."

With Maureen and Kim on one side of the table and Ted on the other, they spread the clear plastic bag against the white enamel top of the table. Even without the use of the magnifying glass, they each saw flecks of some sparkling material. Quartz sand? Quite likely. Gold dust? Hardly. She handed the glass to him. "You go first."

"Thanks." He leaned forward, dodging back and forth, trying to keep his own shadow from getting in the way. "Do you have a flashlight in that drawer?" he asked.

"I'm sure I do." Maureen handed him a pencil-thin South of the Border souvenir flashlight on a key chain. The narrow beam moved slowly across the collected lint.

"See that?" Ted pointed. "It looks sort of pearly, doesn't it? Do we have pearls on our beach?"

"Mother-of-pearl, maybe," she said. "It's on the inside of some of the shells."

"You're right. I've seen it in oyster shells."

"It's in saltwater sea snails too, I think."

He put the glass down. "Kim, are you thinking what I'm thinking?"

"Yes," she said, excitement evident in her voice. "The crushed shells in the Indian mounds."

"Little pieces like that could get trapped in the ridges of Harvey's boat shoes. They're made to grip the deck." Ted clicked the flashlight off. "Maybe it's a good thing these machines are old. A new washing machine wouldn't have let these little crumbs of evidence get so far."

"Evidence," Maureen repeated. "That's what it is. We need to turn this over to somebody who knows what they're doing. Someone who can do a real professional examination. Someone who can compare this with the crushed shells they found on Eddie's body."

Ted nodded agreement. "Like a police lab."

"Woof?"

"Not that kind of Lab, Finn." She pulled the dog close. "I'm starting to get scared, Ted. What if Harvey figures out what we've done?"

By the time Ted and Kim left it was well past midnight and Maureen had started to feel better about the situation. They'd go for their planned run in the morning, and as soon as Larry Jackson's office was open, she'd tell him everything that was going on. Then if Hubbard called about the planned talk with Kim and herself, she'd tell him that she wanted to have her lawyer present.

Maybe, she thought, *just maybe, I should have listened in the first place, when Hubbard said MYOB.*

Chapter 31

By the time she and Finn left to meet Ted in the morning, Maureen had already securely stashed the plastic bag of whatever-it-was in the safe behind the map in her office and left a message on Attorney Jackson's phone that she'd be calling him later.

Ted was already waiting for her just outside the side door. "Are you okay?"

She appreciated the concern in his voice—and in his eyes. "I think so," she said.

"I really didn't want to leave you last night, after you told me you were scared."

I didn't want you to leave either.

Finn stood between them. "Woof."

Ted bent and gave Finn a scratch behind his ears. "I know, boy. I know you take good care of her." He began the usual pre-run stretching exercises. Without comment, she joined him. Stretches finished, they began with a slow jog, picking up the pace when they neared the bookshop. The smell of cookies there was unmistakable. Ted pointed to the shop. "Want to stop now—or later?"

"Later," she said. "Maybe we won't even need the magazines." She moved ahead of him, feet pounding on the sidewalk, her mind racing. *There may be enough evidence in my office safe to incriminate Harvey somehow,* she thought. *There's no point in involving Aster in this mess and possibly putting her in danger.*

The tide was low and the beach was nearly clear of people. She released Finn from the leash and he bounded happily into the water, swimming parallel to the shore where Maureen and Ted ran together on the hard-packed sand at the shoreline.

Finn met them at the sign, shaking drops of water in all directions as he greeted them with wagging tail and joyous woofs. The two rested for a moment. "It'll be good to hand our bag of linty evidence over to Hubbard today," she said. "Then maybe we can relax."

"I'm glad Kim is in on all this. She's the expert on the artifacts."

"You're right. In a way, I wish Kim and I hadn't been so nosy about the yellow bag thing."

"Only in a way?" he asked. "That's how all this mess started."

"But we may have stopped a thief—or even a killer." She took a deep breath and ran a little faster, moving ahead of Ted and Finn. The Casino building was visible in the distance. Tomorrow it would be filled with people coming together to share memories about Eddie Manuel. Unbidden, a different memory popped into her mind. She remembered how, in the darkness of night, a small, patient owl had waited there for a long time under the overhang of the porch, sharp talons ready, to drop silently onto a marauding mouse.

She reached the casino first and began her usual stretches. Ted arrived seconds later, looping the leash around a railing, joining her in the familiar routine. With Finn once again in the lead, they jogged onto the boulevard, past the colorful house with the JACKSON, NATHAN AND PETERS, ATTORNEYS AT LAW sign on it, and past the thrift store, past the one-time Haven summer stock playhouse where Lorna had met her rather ungraceful demise, and past the bookshop where the scent of cookies still lingered sweetly. At her questioning look, Ted said, "We'll see Aster later. I have to get breakfast started. Three-cheese omelets and popovers."

They separated at the side door. Ted headed for his first-floor room. Maureen paused in the lobby long enough to assure Hilda that she'd be back to take over the reception desk in half an hour, then she and the golden hurried up the stairs to the third floor. "I'm not going to wait for a decent hour," she told Finn. "Things are moving too fast. I'm going to call both Larry and Kim right now."

Larry Jackson answered on the first ring. "What's going on, Maureen? I had a call a few minutes ago from Frank Hubbard. He said you'd be calling me—that you've gone and gotten yourself involved in something and that you'd be wanting me with you when he questions you about it and that he's in a hurry to get it over with."

"I want it over with too," she said. "Your office or mine?"

"Yours, I guess. Hubbard said he was heading over there. Want me to come over now?"

"Give me half an hour. We'll use my upstairs office. More privacy."

"Half an hour," he repeated. "But just one thing—should I bring Nora Nathan with me?"

Nora Nathan was one of Larry's partners—the one who specialized in criminal law. Maureen had needed Nora's expertise once before. "No need for Nora this time, Larry," she said—hoping she was right. "I'll meet you in my office in half an hour. If Hubbard is already here, I'll buy him a doughnut and coffee and we'll wait for you."

She called Kim's suite from the shower. "Kim? Hubbard and my lawyer will be here pretty soon. Come on down to the lobby as soon as you can, okay?"

"No time for makeup," she told her mirror image, as she pulled on white shorts and a red silk shirt. She said "see you later" to Finn, then rode the elevator down to the lobby for a change, thinking that being alone for a minute in the glass-and-brass cage might help her collect her thoughts.

As soon as she stepped out of the elevator, she saw Hubbard sitting in a wicker chair opposite the reception desk—he and Hilda ignoring each other. Taking a deep breath, she approached the stern-faced officer. This time, he wore his uniform. *Is that to be sure he'll get the free coffee and doughnut?* She almost smiled at the thought. She paused at the reception desk, told Hilda she could leave, and buzzed the kitchen for coffee and doughnuts—reminding them about the blue packets of sugar substitute.

"Good morning, Frank." She sat in a wicker chair opposite his, the small bamboo table between them. "Larry will be along shortly and I've invited Dr. Salter to join us. When everyone gets here, we'll go upstairs to my office."

"Suite Twenty-Seven? The haunted place?"

Maureen glanced around quickly, hoping no one was listening. "Hush, will you? It's not haunted and you know it. Anyway, I thought you didn't believe in ghosts."

"I don't. Never did. Never will." Gert arrived with a tray bearing two mugs, a cream pitcher, packets of sugar and sweetener, and an assortment of doughnuts. He reached for a blue packet, stirred the coffee, and helped himself to a jelly doughnut. Maureen poured cream into hers and selected a plump cinnamon doughnut. There was no further conversation between the two. There seemed to be a silent agreement that they'd wait for the attorney to join them.

The early-breakfast local regulars began to arrive, filing into the dining room. Jolene was on hand to greet them and hand out menus. The presence of Haven's top cop, eating his second doughnut, drew only a couple of curious glances and a few "good mornings." One thing Maureen had learned about morning people was that they aren't much for conversation before breakfast.

Maureen broke the silence. "I'm going to call Ted and tell him you're here. Something new has come up and you may need to talk to him about it, but you understand that I can't take him away from the kitchen at breakfast unless it's absolutely necessary."

"Doherty," he said, "you have no idea how hearing the words 'something new has come up' from you makes me wish I had gone into banking like my mother wanted me to."

Chapter 32

By seven thirty, with Shelly taking over the reservation desk, Maureen, Larry Jackson, Kim Salter, and Frank Hubbard were seated at the mahogany conference table in the second-floor corner suite. There was no number on the door and hadn't been for many years. A STAFF ONLY sign was the brief designation. Once known as Suite Twenty-Seven, the area had long been unrentable. Guests had run screaming from the bedroom too many times to quiet the growing reputation the well-appointed rooms had of being haunted. Even now, the local part-time housekeepers shied away from entering the sunny, white-walled suite of rooms. The office furniture, desk, bookcase, table, and even the file cabinets were of rich, lustrous mahogany. Maureen knew full well that not too long ago, the handsome rooms *had* in fact been haunted, but thanks to Trent and Pierre, with a bit of invisible help from Lorna, the sad ghost of John Smith had been banished for good. The adjoining kitchen was handy for brewing the occasional pot of coffee, and the bedroom housed extra linens, towels, and china along with far too many extra white wicker chairs.

Maureen sat at the head of the table, the plastic bag from the downstairs office safe, securely wrapped in a white-linen tablecloth, in front of her. "I think we're all ready for any questions you might have for Kim Salter and me, Officer Hubbard."

Hubbard stood, medals on his chest reflecting morning sun. He consulted his phone screen and read aloud the date of the night Maureen and Kim had set out on their "fly on the wall" adventure. "Ms. Doherty and you, Dr. Salter, reported that together you had witnessed a man known as Harvey Album placing a large yellow bag into his vehicle, which was parked in the county parking lot adjacent to the area known as the Forest. Is that correct?"

Both women looked first at the attorney, and at his encouraging nod, each of them said "yes." Hubbard continued. "Shortly after seeing Album place the yellow bag into his vehicle, you reported this action to me, Ms. Doherty, correct?"

"Yes, sir."

"You encouraged me to search Mr. Album's van as quickly as possible because you and Dr. Salter believed he might have stolen artifacts from the Haven Indian Mounds in that yellow bag. Correct, Ms. Doherty?"

"Yes, sir."

"Correct, Dr. Salter?"

"Yes, sir."

"Yet when I promptly acquired the necessary warrant and presented it to Mr. Album within a timeframe that precludes his having returned to the vehicle after leaving the said yellow bag, a thorough search produced no bag and no artifacts of any kind. Is that correct?"

Larry Jackson interrupted. "These women have no direct knowledge of that."

"I stand corrected," Hubbard said. "Moving on. Ms. Doherty, you expressed the idea that someone else must have come and removed the yellow bag from Mr. Album's vehicle. Is that right?"

"Yes. Of course." Maureen tried to hide her impatience. So far, this meeting was a total waste of everybody's time. "If it was there when Kim and I saw him put it there, and it wasn't there when you searched for it—and Album was provably somewhere else—obviously, some other person removed it. We've been over all this before. I can't help you with that part. Do you want to see the new evidence we've found?"

Hubbard frowned, glanced back and forth at the women and the lawyer, then sighed. "All right. Go ahead."

"I'll need to call Ted." She moved to the desk and pressed the intercom button.

Ted's voice crackled over the vintage technology. "Shall I come up now?"

"Yes, please."

Larry held up one hand. "Are you sure this is all above-board, Maureen? Do you want to consult further with me about it beforehand?"

"I think it's important for Frank to have what we found just last night. It could help him answer some questions." She picked at the folded white fabric nervously. "Ted will be here shortly."

"Were you a part of this evidence discovery, Dr. Salter?" Hubbard asked.

"I was," Kim admitted.

Hubbard shook his head, looking dismayed, but didn't comment.

"While Ted's on his way, I'll start by explaining how we happened to find what we're about to show you," she said. "You remember, Frank, when Harvey so willingly offered to go with you to open the van?"

"I was surprised, but he opened her right up. No problem."

"And you remember he asked if he could change his clothes first?"

"He was sweaty. Kind of smelly, actually," Frank said.

202 *Carol J. Perry*

"Ron Treadwell told us tonight that before he left with you last night to search the van, Harvey ordered him to wash and dry those sweaty clothes."

"No kidding?" A half smile crossed his face. "Treadwell took an order like that?"

"He did, and we followed him to the guest laundry and watched him as he took Harvey's shirt, pants, underwear, and sneakers out of the dryer, folded everything neatly, put it in a basket, and carried it away."

"So the man is a sap—doing his boss's laundry. That doesn't prove anything." Hubbard was clearly getting impatient.

Ted entered the room and quietly sat beside Kim.

"After Ron left," Maureen explained, "we took the lint filter out of the dryer." She unwrapped the plastic bag and pushed it toward Hubbard along with the large magnifying glass. "We think you'll find crushed shells along with the lint. Maybe your forensics people can match it up with the shells you found on Eddie's body."

Hubbard held the magnifying glass to his eye and leaned close to the plastic bag, now spread flat on the surface of the table. "Yeah, I see what you mean. No one else has touched this stuff? Are you sure it wasn't already in the lint trap when Treadwell did Harvey's stuff?"

"We're sure," Kim told him.

Maureen followed with the fact that Gert and Molly cleaned the filters conscientiously and that the washing machines were old and not as efficient at getting sand and rocks and shells out of the fabrics—or out of the grooves in sneakers.

Larry Jackson raised a cautionary hand. "Hold it, Ms. Doherty. I'm advising you to confer with me before you continue with this interview." He pointed to the adjoining kitchen. "Could I have a word with my client in private, Officer Hubbard?"

Maureen, surprised by the interruption, looked at Hubbard, who nodded his acceptance. "Could we step into the next room, Maureen?" Larry stood, moving toward the kitchen. She followed.

With the kitchen door closed behind them, the attorney spoke in low, clipped sentences. "Maureen, you've made some unfortunate choices here. So many that I almost wish I'd brought Noreen along after all."

"What do you mean? Every word I've said is true. Kim and Ted will bear me out." She sat on a tall stool at the Formica counter. "I don't understand."

"All right. I'll make this quick. You and Kim claim to have witnessed Album putting a bag into his van."

"It's true. We did."

"Yet when Hubbard obtained a search warrant for the vehicle, Album welcomed the search and found no bag. No contraband of any sort."

"Someone else must have picked it up after we left," Maureen explained once again.

"You and Ted and Dr. Salter then somehow obtained what you think are crushed shells from Album's laundry—without permission, by the way."

"True," she admitted. "Is that illegal?"

"Perhaps not illegal, but did it occur to you that the police might deduce that you and your friends are attempting to make Mr. Album appear guilty of something he hasn't done?" He pointed at her. "Did it occur to you that it might appear to some that you might be trying to shift blame from yourselves? That Mr. Album might consider your interference—your admitted late-night spying on his van, your coercing his employee to let you touch his personal garments—to be objectionable? And I do mean legally objectionable."

"No. I never thought of it that way. I—we—were trying to help."

"I believe you. That doesn't mean you were right to do these things. We can only hope that Officer Hubbard won't think he's investigating some sort of cover-up on your part. Album has been cooperative with the police at every turn, as far as I can see." He slapped a hand onto the counter. "And we can fervently hope that Album himself doesn't file suit against you for besmirching his good name!" He stood up very straight. "Now, with your permission, I'll conclude this interrogation, and you can explain to your friends that they might want to engage counsel as well."

Chapter 33

The walk from the kitchen back into the office seemed very long indeed, as thoughts—not pleasant ones—raced through Maureen's head. Had she unwittingly made herself and her friends look as though they were deliberately trying to make an innocent—if unlikable—person look guilty of something he hadn't done? They'd all been so sure that Harvey Album had been for some time—many years, actually—involved with buying, selling, trading, or actually stealing Indian artifacts from sources all over the country, and covering his tracks with the popular bird-watching magazine excuse.

Larry Jackson, as he'd promised, brought the meeting to a close, citing a need for more fact finding regarding the likelihood that someone else had seen the transfer of the yellow bag into Album's vehicle. Maureen could only hope that he was right.

Surprisingly, Hubbard agreed immediately. "Yes," he said. "I've been looking into that possibility also. Some video information might be forthcoming soon."

Video information?

Does Hubbard know something I don't know? she wondered, but expected no immediate answer. Maybe Hubbard would announce such a miracle eventually. She could only hope so. Meanwhile, as the attorney had told her, she'd have to explain to her friends that they might all be in a real legal pickle.

Hubbard gathered up his phone and notebook and bid her and the others a reasonably polite goodbye. "I'll call you later, Doherty," he said, and headed for the elevator.

Larry Jackson asked Maureen to call his office later in the day to make an appointment with himself and Nora Nathan. "Sooner rather than later, Maureen," he said, his tone urgent. "We need to get on this right away, and for God's sake, stop playing sleuth."

Kim and Ted remained at the long table, looking somewhat lost in the expanse of polished wood. Ted spoke first. "What's going on? What was all that about? Has Larry found a witness to the bag exchange?"

"It sounds encouraging, doesn't it?" Kim smiled. "Hubbard is looking into it too. Where could they have found a video?"

"Where could there possibly be a video?" Maureen spoke quickly and knew she was right. "The truck! The eighteen-wheeler! The trucker whose dashcam caught us on video must have caught another car when he passed the Forest parking lot."

"Of course. Why didn't we see that?" Ted said. "He could have recorded the vehicle that stopped and maybe even the person who picked up the yellow bag. That has to be it."

"I hope so," Maureen said. "That would be good news. Meanwhile, I have some really bad news to give you guys."

Ted looked at the clock on the mahogany sideboard. "I hope it's not *too* bad. I have to get back to work and get the prep work for lunch started." He didn't look as worried as Maureen thought he would be.

"I'll try to make it fast," she promised, "and it's pretty bad."

She didn't try to sugarcoat anything Larry had told her, including the idea that Kim and Ted each might want to hire lawyers. "Larry thinks it's possible that some people could think that our interest in finding evidence to incriminate Harvey could be a means to divert suspicion from ourselves," she finished.

Their astonished faces told her that they were each as shocked as she'd been at the very idea that they might have had a hidden motive in their admittedly unorthodox methods.

"But we're right," Kim protested immediately. "Our old friend Harvey is involved in illegal involvement in buying or selling artifacts stolen from protected land, and we all know it. Everything points to him."

"Knowing it isn't proving it." Ted's voice was calm, reasonable. "Maybe we could have been much more careful. Larry is right. Every single thing we've discovered is circumstantial—if it's even anything at all. After all, we *could have* put some broken shells into any old ball of lint and said it was from Harvey's clothes. The yellow bag story could have been made up of whole cloth"—a brief flicker of a smile—"no pun intended."

"What about Tommy Manuel? Is she actually in danger from Harvey? The memorial service is tomorrow. She'll be taking Eddie's ashes out on the *Tightline*. Should we ask Hubbard for some extra protection for her, just in case?"

"Frank said he'd call me later," Maureen said. "I don't mind asking him about assigning that plainclothes cop who used to be a mate to go along on the memorial boat trip."

"Do you think Hubbard still maybe believes us?" Kim asked.

"It's not his job to believe us," Maureen said. "He's supposed to just follow the law, ask questions, determine what's a crime and what isn't. I don't think he *disbelieves* us, though. Especially if he finds that we were right about someone else picking up the bag."

"I hope you're right about the trucker's dashcam," Ted said. "That makes us pretty darned credible. I have to leave now. Okay?"

"Of course. See you later."

"For sure."

"I need to go back down to my other office," Maureen told Kim. "I saw that a few more packages have arrived for the gift shop. If you have time, I could use some help putting price tags on the merchandise before the official soft opening tonight."

"I'd love to help."

"I appreciate it. It looks as if the tournament is set to go off as planned. Trent's birthday celebration needs some more work. I'm thinking having some live music would be fun. I want it to be special. I owe those guys a lot."

"For the wonderful designs they gave you," Kim said. "That was an amazing gift. They are special friends, aren't they?"

More special than you'll ever know! Maureen looked around the handsome office that had for years harbored a melancholy ghost. In addition to their design talents, the two men had helped to free that spirit.

The women left Suite Twenty-Seven and took the elevator back down to the lobby. A wide-eyed Shelly greeted them. "This phone has been ringing off the hook," she said. "I think I've booked more than half of the suites and all but one of the rooms for the tournament and some for both the fishing and Eddie Manuel's send-off. All the first-floor rooms would be booked, but one of the guests just checked out. Mr. Album. There are a bunch of inquiries on the inn's website as well. It looks like it's going to be a totally good week."

"Mr. Album checked out? Any problem?"

Shelly gave a one-shoulder shrug. "Nothing serious. He says he saw a cat outside of his room and he hates cats."

"Oh, dear. It was probably Bogie. He loves to wander. I'm sure we'll have no trouble filling the room."

So Album had checked out. It wasn't too surprising, considering the man was so tight with a dollar. Seeing the cat was a handy excuse. The room would be booked quickly, no problem. The encouraging words from Grandmother's Prophecies came to mind. Maybe that long ago precursor to Zoltar was right. Would her battle against bills soon be over? Could be, but she reminded herself, Grandmother hadn't said anything about a battle with the law!

She tried to shake the bad thought away. All of the trophies for the tournament had arrived, silver pieces polished and engraved, fishing equipment prizes attractively packaged, jewelry secured to blue velvet pillows, traditional handled metal cup trophies and shiny plaques ready to be presented to lucky winners. She'd decided to display all of them on a long table in the dining room. Sam had already put the table in place, and Molly and Gert had draped a bright blue tablecloth over it and placed a colorful EDDIE MANUEL MEMORIAL KINGFISH TOURNAMENT sign on the front.

The awards had been stored temporarily in the stock area of the new gift shop. Maureen hoped she'd be able to retrieve them without starting another soft opening for observers, similar to the previous evening's unexpected sales event. She'd just have to be more firm about saying no. She wished now she'd said a firm no to the fly-on-the-wall adventure.

She carried the key to the gift shop in her shorts pocket and ventured onto the porch. She recognized the few guests on the porch with a "hi" or "hello" or "good to see you," hoping no one would insist on a gift shop visit. She was pleased to see George in his usual top-of-the-stairs position. If he helped carry the awards, they could get the display done in one or two trips. The other three seniors were missing.

"George, want to give me a hand with a few tournament trophies?"

"Sure thing, Ms. Doherty. From the word around town, it's going to be a big deal."

"Let's hope so." She unlocked the door. "Everything is in boxes in the stockroom. Grab what you can carry, and I'll do the same." She closed the door behind them and followed George, who within minutes had gathered the variously shaped boxes into two neat piles. "Can you manage the small pile, Ms. Doherty?"

"I think so," she said. "You go first. I'll carry mine onto the porch, then I'll have to lock the door. I'll be right behind you."

The plan was a good one. They made it into the dining room with only one or two dropped boxes. After arranging—and rearranging—the prizes several times, Maureen stood back and pronounced the display satisfactory. There were items plainly marked for first-, second-, and third-place youth angler, lady angler, single outboard engine division, and overall kingfish division winners. There'd be a cash award too, depending on the number of paying anglers. "I think there'll be enough money in the kitty to give the big winner a thousand dollars and have enough money left over for a big fireworks display on the beach on the last day to celebrate the end of the tournament," she said.

The two walked back onto the porch and George reclaimed his rocking chair. "I really appreciate your help," she told him. "Between the shop and the tournament, it looks like we might have a full house. Shelly says all but one of the first-floor rooms are reserved."

"It looks like you've got a cancellation coming," he said.

"What do you mean?"

"That photographer guy, Ron. He told me he went over to the Quic Shop to get a few things and his credit card was declined." George frowned. "He hasn't got enough money to pay for the room for another night, so he packed up his stuff and he's walking over to the Forest where that friend of his has a van he might be able to sleep in."

"Walking to the Forest? That's a good five miles away." She thought of how there'd been a mix-up earlier about the *Watching Birds* card. "I'm sure that card is okay. I checked it myself a day ago. When did he leave?"

"Right before you came out to get me. He said he had the guy run the card twice. Declined. He was embarrassed about it."

"I'll bet he's carrying that heavy equipment bag too," she said. "Why don't you take the truck and catch up with him and give him a ride over there? I feel sorry for him. It won't take you long."

"No problem. He's a nice guy. Thanks, Ms. Doherty. I'll do that." George hurried down the stairs and around the corner to the back parking lot. Within a few minutes she heard the toot-toot of the truck's horn along with the engine misfiring and a loud exhaust noise. Bad muffler? More expense. She walked slowly back into the lobby. Maybe her battle with the bills would take a little longer than the grandmother had prophesied.

Chapter 34

It was with a feeling of satisfaction that Maureen opened the most recent shipment of merchandise for the gift shop and, with Kim's help, began the task of attaching price tags and folding and hanging attractive beachwear and novelty items she was sure would please customers. Talk between the two women about the merchandise soon turned to concern about Larry's warnings of legal consequence from their impulsive—and admittedly amateur—attempt at proving Harvey Album guilty of . . . of what?

"We don't even know *exactly* what he's been doing—except that he could be involved somehow in robbing a number of Indian mounds around the country," Maureen said. "We don't know what we're doing, and we're trying to make a federal case out of bits and pieces of random happenings."

"If we're right, though," Kim said, "it actually *is* a federal case. In 1979 the government passed the Archaeological Resources Protection Act."

"Meaning?" Maureen paused in tagging a sweet Gigi Moda crop top.

"Meaning unpermitted excavation or removal of objects from public archaeological sites—like Haven's Indian mounds—can bring fines and imprisonment. Sometimes big fines and long imprisonments."

"So, if we're right, and I'm sure we are—and if we somehow can *prove* we're right, Harvey can go to jail?"

"Yes, indeed." Kim sounded confident. "We need to prove it, though."

Larry Jackson's recent admonition came to Maureen's mind. *"For God's sake, Maureen, stop playing sleuth!"* And hadn't Hubbard warned her more than once to mind her own business?

"I think we need to leave the detecting up to the professionals at this point," Maureen said. "If Hubbard has something on video that can help us, that's great. I'm still worried about Tommy Manuel's safety, though. Maybe we can keep an eye on her somehow without getting in anybody's way."

"Good idea. Did I ever tell you I'm a pretty good fisherman?" Kim smiled. "What if I even fish the tournament aboard the *Tightline?*"

"I don't think anybody can find fault with that," Maureen agreed. "You'd just be observing and fishing at the same time. I like it."

"I'll do it, then," Kim declared. "I'll call the fishing dock right now." She reached for her phone, then looked up. "What's that noise?"

"It sounds like George is back with the truck," Maureen said.

"Loud muffler?"

"I'm afraid so. He was giving Ron Treadwell a ride to the Forest. It seems that Ron's *Watching Birds* credit card isn't working, so he thought he'd better not stay another night. He's planning to see if he can sleep in Harvey's van until it gets straightened out."

"I hope that works out for him," she said. "After I tag the last few scarves, I think I'll go up to my room for a little beauty nap before dinner."

"I'll see you at dinner, then. Right now I need to go inside and man the reservation desk, but first I think I'll check with

George and find out what happened." Maureen tagged a wonderful Mary Frances cross body bag, hung it from a brass door handle on the wall, and stepped out onto the porch in time to see the truck rolling into the driveway. There were two men in the front seat. George had brought Ron back to the inn with him. The photographer's heavy bag and small suitcase were visible in the truck bed. She hurried down the ramp at the side of the building and followed the pickup into the parking lot.

"What's going on?" she asked as George stepped down from the cab. "Couldn't Ron stay in the van?"

"It isn't there."

"Album's van isn't there?"

"Right. His regular parking place is empty—the ground swept clean as a church—not a sign of him anywhere. I couldn't leave Ron alone in the Forest, so I brought him back. I thought maybe you could find something for him to do—to earn his keep for a little while, you know?"

Maureen thought fast. "Actually, that is a very good idea, George. What, with the tournament and the renovations and the gift shop opening, I could surely use a professional photographer around here." She waved to Ron, who was still sitting in the truck. "Come on out here, Ron. Let's make a deal."

It didn't take long for the arrangements to be made. As they discussed the room-for-work proposal, she liked the idea better every minute. She could have postcards made with Ron's photos of the front of the inn, the handsome bar, the dining room, the porch with its inviting rocking chairs, the interior of the gift shop, and more. Ron could cover the tournament with publicity shots of all of the winners. How about real professional pictures of some of Ted's best specialties for some new menus—the real laminated kind, not paper handouts like she'd been using? Trent's birthday party deserved some photos too. Oh, yes. Ron Treadwell might be a truly good addition to the Haven House Inn's room-for-work household staff. She hurried back to the lobby, making sure that his room was still available. It was. The one Harvey had vacated had already been booked. He'd left it so immaculately clean that the housekeepers had barely had to do anything but replace the linens and towels. "I can put you to work right away, Ron," she said. "I'll be opening the gift shop for a while after dinner tonight. I'd like you to cover that. All right?"

The photographer agreed readily.

"Do you have everything you need for photographing things around here, Ron?"

"I think so. I take good care of my work tools. Camera accessories don't come cheap, you know. I think the only time Harvey ever paid me back for anything was when he borrowed one of my rope bags and then lost it. He wanted to trade me an old class ring for it. I told him he'd better replace it or look for another tree-climbing bird photographer."

"He replaced it?"

"Sure did. Bought me a brand-new one."

Interesting. Harvey's room and parking place are both vacant, she thought. *If Harvey has really skipped town, I'll bet he did cancel Ron's credit card. I doubt that he's away on birdwatching business without the photographer.* Was this a "feeling?" She called Frank Hubbard.

"What's going on, Doherty?"

"Harvey Album checked out of his room this morning," she said, "and I just learned that his van isn't parked at the Forest. I thought you should know."

"Thanks. We're on it."

"You've been watching him?"

"I don't totally disbelieve the things you suspect about him, Doherty," he said. "I just don't like the way you go around meddling in other people's business. Just please MYOB. Let me handle this."

"I will," she said, meaning the promise sincerely. "If you don't mind my asking, did the video you mentioned make you think I've been telling you the truth?"

"Yes. Now stay out of it."

"I will. I am. I-I mean, I'm trying to," she stammered. "But I'm still so concerned about Tommy Manuel's safety. Do you . . . have you . . . can you arrange some kind of protection for her?"

"We're on it, Doherty. Run your hotel. Let me run my police department. Got it? Goodbye."

The ending of the conversation was abrupt, but she felt good about the call anyway. Hubbard admittedly had video from somewhere—she was pretty sure it was from the eighteen-wheeler's dashcam—that showed someone in the parking lot after she and Kim had been there, but before Hubbard searched the van. *Besides that,* she thought, *he says "we're on it" about Tommy too. Maybe I can relax and actually mind my own business—and my business needs a lot of minding—starting with getting all the plans in motion for Trent's birthday party.*

Molly had already designed a wonderful birthday cake in the shape of the Haven House Inn. She'd even found some miniature dollhouse-sized rocking chairs for the porch. They'd decided to have the party during a regular dinner hour so that all the diners would feel included, but not obligated to bring a gift. The special menu would include prime rib with all the fixin's. The date of Trent's actual birthday fit in nicely too—the day after Eddie's memorial and the day before the kingfish tournament. She'd thought about serving Penelope Josephine's famous drink—the Celebration Libation, complete with American flag and lighted sparklers, but the unfortunate death of a previous guest after drinking one had caused her to remove it from the beverage menu—even though the drink itself was not really at fault. She'd hired a local banjo player to strum along with the player piano—with the hope that Billy Bedoggoned wouldn't take off on a noticeable riff of his own. She was quite sure that Pierre could coordinate Trent's vacation schedule so that he'd be surprised when he walked in to dinner on his special night.

The stock we have now in the gift shop will easily be enough to hold the soft opening after dinner tonight, she thought. With Gert operating the register and Kim helping her wait on customers, it should serve as a good dress rehearsal for permanent business hours. Then as soon as the rest of the merchandise she'd ordered arrived, she'd be ready to advertise the new shop to the general public. By then the Quic Shop probably would have spread the word all over Haven anyway.

With Ron Treadwell happily and gratefully reinstalled in his first-floor room, and with her mind more or less at ease about Hubbard's assurance that he was "on it" regarding Tommy Manuel's safety and Harvey Album's whereabouts, Maureen decided to allow herself another peek into Penelope Josephine's trunk before Finn's afternoon walk. With the office door open, giving her a clear view of the desk and the lobby, she lifted the lid of the trunk.

Chapter 35

Maureen moved the brown envelope with the word "Trevaney" on it to one side. For now, she'd had quite enough information about the woman who'd given the inn to Penelope Josephine. She was curious about the other things her benefactor might have stored there for a planned book. *Of course, she saved a lot of things that had no apparent use at all*, she told herself, *but surely there'll be* some *items here that will tell a story about Haven—about my inn.*

Maureen had noticed that there were often newspapers between the layers of items the old woman had chosen to preserve. At first she'd thought they were there to cushion the more important memorabilia, but when she noticed a headline announcing President Kennedy's assassination, she'd realized that each of the intact newspapers had special meaning—at least to Penelope Josephine. She selected two papers, the first, a yellowed, August 1992 edition of the *St. Petersburg Times* with a front-page story about Hurricane Andrew. It was easy to see why that one had been saved. Second was a *Tampa Tribune* from mid-June 2000. The lead story was about a drought-caused sinkhole that had drained Tallahassee's Lake Jackson dry, stranding hundreds of turtles.

Sad, but why was it important to Penelope? she wondered. *I've never seen anything about turtles within her enormous hoard—like turtle figurines or turtle books or even pictures of turtles. Maybe there's something in the inside pages that had meaning for her. It's dated close to the time of the first fishing tournament. I'll bet there's something in here about it.*

Maureen put the paper on her desktop, and carefully spread it open to pages two and three, realizing that she'd have to read every word. After half an hour, she'd learned that *The Perfect Storm,* starring George Clooney and Mark Wahlberg was playing at the State Theater in St. Petersburg, and that the price of a dozen eggs at Albertson's was ninety-six cents.

The photo on the front page of the sports section answered her question. It was a photo of Penelope Josephine herself awarding the King of the Beach trophy to a smiling man. The copy under the photo said that Penelope Josephine Gray, proprietress of the Haven House Inn and major sponsor of the event, had donated the trophy as well as the thousand-dollar cash prize to the lucky recipient. *I wonder, how soon after that photo was taken was Mr. Sherman's body found?* she thought. *There'll probably be another newspaper in here detailing that sad happening.*

The article about the tournament answered the question of why Penelope had saved that particular edition of the *Tribune.* Maureen refolded the paper with care and looked into the trunk to see if there were other copies dated June 2000. In typical Penelope fashion, though, there was nothing else in the immediate area bearing a June date. The pile, however, yielded several other papers of interest, ranging from a yellowed *New York Times* for May of 1945 marking Victory in Europe day, when Germany surrendered unconditionally, to a 2004 *Boston Globe* marking the first Boston Red Sox World Series win since 1918. Both stories were worth saving.

Maureen kept the King of the Beach issue on top of her desk returning the others to the trunk with a silent vow to search the trunk for more of Penelope Josephine's preserved newspaper collection when she had more time. Reading the article with the photo of Penelope Josephine didn't offer any more information. It did, however, give the names of the winners of all of the other, lesser categories, and the name Harvey Album stood out as the third place winner of the single outboard division. So Harvey had fished from an outboard motorboat, not one of the charter boats with a full crew. Exactly what did that mean? Was it because he was, even back all those years ago, tight with a dollar? She checked the current rules for this division. The boat operator would have been designated as the "captain" and could carry one or two anglers. Maureen guessed that Harvey had fished alone. He was a loner even back then.

That was then, this is now, she told herself again. It was time to concentrate on *this* tournament—not one that happened decades ago. Digging into Penelope's old trunk was becoming a distraction. She returned the newspaper to the trunk, closed the lid firmly on Penelope's past, and tried hard to envision her own immediate future in Haven.

The first duty on *that* list was walking Finn. She buzzed the kitchen to see who was available to watch the desk for a while. Ever-faithful, hardworking Shelly volunteered, and Maureen climbed the two flights to her suite. The strains of "Monday, Monday" by the Mamas & the Papas told her that Lorna was in a reminiscent mood. She opened the door to a tranquil scene. Finn had his head on Lorna's somewhat translucent lap, while Bogie and Bacall snoozed on their respective levels on the cat tower. Bogie blinked once or twice, Lorna opened her eyes, and Finn stretched, then wagged his tale and gave her a proper greeting. "Woof," he said.

"Woof to you," she said, and headed for the kitchen to get the leash. "Time for a nice walk, then I need to change my clothes for dinner and the opening of the shop."

"You've got some nice stuff down there," Lorna enthused.

"I've tried on almost everything. I especially like the cro-cheted string bikinis. You could use some of those nice big sunhats, though."

"Good idea," Maureen agreed. "Come on, Finn. Time for walking." The golden followed her happily, and the two raced down the stairs to the side door and out onto the boulevard. They'd almost reached the Coliseum before she noticed the unmarked but familiar cruiser in the old building's driveway beside the play area with the swings and seesaws. Frank Hub-bard was behind the wheel, coffee cup on the dashboard, looking in her direction. *Now what?*

He rolled down his window as she approached. "I thought it might be time for you and the mutt to take a walk."

"Are you watching me for some reason?" Annoyed, she approached the window. "I know you're worried about where Album might be." He shrugged. "I just want to let you know that he's nowhere near here, in case you've been looking over your shoulder."

She had, in fact, been figuratively, if not literally, looking over her shoulder—half expecting and certainly dreading see-ing Album close behind her.

"You've found him?"

"Not exactly," he admitted, "but we know he's in his van on U.S. Route One, heading west, away from Florida."

She remembered how Hubbard had tracked her phone. "You're tracking him?"

"No. He doesn't have his phone with him. We tracked it to a dumpster in Orlando. He ran a toll booth just outside of Knoxville. They got a picture of his number plate."

He probably didn't want to pay the toll, she thought, but didn't say so. "Do you have any idea where he's going?"

"We do. The car the trucker caught on his dashcam has out-of-state plates. He could be heading there. We'll be checking with toll gates as he goes along."

"Okay. So where is he going?"

"That's on a needs to know basis and you don't need to know. You've got a lot going on. Let me worry about Album. He's long gone from here." He began to roll the window up. "You and the mutt have a nice walk. I've got this."

"Thank you," she said.

"No problem." He backed the cruiser out of the driveway.

Chapter 36

Lorna was still in the suite when Maureen and Finn returned. "You ought to model something from the shop for your opening tonight," she advised. "You tuck the tags inside, don't spill anything on it, and put it back in stock later."

"Good idea," Maureen said. "I'll do it. There's a halter-top Tiare Hawaii midi in a hibiscus print with pockets that's in my size."

"A perfect choice for you," Lorna said. "I've been thinking about wearing that one myself to the luau at Graceland next month."

Thinking that the print would translate well into black and white, Maureen echoed Lorna's statement. "A perfect choice for you too. I'll run downstairs now and get it."

"I'll be here. I want to tell Finn about a cute girl corgi I met in London, and, hey, be sure that photographer gets a nice picture of you in that dress. It will be good for advertising the place."

"I'm on it," she said, borrowing Hubbard's often-repeated phrase.

By dinnertime Maureen, in the colorful and perfectly fitting midi, tags skillfully tucked inside the halter top—passed through the lobby on the way to the dining room. Hilda was already in her place behind the reception desk. "Wow," the night manager commented. "That is simply stunning on you."

Maureen attempted a model turn. "I'm glad you like it. It's from the new gift shop."

"I like it too. Very much." Ted spoke from the dining room entrance.

Maureen felt her cheeks flush pink. "It's from the gift shop," she repeated, feeling embarrassed and pleased at the same time.

"I wanted to ask if you'd like some celebratory champagne for your guests tonight."

"Don't spill anything on it," Lorna had warned.

Maureen had a fleeting vision of happy, slightly tipsy customers crowded into the shop holding Penelope Josephine's crystal flutes overflowing with champagne. "Maybe on the porch, after they leave the shop," she suggested.

Ted caught on immediately. "Spillage," he said, flashing his wonderful smile.

"Exactly."

"Champagne on the porch it is," he said, "and maybe we can arrange another late date in the bar after your guests leave. The last time was—interesting."

She blushed again. "Quarters," she said, "and laundry. And I almost led us all into legal trouble over that big idea." She raised her right hand. "I promised Hubbard I'd mind my own business from now on. No more trying to figure out what Harvey Album is up to."

"I understand," he said. "We all got a little carried away, didn't we? But it was fun sharing an adventure with you, Maureen."

She giggled softly. "It was fun, wasn't it?"

"Maybe we'll skip the Fairy Godmother this time."

"Good idea. Maybe a nice Irish coffee instead." She paused and looked around. "One more thing about Album, though. Hubbard told me that he's heading west on Route One and they're keeping track of him, so we don't have to worry about him bothering Tommy."

"That's a big relief," he said. "See? The professionals are handling it all just fine. I need to get back to the kitchen now. I'll meet you in the bar after the gift-shop opening."

"See you then," she agreed happily.

She'd asked Gert and Kim to join her in the shop before dinner for a brief rehearsal on cash register operation and sales techniques. Each had opted to wear one of the colorful Haven T-shirts with their own jeans for the event. She'd offered both of them the option of wearing something from stock, but, as Kim said, "If we're wearing it, you can't sell it. You have plenty of T-shirts on hand and they're so pretty."

By the time the dinner guests had begun to leave the dining room, the door to the brightly lit shop was opened wide and colorful bunches of balloons decorated the entrance. Ron Treadwell was on hand with his camera, and George had rigged a speaker to play island music for the occasion. The three smiling and slightly nervous women stood ready to welcome shoppers inside.

Even before dinner had ended, customers began to arrive, filling the parking lot behind the inn and using most of the metered spaces on the boulevard. Maureen hadn't advertised the soft opening anywhere, but it was obvious that between the Quic Shop and word of mouth, the news had spread throughout the community. Within the first half hour she knew she'd be on the phone with suppliers in the morning reordering merchandise.

As customers left the shop, most of them carrying at least one pink-and-purple shopping bag, Jolene served champagne from a round table with a pink umbrella at its center. It was apparent when Maureen closed the shop doors at midnight that—as the old newspapers used to report—"a good time was had by all." She could hardly wait to see the pictures Ron had taken.

"You must be exhausted," Kim told her. "I'll bet you're ready for a good night's sleep. Pleasant dreams."

"I'm too wound up and excited to sleep," Maureen said. "So, fortunately, I have a late date with a handsome chef."

"Oooh! Pleasant wakefulness, then! I'll see you tomorrow."

Maureen thanked her helpers sincerely, giving each of them one of the sterling-and-shell craft bracelets. Checking her reflection in the wonderful dressing room mirror, adding a touch of lipstick, locking the shop door, and heading inside her inn. With a wave and a smile to Hilda, she pushed open the louvred dining-room door and, skirt twirling, headed for the bar. Ted was already there, on the same seat he'd had last time, watching her cross the room. He patted the seat beside him, then held out his hand to her.

Maureen grasped Ted's hand and, with another little twirl, sat beside him. "You look happy," he said.

Lennie placed a steaming whipped-cream-topped Irish coffee in front of her. "Here you go, Ms. Doherty." He repeated Ted's observation. "You look happy."

"I feel happy." She hadn't let go of Ted's hand. "The gift shop is going to be a success."

"I know," Lennie said. "Jolene reported back to us that the customers gave glowing reports about everything—the clothes, the decorations on the walls, even the dressing room mirror. This old inn is happy that you're here to save it."

"Not just me," she insisted. "It's everybody—you and Ted and Molly and Gert and George and Sam and the Gaudettes and Jolene and Shelly and—and everybody."

"It's a happier place since you came," he said, then—perhaps noticing the clasped hands—moved to the far end of the bar, busying himself slicing lemons and limes.

"You've checked off an important box in this busy week,"

Ted said. "Next comes Eddie's memorial tomorrow and then the tournament."

"I know." She sipped the hot brew. "It's all moving so fast. How are the plans for the memorial coming along?"

"It looks as though it's going to be huge. The other restaurants in the area as far away as Clearwater are going to contribute food—not just us. Eddie had a lot of friends."

"I wish I had known him," she said.

"I wish you had too. A sweet guy. We'd been friends a long time." He gave her hand a squeeze, then picked up his own drink. The player piano tinkled a brisk rendition of Cole Porter's "Friendship."

A coincidence? *Not a chance.* She lifted her glass in Billy Bedoggoned's direction.

"Shelly says it looks like we'll have a full house for the tournament," he said. "A big boost for the June figures. Like Lennie says, 'This old inn is happy that you came to save it.'"

"Some thanks for the recent happenings go to Penelope Josephine," she remarked. "The idea for the fishing tournament came from her old trunk full of odds and ends of local memorabilia, and most of the décor for the gift shop came from her hoard."

"Maybe, but it took you and your imagination to put it all together." He leaned toward her and their eyes locked for a long moment. "You're so beautiful," he whispered.

"Ted!" Lennie shouted from the end of the bar, the house phone to his ear. "Molly says come to the kitchen right away. The kittens are coming!"

"Molly's still here?" she asked.

"She wouldn't leave Momcat tonight," he said. "Come on. We're having kittens."

Together, they ran for the kitchen entrance, around the long counters, refrigerator and freezer, past Ted's office space, and into the alcove between the kitchen and outer door. Molly was on her knees beside the big FedEx cardboard box that was lined with blankets and contained a small but very pregnant tiger cat emitting faint little mews.

Molly looked up at them. "Any minute now, we should see the first one," she said. "Come on, Momcat. Push."

"She looks so tiny," Maureen said.

"Yes. She's young. We'll need to get her spayed after this. Maybe Bogie and Bacall's vet would do it."

"I'm sure she will," Maureen said. "I'll be happy to pick up the tab for the surgery."Maureen was sure that Momcat cast a grateful look her way.

The first kitten was a little tiger, just like the mother cat. Momcat licked the baby, then expelled the yucky afterbirth, which she promptly ate while everybody present except Molly looked away. Three more identical little tigers appeared, about thirty minutes apart. With Momcat's guidance, licking, and nuzzling, all four babies soon began nursing. Molly and Maureen cleaned the area and tucked fresh blankets into the box while the men plugged in an electric space heater to insure the warmth of the improvised nursery.

"Now we need to think up names for them all," Maureen said.

"I thought of names for all four when the last one was born," Molly spoke quietly, still stroking Momcat's head." I think they might be sisters. Four little sisters. What do you all think of Meg, Amy, Jo, and Beth? If I'm wrong, we can change the names later.

The men exchanged puzzled glances.

"Perfect," Maureen exclaimed. "*Little Women*. One of my favorite childhood books, I love that idea!"

Chapter 37

Due to the late-night arrival of the kittens and the needed
last-minute preparations for Eddie Manuel's memorial, Maureen and Ted cut their morning run short. Both were at their
respective positions at the inn by six thirty, Ted serving breakfast and Maureen manning the lobby desk, answering question after question about the upcoming kingfishing tournament
on one phone and ordering overnight shipments on merchandise for the shop on the other.

The event at the Coliseum turned out to be a memorable
one for sure. The old building was packed, with overflow
guests on the wide porch and some even standing on the
beach outside. A row of tables and even a few volunteered
food trucks from St. Petersburg offered light refreshments to
the crowd. Loudspeakers had been attached to the overhang,
so the many spoken and musical tributes were audible
halfway down the boulevard. Maureen and a veritable skele-
ton crew manned most of the positions at the inn. Ted,
Molly, Gert, George, and Sam had all been Eddie's friends, so
they attended the ceremony while she, Shelly, Jolene, Lennie,
and a couple of the part-time high school kids kept things
running in their absence. Kim, ever curious, had attended the
memorial, "just to keep an eye on who's there," and Ron

Treadwell went along to make a video of the spoken and musical tributes for the Manuel family.

At noon, family members and a few of Eddie's closest friends were invited to join Tommy and her mother and grandmother to accompany his ashes out into the gulf. Ted was honored to be among them.

When the *Tightline* returned to port after Eddie's final voyage, Ted told Maureen that he'd recognized the plainclothes cop serving again as mate and that there'd been another man who'd stayed close to Tommy the whole time. "That one looked to me like a security guard," Ted said. "I'm sure Hubbard is taking no chances with Tommy as long as Eddie's killer is missing."

"Harvey Album is missing," Maureen said.

"Hubbard is working on it." Ted reached over and ruffled her hair. "Like the man said, leave all that to the professionals. There's more than enough going on around here. The captains' meeting will be held here in the bar to be sure everybody understands all the rules before the start of the tournament. Besides that, Momcat and the babies are still living in the birthing crate, and Molly and Gert are hovering over them like a couple of elderly helicopters."

Maureen frowned. "Are the cats safe in the box? Can a predator get to them? I remember what you said about 'the circle of life.' That's scary."

"We've done all we can for them for now," he said. "Mother Nature will take over from here."

"Should we block the cat door so nothing bad can get in at them?" Maureen worried aloud.

"Nope. Remember, Momcat isn't used to being indoors. She isn't litter-box trained. She needs to go in and out. She'll want to take the kittens outside too, as soon as she thinks they're ready."

Maureen made a face. "Molly and Gert aren't about to let *that* happen to their little women. I'm betting they have new homes picked out for Beth and Jo and Meg and Amy already."

"You're probably right," he said. "But anyway, we don't need to mess around with police business. Frank Hubbard knows what he's doing. Like he told you, Harvey is headed far away from here." She knew that what Ted said was surely correct and tried to erase the image of a menacing Harvey Album from her mind.

Kim had heard about the kittens at the Quic Shop and came into the kitchen to see them. After the prerequisite oohs and aahs, she reported that she'd "taken a quick side trip" over to the Forest after the ceremony. She held up both hands. "I know! I keep thinking about the connection between Eddie Manuel and Harvey. I'm overly curious about everything. I went over to take a look at *our* Indian mounds. Something's not right."

"What do you mean? What something?" Maureen wanted to know.

"There's a sunken area on the east side of the mound that wasn't there last time I climbed it."

"Sunken?" Ted asked.

"Definitely. The topography has changed. Remember, Maureen, when I told you about the patch of white clover where Bitter Blue grass used to be? That's where there's a hollow spot."

Maureen remembered. "You were going to ask the county extension service about the clover."

"I did. It's not an uncommon weed, but it's not something that typically grows in that area. I've contacted the Florida Fish and Wildlife Conservation Commission and asked permission to excavate."

"You can do that?"

"As a licensed archaeologist, I can. And I will. I believe something has been removed recently from the mound in exactly that spot. An officer from the Fish and Wildlife division will be with me. The park will be closed to visitors while we're working there."

"You think Harvey took something from the mound," Ted said. It was a statement, not a question.

"I think someone did."

"Frank Hubbard says Harvey is heading west on Route One in his van," Maureen told her.

"Good. He won't know what I'm doing, then." There was a hint of relief in Kim's voice.

She's afraid of him too.

"Kim, would there be any objection to having Ron photograph the excavation process?" Maureen asked. "Frank Hubbard will probably want photos anyway, and Ron is anxious to be useful because of the room-for-work arrangement we have."

"I'm sure Fish and Wildlife has notified Hubbard," she said, "but even if he has a police photographer there, I can authorize Ron to cover it for my personal records."

"If Frank knows anything about all this, I'm surprised that he hasn't called me." She aimed a questioning look in Ted's direction.

"He's handling it without your input, remember?" Ted spoke with a kind smile. "It's okay."

She sighed. "I guess so. I don't suppose I can come along with you, Kim?"

"I'm afraid not," she said. "This is official archaeology business. Ron can ride with me. Is he here now? I'd like to leave a little bit early, say—in half an hour?"

"I'll buzz his room."

Ron Treadwell, with full camera gear, arrived in the lobby precisely on time. "Glad to have you aboard for this," Kim told him. "There won't be any tree climbing this time, so you probably won't need all of your special equipment."

"No problem," he said. "I just had a text from Harvey that one of the bird-spotters thinks he saw and heard a grasshopper sparrow in the Forest. Harvey says for me to get over there right away. Then you called. What a coincidence, huh?"

"Harvey texted you?" Ted spoke first.

"A grasshopper sparrow?" Kim sounded incredulous.

"Where is Harvey calling from?" Maureen demanded.

"Wait a sec!" Ron laughed. "One question at a time. He didn't say where he was, but he's real anxious to get that picture if the report is true."

"I should think he would be," Kim said. "According to *Funky Florida Facts,* that bird is the most endangered critter in Florida. The spotter must be wrong."

"I know," Ron said. "I don't think it's possible either, but that photo would make me famous. It's still early afternoon and the light is perfect. As long as I'm going to be in the Forest anyway for Kim, why not look around? Right?"

"Hubbard said that Harvey dumped his phone in Orlando," Maureen said. "Did you get the number he called from?"

"I suppose it's on my phone somewhere. I didn't look."

Maureen had already picked up her own phone and hit Hubbard's number.

Chapter 38

"Don't let that guy leave with his phone," Hubbard's voice was so loud, everybody in the lobby could hear it. "It must be a prepaid burner, and I need that number before Harvey tosses it."

"They have to leave now. They're meeting the Fish and Wildlife people at the Forest."

"What the hell has Fish and Wildlife got to do with anything? What have you gotten yourself into now, Doherty? Never mind. I'll meet them at the Forest." Boom. The call had ended.

Ted and Maureen watched from the porch as Kim's Audi pulled out of the driveway. Ron waved from the passenger seat. "Kim's hoping that digging a hole in the mound will prove that Harvey is connected to Indian artifact thefts, and Ron is hoping that an endangered bird is actually in our Forest," Maureen suggested. "I hope they both get their wishes."

"Hubbard is hoping he can catch up with Harvey," he said. "I'm hoping Molly's cake will be finished in time for Trent's birthday party tomorrow and that you and I can spend some time together after dinner."

"For sure," she agreed. "But let's not stay up all night again."

Ted looked around, as though making sure they were

alone, and gave her a quick peck on the cheek. "It was fun, though, wasn't it?"

Surprised by the kiss, she touched her cheek and agreed. "It was fun." She watched as he dashed through the green door, then she sat in the nearest rocking chair. *This is very pleasant*, she thought as she rocked. *I'll bet this is a good place to spend a vacation.* It was too early for Finn's afternoon walk, she had no desire to get sidetracked by delving into Penelope Josephine's trunk, and no new gift shop merchandise had arrived to be unpacked. Shelley was on duty in the lobby. There wasn't any reason why she shouldn't sit in that chair and simply rock for a while. It was a good feeling. She watched the cars move along the boulevard and shoppers stop to look into store windows. She waved to the newspaper boy as he tossed the weekly copy of the *Beach Beacon* onto the front steps.

Maureen realized that she must have dozed off when flashing lights startled her awake. They were from the cruiser parked in front of the inn. Hubbard got out and took the stairs two at a time. She brought her chair to an abrupt stop. "What's going on?" she demanded.

"The SOB must have turned around before he got to Utah. He ran a toll in Valdosta. He's on his way back here. I thought I'd better let you know."

"Utah?"

"We figured he'd be heading there. Because of the car the trucker captured on his dashcam, you know?"

"I didn't know."

"Well, never mind that now. It had Utah plates. I'll tell you about it some other time." He spoke into his phone. "Yeah. Doherty's here. She's okay. Did you catch up with the doc and the Fish and Wildlife guy?" He nodded a couple of times. "Yeah, I figured it was a burner. Anyway, keep an eye on them and the photographer." He put the phone into his pocket. "My deputy says the phone Harvey used got trashed—probably in water—the minute after he sent the text. Doc is digging a hole in the small mound. You know what that's all about? She's not talking and neither is the tree climber. The Fish and Wildlife man is armed. He's going to follow the doc and the photographer back here."

Kim needs an armed guard?

"That's good. She's looking for proof that the mound has been robbed. She's found the spot where Harvey, or somebody, took something out of there very recently. She has permission to do it. You're worried about Harvey doing—something—to me or to Kim?"

"Of course I am. You two are the only witnesses to—to whatever it is that he's up to, and whatever that is must involve a lot of money. The owner of the car that picked up the yellow bag is a major suspect in a pile of stolen antiques—paintings and jewelry and especially Indian relics. Big-time crook, but they haven't been able to pin anything on him. Then you, Ms. Nosy, you and your gal pal have linked him to Album, so I'm thinking he's told Harvey to clean up his mess—or else."

"I'm part of the mess." Her voice was hesitant. "And so is Kim."

"Yes."

"What should I—we—what should we do?"

Maureen felt suddenly cold. Frightened.

"Stay close to home. Don't go anywhere alone. I'll have a cruiser do regular drive-bys but I don't have enough staff to assign anyone to protect you or the doctor. Anyway, there's not a lot I legally *can* do. He hasn't broken any laws here. He's been perfectly cooperative when I wanted to search his van. Hell, he doesn't even litter! Does anyone else have access to your suite?"

"Of course. The housekeeping staff has keys to every door

in the inn." She tried to shake off the fear. "What should we do?" she asked again.

Hubbard's voice was calm. "Hey. There's no need to panic. He must still be driving that big black van of his. I've posted the license number and description and a picture of that model vehicle." He handed her a flyer. "I'll be notified if he's spotted anywhere. Have George install a deadbolt on your suite and one on the doctor's. As far as I can see, you're never alone anyway. Relax. The inn is full. People you know are around you all the time except when you're in your own apartment—and you have the mutt with you then."

. . . along with a couple of ghosts and two cats.

"I'll try to relax, but Frank—it's possible that Harvey is the one who killed Eddie Manuel. It's possible that killing isn't new to him."

"We're well aware of that. Just be careful. Stay home. Stop being so nosy. Lock the doors. Tell the doctor to stay away from the mounds. Never mind what's in them or missing from them. She can work on that later. This will all be over soon. I'm sure of it." He gave her a tentative, fatherly pat on the shoulder. "You can start by staying home today. All day. All night too. And you'd better stop the morning runs with the bartender. You'll get used to it. Call me anytime. Day or night."

She watched as the cruiser pulled away, not feeling one bit relaxed. She wasn't alone on the porch now, for sure. A police cruiser with lights flashing will always draw a crowd. Within seconds she was surrounded by caring, friendly, concerned faces.

"Is everything all right, Ms. Doherty?" the Louisiana lady asked.

How was she to answer the obvious questions? She couldn't very well tell the truth about Harvey Album. Telling paying guests that a would-be killer might be stalking her would surely cause a mass exodus from Haven House. She held up the paper flyer. "Officer Hubbard is distributing these around town. He asked me to post it prominently because the owner of the van once stayed here. If any of you see it around Haven, please call the phone number, but don't approach the driver."

"What did he do?" someone asked.

"Maybe nothing. He's wanted for questioning about some stolen property," she answered truthfully.

"Maybe you should make some copies of that," the Louisiana lady suggested, "and put them around, like in the laundry room and the elevator."

It was an excellent suggestion. "I'll do it right now," Maureen said, and headed for the green door to the lobby.

Chapter 39

The flyers with pictures of the 2015 Hyundai cargo van had been copied and tacked up on the bulletin board, in the laundry and in the elevator and in the public bathrooms. When Kim walked through the front door, Maureen realized that she'd almost been holding her breath, waiting.

"Kim. Are you all right?"

"All right?" The woman's smile was dazzling. "All right? I'm on top of the world! I excavated the sunken part of the mound and I was spot-on! Something has been recently removed—something that's been buried in the mound in a deteriorated canvas bag for a very long time."

"Can you tell what was in it?"

"That kind of analysis is above my pay grade, I'm afraid," Kim said. "I suspect, of course, that whatever was in it was Harvey's stash of stolen artifacts. I've called an expert from the Florida Museum of Natural History to come and pick it up." She held a large green plastic trash bag over her head. "It's all in here. I want to thank you for sending Ron along. He photographed every bit of the excavation and the discovery. I'll bet we'll have a spot on YouTube before long! What a great day."

"I guess Ron didn't find the rare grasshopper sparrow."

"He didn't, but I think he enjoyed crawling among the palmettos and climbing the skinny palm tree to get a new shot of the baby ospreys."

Maureen realized that Kim hadn't yet been informed of Harvey's change of direction—and the possibility that she and Kim were in danger.

"Would you like me to put the bag in my safe until the expert arrives?" she asked.

"That would be great. It must be pretty important." She handed the bag across the counter. "Ron and I had an armed guard following us home to be sure it got here safely."

To be sure you *got here safely!*

"I'll put this away right now," Maureen promised. "Then will you come back down and tell me all about your day? Frank Hubbard stopped by and I need to discuss something with you."

"Of course. Let me shower and change and I'll be right back."

Maureen watched as Kim entered the elevator. *I'll bet she'll be surprised by the new deadbolt on her door*, she thought.

Very much aware of the new restrictions Hubbard had imposed, Maureen had to reconsider her involvement in the rapidly approaching fishing tournament. She'd promised to be careful, but she couldn't very well be expected to deadbolt herself into her room and hide until Harvey was apprehended—and neither could Kim.

There was Trent's birthday celebration tomorrow, followed the next day by the much promoted, much needed for business—Eddie Manuel fishing tournament. Kim would have to be talked out of actually fishing it, but Maureen herself, as the main promotor of the event, needed to see—and be seen. *I'll just have to figure out how to do everything from here*, she promised herself, *and if that's not possible—for instance when I walk Finn—I won't go anywhere alone, and*

I'll lock all the doors and I'll be really, really careful. I'll have to cancel the runs with Ted too. That'll be the hardest part.

The details of Trent's party had been well planned. She was sure he'd be surprised, and that her gift to him—a certificate for a week's stay for two for the following year—would be happily received. She was also sure that there'd be no need for her to move very far from the inn, so Hubbard needn't worry about her tomorrow. She'd be sure to keep Kim inside too. If her rush orders for the shop arrived as planned, the two of them would spend much of the day unpacking, pressing, hanging, and arranging wonderful new things for the shop opening. Even with the threat of possible danger, she had a lot of good things to look forward to—beginning with another late date with Ted. Maybe she'd wear another stick-the-price-tags-inside outfit from the new stock she'd ordered. Something glamourous maybe, to make the news about canceling the morning runs less disappointing.

By the time Kim returned to the lobby, Maureen had carefully rehearsed the words she'd use to soften the bad news about Harvey's change of direction, and the possibility that he might be looking for the two women who'd witnessed the transfer of the yellow bag to a Utah-licensed, crime-connected vehicle. She'd quote Hubbard's assurance that the van would most likely be stopped before it got anywhere near Haven. She'd make sure Kim understood that staying within the boundaries of the inn for a short time would be the safest course to follow and that she herself had no problem with doing so.

"I guess the shiny new lock on my door has something to do with the reason that Frank Hubbard stopped by," Kim announced. "What's going on?"

"I should have told you as soon as you got back from the Forest," Maureen admitted, "but you were so happy, I didn't want to spoil your fun. Anyway, come into my office and have a seat. This won't take long."

It took only a few minutes for Maureen to deliver the un-settling news about Harvey possibly making a fast return to Haven from Utah. "Frank wants us both to lie low until Harvey is apprehended, starting right now. Today. That means we're unofficially pretty much restricted to the inn property. That means no fishing tournament for you, and not much of anything outside these walls for me."

"That sounds serious."

"It might be."

"Harvey wants us dead." Arms folded, Kim looked defiant.

"N-nobody has exactly s-said that," Maureen stammered.

"Harvey wants us dead," Kim repeated. "Why wouldn't he? We can send him to jail for a long time."

"That's true. That's why it's so important for us to be care-ful—to do as Frank says—to stay right here and to lock our doors until they catch him." Even as she spoke the words, Maureen knew how hollow they sounded. It was against her every instinct to hide, when all she wanted to do was help to punish this evil, cowardly thief of some of Florida's most sa-cred history.

"Well then," Kim said, "we'll simply have to figure out a way to nab Harvey without wandering far from the comforts of home."

"I'd hoped you'd see it that way." Maureen couldn't hide her grin. "Let's get started. I promised Frank I wouldn't go anywhere alone, so you'll have to come with me when I walk Finn in the daytime. I'll get one of the men to take him out after sundown. Okay?"

"My pleasure," Kim said.

The remainder of the day passed just about as Maureen had planned. There was no pressing need to leave the com-fort and relative security of the inn. She placed orders for some of the items she'd been meaning to get for the bar—coasters and cocktail napkins with "Haven House Inn" in-

scribed in purple script. On a whim, she ordered plastic cocktail picks in the shape of palm trees. Lennie would like them.
She sent the first of Ron's photos of the front of the building
to an online printer of glossy postcards. If that one turned
out well, she'd order others for the gift shop. With final
touches for the birthday party in place, Maureen had time to
do a little tidying in her suite. Although the housekeeping
staff kept everything vacuumed and dusted, she preferred to
arrange her desk and bookshelves, cat and dog toys, cosmet-
ics and toiletries herself.

Lorna was already seated on the couch, Finn at her feet,
when Maureen turned both locks on her door, using a shiny
brass key for the new deadbolt.

"What's going on with the heavy security?" the ghost wanted
to know. "I haven't noticed anything around here that's worth
stealing."

"Thanks a lot," Maureen said. "Our favorite local cop
seems to think a bad guy is after me."

"The creepy old guy with the bird magazine, huh?"

"Right." Maureen approached the cat tower, examining
all of the shelves. "Where are the cats?"

"Look outside." She pointed. "They're both sitting in the
tree beside the little balcony. Just sitting. They've been there
for an hour. Cats are weird. If I could, I'd open the window
and let the darn fools in." She held up pale, perfectly mani-
cured, shimmering hands. "Can't do it."

Maureen knew that sometimes, for reasons of their own,
the cats occasionally liked to enter the suite via the window
instead of the cat door. In fact, when she'd first met the cats,
they'd been sitting outside on the oak tree branch in exactly
the same positions. "I've got it." She turned the crank that
made the two panes swing inward.

Bogie, the big yellow tiger cat, moving carefully from the
tree branch onto the narrow balcony, entered first, crouching
on the middle platform of the tower. Bacall followed, one

dainty foot after the other, onto the top tier of the carpeted structure. Each cat lay down on its chosen spot, eyes closed, feigning sleep.

"Cats are weird," Lorna said again. "Now tell me what's going on with the cop."

Maureen synopsized, as best she could, the story of how Harvey had appeared on the scene, how Kim had come to suspect him of robbing Native artifacts, and how she and Kim had witnessed the possible transfer of stolen property into Harvey's van. She wound up with Hubbard's own words: "He's told Harvey to clean up his mess."

"You and the well-dressed doctor are the mess," Lorna said.

"I'm afraid so."

"Maybe you'd better do what the cop says," she offered, "and I'll keep an eye on things around here. Reggie and—um—some of the others will too."

Some of the others?

She didn't ask.

Chapter 40

Maureen and Kim walked together with Finn for his regular four-o'clock outing. It would be one of their short walks, not involving a run for Finn on the beach, but that was not particularly unusual. She didn't want to do anything to indicate that something was amiss at Haven House.

"Just two friends chatting together and walking a beautiful golden on a pretty afternoon," she said. "No one would guess we had a trouble in the world."

"Normal as apple pie," Kim agreed. "Have you told Ted about what Frank said yet?"

"He's been busy all day with food prep and party food and the kittens in the kitchen, but we're meeting after dinner tonight. I'll tell him everything then, including the part about canceling our morning runs on the beach."

"He's going to want to protect you," Kim said. "Maybe now's a good time to invite him to spend the night."

"What on earth gave you that crazy idea?" Maureen was shocked, and didn't try to hide it.

"Woof." Finn stopped walking and looked up at Maureen. "Woof woof."

"See? Finn agrees. Everybody who sees you two together knows what's going on." She giggled softly. "You aren't fooling anybody around here."

Maureen didn't know what to say. The very idea was out-rageous. Or was it?

When in doubt, change the subject.

"I'm wondering if any of the new stock I ordered will arrive this afternoon," she said. "I might find something special to wear to dinner."

"Yes." Kim's expression was solemn. "The occasion calls for something special."

"Something glamorous," Maureen offered.

They'd reached the Coliseum, turned and headed back down the boulevard—two friends walking together on a pleasant Florida evening, chatting now in low tones about a way to nab a thief without leaving home—and without getting themselves killed in the process.

Both were pleased to see four Amazon cartons smiling at them from the front porch.

"I'll bet there's something special in there for you to wear tonight." Kim dashed up the stairs toward the boxes.

Maureen was right behind her. "Something glamorous," she said, thinking that maybe, just maybe, there *was* a chance that she and Ted might be alone together in her suite this very night.

She nearly laughed aloud at her next thought. *Sure. All alone with a dog, two cats, Lorna, Reggie, and—uh—"some of the others."*

A sleepover at my place is not happening anytime soon.

With each of them carrying a couple of boxes, Maureen opened the shop. They put the boxes on the counter and she quickly locked the door behind them. "I'm feeling paranoid, looking over my shoulder, jumping at noises. You too?"

"Pretty much," Kim agreed. "I like being in here with the door locked, though. Cozy."

"Me too. Hilda came on at five o'clock, so we can work in here undisturbed for as long as we want—or at least until we get hungry and break for dinner." She opened the first package. "We need a plan, you know. We can't just depend on Frank Hubbard to get us out of this mess."

Kim lifted a lacy white blouse from the box and put it on a velvet hanger. "These are super cute. The pastels look great too. I'm thinking of some kind of trap to capture the creep."

"They look good with the flowered palazzo pants. With us as the bait?"

"Let's put a set in the window," Kim said, "with a big white sunhat. Sure, but we'll have to have some kind of protection from him."

Maureen paused in clipping a tag onto a Joseph Ribkoff scarf. "What kind of protection?"

"I love the colors in that. Is it real silk? That's the part we need to plan. Really carefully."

"It's silk. You have to handwash it," she said. "We can't afford to involve anyone else. Too dangerous. We'll have to do it all by ourselves."

Kim opened the next box. "Oh boy. This might be the dress you should wear tonight. Don't you want to involve Hubbard?"

Maureen stood, holding the slim-fitted silver tube dress against her body. "It's pretty simple."

"The plan?"

"No. The dress."

Kim smiled. "Sometimes less is more."

"I'll wear it." She slipped the dress into a pink-and-purple bag. "We'll have to be sure Hubbard knows where we are all the time—but maybe not exactly what we're doing."

"Wear your silver sandals and one piece of jewelry. We'll let him know just enough to keep him in the loop but not enough to freak him out."

"A single shell on a silver chain," Maureen decided. "This isn't going to be easy."

"A miniature, pearly, chambered nautilus." Kim smiled and winked. "We'll be close to home. Harvey will have to come into our territory if he wants to get to us."

" 'Come into my parlor,' said the spider to the fly." Maureen returned the wink.

"Exactly."

"We already know that Harvey is a creature of habit," Kim pointed out. "He likes things neat. He likes patterns. Time patterns. For instance, he knew exactly what day the county inspector would show up every month, so he must have done all his mound digging the rest of the time."

"Except that Eddie Manuel made random visits by water to the Forest and must have caught Harvey with the mound opened," Maureen realized. "That's why Eddie had to die. That's how come they were both on Eddie's ski."

"Then Harvey ditched the ski and walked back to his van, cut through the gate, got the ski he'd rented and left on the beach. He returned it on time—charged to *Watching Birds*." Kim was excited. "Time is important to him. Let's give Harvey a nice, neat time pattern." They exchanged high fives and continued with the tagging, folding, hanging, and displaying task at hand, and continued to chat—as good friends do.

When the two women left the gift shop, they brought with them from the new inventory two identical beach chairs. "It looks as though it'll be a beautiful sunset," Maureen said. "As soon as I put my dress in my room, I'll meet you out in the side yard under the oak tree."

"I'll set up our beach chairs," Kim offered. "We have to stay clearheaded, totally alert. Since you own the place, you can bring the beverages."

As agreed, within a short time, Maureen—carrying two glasses of diet ginger ale in Penelope Josephine's second-best stemware—left the inn via the side door and joined Kim in the beach chairs, their backs against the sturdy oak tree, facing the glowing sun setting over the Gulf of Mexico. Each of them wore beneath her cute top a special necklace, much like something one would wear if one had fallen and couldn't get up, like a medical alert necklace. A touch of a finger on either necklace would summon a cop instead of an ambulance. Frank Hubbard had personally delivered them to Maureen one recent afternoon at the gift shop. "Just a precaution." His voice was gruff. "They're not expensive, but I have to bill you for them. The city can't pick up the tab for such things. It makes me feel better, knowing how much trouble you two can get into." Maureen had silently, and gratefully, written a personal check.

"It's very pleasant here, drinking make-believe champagne, isn't it?" Maureen raised her glass. "We should make a habit of doing this."

"What a remarkably clever idea," Kim agreed. "Let's definitely do this every evening."

"For as long as it takes," Maureen said. They tapped their glasses together, toasting the sunset.

The silver dress, with tags artfully hidden, was a definite hit at dinnertime. Maureen sat with Trent and Pierre, who both enthused over the dress's fit and fabric. They were soon joined by several of the newer guests, most of them there for the tournament. Kim arrived shortly and sat beside Maureen. Soon fishing, not fashion, was the main topic of conversation. Enthusiasm for the event was obvious, and she was impressed with the knowledge of the intricacies of the sport on display by her dinner companions. This was clearly going to be a competition between experienced anglers.

Ron Treadwell roamed amid the tables, snapping pictures that would be posted on the office bulletin board and the inn's website. The lively table conversation and the beautifully presented food gave Maureen a new sense of pride in what she'd accomplished so far in her unfamiliar role as innkeeper. The happy glow was short-lived, as the phone in her silver evening bag vibrated. Caller ID showed the Haven Police Department.

"Please excuse me." She stood. "Business call," she apologized. The closest exit was through the kitchen door. Careful to avoid collision with a server—cognizant of what a splash of onion soup or a blob of salad dressing from a server's tray would do to the dress—she checked the round window before pushing the door open and spoke into the phone. "Hello. This is Maureen Doherty." She stepped out of the way of kitchen traffic, into a small space beside one of the freezers.

"Doherty, you can deep-six the flyer on Album's van. He's ditched it," Hubbard announced.

She literally felt her heart skip a beat. "Where is he?"

"He abandoned it in an RV park just over the state line from Georgia."

"So where is he now?" she asked, her voice urgent.

"I don't know. He could have rented a car, he could have stolen one, he could be hitchhiking. Anyway, he's on his way here. Listen, Doherty, you stay put. Hear me?"

"Other than a daytime dog walk on the boulevard in plain sight of the whole town, I'm staying put," she promised.

"No morning runs on the beach either," he ordered.

"I know." Hubbard's words echoed in her mind. *"He's on his way here."* She wasn't prepared for the chill of genuine fear the words brought.

"Stay in touch, Doherty."

"Frank, I'm taking this seriously. If you get a hurry-up call from us on our necklaces, you come a'runnin' okay?" She kept her tone light. "Just in case he shows up."

"No problem there, Doherty."

She slipped the phone back into her purse, willing her hands not to shake.

"Wow! Look at you!" Ted's voice was warm, low, and—

dared she think—intimate. "You light up my kitchen. Did you come to see me?"

"I—I had to answer my phone." She tried to smile, to pretend everything was normal.

Ted wasn't fooled. He moved closer to her. "What's wrong?"

"It was Hubbard on the phone," she told him, willing tears away. "Harvey ditched the van in Georgia. He could already be here in Haven. Right now."

"You need to stay here. Inside the inn. With me. Can Hubbard offer you any protection?" He handed her a paper napkin.

She wiped her eyes. "Not officially. Remember, Harvey hasn't broken any laws that we know of. He's been cooperative with the police. He pays his bills. He keeps his area clean." She tried to muffle a sniffle. "Frank says I can't even run on the beach with you mornings anymore."

"That's okay. They'll catch him soon. We'll be fine. Was Kim with you in the dining room?"

"Yes. I haven't told her about this yet, but we've already agreed to stay within sight of the inn until this mess is over."

But we're the mess Harvey means to clean up. Kim and I are the mess.

"I have to get back to work." He gripped her by the shoulders pulling her close. "I'll meet you in the bar as soon as I can after dinner. We'll figure this out."

"Okay," she said, moving toward the door to the dining room.

"Maureen," he said.

"What?"

"You look beautiful."

She managed a smile, and motioned to Kim to join her beside the kitchen door. In a few words, she relayed Hubbard's chilling message. The two rejoined the table full of friends and fishermen, now engaged in a loud, friendly discussion about the merits of the various boat captains, the speed of the vessels involved, their preference of baits—live or artificial. Maureen was surprised to learn that Pierre was an avid fisherman and planned to fish the tournament aboard one of the largest party boats, while Trent, pleading seasickness, had volunteered to help at the weighing station.

Maureen was pleased when Kim, who'd already booked a spot aboard the *Tightline,* came up with a ready excuse to stay at home—indefinitely. Kim held up her right hand, the wrist at an awkward angle. "I just called Gert to run over to the Quic Shop to get one of those black wrist braces for me. I seem to have strained my wrist somehow—the one on my reel-cranking side. I'll call Tommy and cancel after dinner."

"No kidding?" One of the men pushed his chair back. "If there's going to be a spot left with Tommy, I'm going to call and try to grab it."

Maureen put on a sad face. "I'm sorry, Kim. I've had you putting price tags on merchandise all week. Is that what's hurt your poor paw?"

"Don't worry about it!" she said. "I'm enjoying handling all the beautiful things for the gift shop. I can hardly wait for the opening." She neatly changed the subject from fishing to shopping.

All the rest of the dinner conversation went smoothly. Maureen said good night to her tablemates, asking Kim to join her in the lobby office. They renewed their pact to stay vigilant and had a brief, whispered chat—something about spiders and flies—before Kim took the elevator up to the Joe DiMaggio Suite, where, she claimed, the scent of Chanel No. 5 was now present every day.

Maureen locked the office, stepped out onto the darkened front porch, and made a fervent wish on the North Star just as a Haven PD cruiser rolled by. She took the time to remove the flyers with the photo of the cargo van from the bulletin board, the laundry room, the public restroom, and the elevator. Then, sipping ice water at the busy and bustling pretournament bar, she waited for Ted. The piano plinked out "Anchors Aweigh" while Lennie mixed, stirred, blended, shook, and muddled with all the flair of a Vegas showman. *All this hustle is great for business*, she thought, *but not so good for a serious conversation.*

She put the silver purse on the seat beside hers, indicating that she was waiting for someone, and watched the angelfish swim in circles.

Chapter 41

It wasn't long before Ted arrived. "They say watching fish in an aquarium for fifteen minutes lowers your blood pressure and lightens your mood," he whispered.

"Good therapy," she said. "I'm glad you're here."

"I left the girls in charge of tomorrow's breakfast prep," he explained. "Neither one of them will leave the kittens anyway, so it's all in good hands." He kept his voice low, although the crowd had begun to thin out. "How're you doing? Did you tell Kim about Harvey being closer than we thought?"

"I did," she said. "She'll do what Hubbard wants us to do right along with me. She's not going to fish the tournament after all. We'll be practically Velcroed together until all this is over." She raised the water glass. "We've agreed to stay as alert as we can. So no Fairy Godmothers or even Irish coffee for now."

"That's a good plan," he agreed. "Count me in. I wish I could be with you every minute." He reached for her hand. "I wish we could tell the girls and George and Sam about Harvey. They'd all have your back. In fact, everybody who works here cares about you more than you know."

"They're all good people and I appreciate every one of them, but they can't be involved in this. Hubbard kept his word about a police car doing random checks. I just saw one pass by out front. Kim and I will walk Finn together in the daytime, and I'll ask George or Sam to walk him later." His hand on hers was comforting. "We'll get through this soon. I'm sure of it." If he hadn't been holding her hand, she'd have crossed her fingers on that giant fib.

"You know, Maureen, nobody would blame you if you went to California to stay with your folks until this blows over. Would you consider doing that? Harvey would never find you there."

She couldn't say that the thought had never occurred to her, because it had. She'd dismissed it quickly, though. There were too many people—too many friends—depending on her now. She had an inn to run, a birthday to celebrate, and a fishing tournament to coordinate, along with a pretty darned good plan to catch a thief. Leaving out the part about the plan to catch Harvey, she told him so. He didn't bring the subject up again.

Instead, he told her he'd pick Finn up every morning and take him along on his own run, that he'd make sure the golden got plenty of exercise. "We'll start tomorrow morning. I'll come up and get him. Just leash him and hand him out your door."

"I'd appreciate that so much," she said, "and so will Finn, but you can't be seen coming and going from the third floor, dog or no dog. That'd be all over the Quic Shop in minutes."

"True," he said. "I guess you'll have to hand him over to me in the lobby."

"That's okay. It'll give me an early start on my day."

With the subjects of Harvey getting closer to Haven, the impossibility of Maureen running away to California, and the assurance of a daily morning run on the beach for Finn behind them, the conversation became lighter and perhaps a bit more intimate. They lingered over diet sodas until the bar was nearly empty. It was after one o'clock when he escorted her to the elevator, then stood close beside her while the beautiful door slid open. Their eyes met—and under the obvious stare of the night manager—he gave her a decorous peck on the cheek. "See you in the morning," he said.

As soon as she walked down the third-floor hall she heard Finn's welcoming woofs. "It's a good thing to have a dog to come home to," she said aloud as she unlocked the dead-bolted door and knelt to accept the golden's happy kisses and excited tail wagging before relocking the door behind her. The cats were in their usual spots in the tower, and neither acknowledged her homecoming. "I know you're glad to see me," she told them, "even if you pretend I'm not here. You like me well enough when I feed you."

There seemed to be no ghostly presence around to chat with, so she prepared for bed. Finn assumed his accustomed sleeping spot, and after a while Maureen fell into an uneasy sleep. She needed no alarm clock to wake up in time for the morning run on the beach—the one Finn would enjoy without her that day—and for an unknown number of days in the future.

As planned, she handed the properly fed and leashed Finn over to Ted just before sunrise. She watched from the top stair on the porch as the two jogged along the boulevard toward the beach, then, regretfully returned to the lobby under Hilda's watchful gaze. "No run for you today?" the night manager asked.

"Nope." She pasted on a fake pout. "I have way too much to do today and probably all the rest of the week, what with Trent's party and the fishing tournament and all."

"Understood," Hilda said. "If you need me for any extra hours this week, just call."

"Really? Thank you so much. That's awfully kind of you." Maureen, surprised by the offer, remembered what Ted had said. *"Everyone who works here cares about you more than you think."*

"No problem. Anytime." The woman smiled. "I love working here."

Maureen unlocked her office door, pausing before going inside. "So do I, Hilda," she said. "So do I." She left the door ajar, sat in the uncomfortable white wicker chair, and glanced up at the old map of Haven over the desk—the map covering the office safe. *That dirty old canvas bag is still in there*, she thought. *Maybe the Florida Museum of Natural History people will come today to pick it up. Would an old canvas bag still have fingerprints on it?*

Maureen hadn't been altogether kidding when she'd claimed she had a lot of work to do. She'd checked her email and was only halfway through outlining the speech she'd have to give when she handed out the winning tournament trophies when she heard a familiar "woof" from the front porch. Ted and Finn were back from the beach. She came out into the lobby to greet them.

"We had a good run," Ted told her. "Finn chased a heron. We ran all the way down to the docks, and the fleet looks great, banners flying everywhere. All their trucks and cars have been washed and polished and more than a few of them have FISH EDDIE'S TOURNAMENT WITH US signs on them. The weather is going to be fine for fishing. It's going to be a perfect weekend."

He handed her the leash. "See you at breakfast?"

"For sure," she said. "Breakfast and lots of coffee. I'll be in the dining room as soon as Kim comes downstairs." Ted headed past the brochure rack toward his first-floor room, looking confident that it would, indeed, be a perfect weekend. Maureen most sincerely hoped he was right.

When Kim arrived in the lobby Maureen had already confirmed the number of registered anglers with the Coast Guard, checked with the banjo player about music for Trent's party, and said goodbye to Hilda and hello to Shelly, who'd signed up for the morning reservation desk shift. Maureen wished

Kim a good morning, and the two joined the early break-
fasters in the dining room, taking seats at one of the smaller
cocktail tables. Over warm oatmeal muffins and hot coffee,
they discussed their own plans for the day ahead.

"We can do some stock work in the shop," Maureen said,
"but I can't stay in there all day, and we've got to stick together somehow. Maybe after we walk Finn together, you
can relieve Shelly at the reservation desk while I take care of
business in my office. Would you mind that? You're a paying
guest and I'm asking you to work here. It doesn't seem
right."

"Are you kidding? I love working here." Kim gave a broad
wink. "And I certainly look forward to our sunset champagne break."

Does everyone really love working here?

By afternoon it seemed to Maureen that maybe everyone
did enjoy their jobs. Gert and Molly took turns in the
kitchen, insisting that one or the other needed to be there for
Momcat and the kittens. Whoever wasn't on cat watch,
along with some of the part-time neighborhood women, took
care of the indoor housekeeping duties while George and
Sam did the usual errand running and outdoor maintenance.
All four found time between duties to rock together in their
top-of-the-stairs porch spots.

The Florida Museum man arrived to pick up the canvas
bag. He and Kim put on blue latex gloves and transferred the
shabby thing into a clear plastic case, with the museum guy
carrying it off as if it was made of gold. Maureen, happy to
see it leave, vacuumed the inside of the safe and sprayed it
with pine-scented antibacterial deodorizer.

George, as he'd promised, took Finn for an afternoon
walk. Some more Amazon boxes arrived and were placed in
the stockroom for unpacking. At the appointed hour Kim
and Maureen, having pressed, tagged, and displayed the

newest inventory, dressed in shorts and crop tops, carried their beach chairs and wineglasses out to the old oak tree and proceeded to enjoy a Florida sunset, smiling, posing prettily, and chatting as good friends do—even though most good friends don't chat about killers and thieves and the belongings of long-dead Tocobagans.

Chapter 42

When the filled-to-capacity dining room burst into a full-throated, if slightly off-key version of "Happy Birthday," accompanied by both piano and banjo, the look on Trent's face made all of the planning and preparation worthwhile—and then some. He was so genuinely surprised and delighted that Maureen's eyes grew misty. The dinner was expectedly excellent, with Ted presiding over the prime rib carving, Gert and Jolene serving vegetables and side dishes. The towering birthday cake was greeted with spontaneous applause from the crowd, and Molly was called in from her self-imposed kitten watch in the kitchen to take a much-deserved bow.

Maureen, in another tag-tucked Tiare Hawaii number, this one side slit with a red-amaryllis pattern on white linen, table-hopped the room, making sure everyone was well-fed and happy. When the dessert was served, she and Kim shared a good-sized piece of the cake—the part with a lot of chocolate frosting on it—and quietly discussed the progress of their plan for the spider's web.

"If he's anywhere around here, and I feel sure that he is, he's watching us establish certain patterns. The dog walking is erratic timewise and happens in public," Maureen said, "so that won't interest him."

"The pre-sunset champagne break is definitely the one for

him to concentrate on." Kim picked up a forkful of cake. "OMG, Maureen. This may be the best thing I've ever eaten in my whole life."

"I know. Molly is a gem. My whole staff is amazing. I kind of wish we could let them in on this." Maureen sipped her after-dinner coffee. "Frank's idea of the necklaces makes me feel much better about the whole plan. With our backs to the building and the oak tree, chances are we'll be able to see him coming, to alert Hubbard in time."

"How do you think he plans to—um—to eliminate us?"

"He has to get us to go with him somewhere else. He can't just leave us dead and bleeding in our beach chairs."

"Do you have to be so graphic?" Kim shuddered slightly. "He'll have to kidnap us somehow. Get us to go with him to someplace else."

"I agree. That's the way he'll do it." Maureen savored another bite of cake. "He has to make it look like an accident. Like he tried to do with Eddie."

"Most everybody still thinks that was an accident," Kim reasoned. "Nobody has proven that it wasn't."

"He seems to be good at everything he does," Maureen admitted. "Magazine editing, bird-watching, fishing, cleaning, Jet Skiing—and probably stealing and killing."

"Do you think he was watching us from somewhere when we were in the beach chairs this afternoon?"

"It's pretty likely. He can be using binoculars from somewhere on the boulevard," Maureen said. "He could even be spying on us with a drone. He has one. Ron wanted him to use it to spy on the ospreys."

"That's beyond creepy."

"I know. Look. Here comes Ted."

Ted had shed his chef's coat, and his white shirt was unbuttoned at the neck. As always, he looked cool and comfortable. "Hello, ladies. May I join you?" He pulled one of the ubiquitous white wicker chairs up to the small table.

"Of course. Ted, the birthday party was a huge success. Did you see Trent's face when they sang 'Happy Birthday'?"

"It was worth a million dollars," he said. "I have to get back to the kitchen right away, but I need to know that you two are okay—that you're being careful every minute. Have you heard any more about Album? Where he might be?"

Maureen and Kim exchanged glances. How much should they share with Ted? Maureen began. "It's quite likely that he's already somewhere in the area, maybe even in Haven. We're both taking it seriously. We will be here on the inn property all the time, except when we're walking the dog in plain sight of everyone on the boulevard." She looked into Ted's eyes. "We're practically under house arrest. We'll be okay. If Harvey shows his face anywhere, Hubbard will find a reason to detain him." She hoped with all her heart that it was true.

Kim added more information. "You know how we like to sit outside and watch the sunset? Even then we're on the property, and we each have panic buttons hooked up to Hubbard's number. He'll know right away if we're in trouble."

"Thanks for telling me. I've worried about that. I need to know that you two aren't on some kind of all-girl crusade to catch a thief." He managed a wry smile. "I'm glad you're not taking crazy chances—like staking out the Forest parking lot or invading his laundry basket."

"Nothing like that, I promise," Maureen told him, somewhat truthfully. This plan was *quite* different.

"Okay, then. I'll try to stop worrying." He stood and glanced at the nearly empty cake plate. "How about that cake? Molly is a wonder. Doing all her regular jobs and being a grandmother to four kittens at the same time. Will I see you later tonight, Maureen?"

"Same time, same barstool. I'll be there," she promised, watching as he headed back to the kitchen.

"You two make such a cute couple," Kim said. "I'm sorry you think you have to keep it under wraps."

"It doesn't look right, you know? Business owner and employee?" She made a silly face. "Maybe someday. Want to go out and sit on the porch for a while?"

"Do you think he can see us when we're on the porch in the dark?" Kim whispered as they left the dining room.

Maureen knew she meant Harvey Album. "I wouldn't be a bit surprised." She pushed the green door open. "Creepy, huh?"

It was a pleasant night to be on the Haven House porch. A soft Florida breeze stirred the air, and there was a delicate fragrance coming from the lantana plants hanging in baskets from the hooks that once held the old VACANCY/NO VACANCY signs. Many of the rocking chairs were occupied, but conversation was muted. The two women rocked together in silence for nearly an hour before Kim excused herself and left for the Joe DiMaggio Suite while Maureen made her way to the beautiful bar where she could watch angelfish swim, hopefully lowering her blood pressure and lightening her mood while she sipped ice water and waited for Ted.

He arrived a little earlier than usual, sliding easily onto the barstool next to hers. "They shooed me out of the kitchen," he said. "Told me to relax."

"It's a good idea," she agreed. "You can help me watch fish swim."

"I like watching you," he said. "I like that dress."

"I like it too. I'm thinking about buying it."

If the answer puzzled him, he didn't show it. "So tomorrow the tournament begins," he said. "So far it looks like it's going to be a huge success. There was a spot on the Channel Nine late news showing the charter boats all decked out and ready to go." He signaled for the bartender and ordered a Diet Coke.

"I saw it," she said. "Did you notice the photo credit? Our

own Ron Treadwell shot it. I'm proud of him. We have a full house, and the captains' meeting tomorrow morning should tie up any loose ends. The weather is going to be good all weekend. For our first attempt at anything like this, I think maybe we've nailed it."

"Fingers crossed," he said. He held up his hand displaying his own crossed fingers.

She crossed her own, holding her hand up to meet his. "Fingers crossed."

He grasped her hand in his, bringing it to his lips. The expected kiss never landed. The door leading to the kitchen burst open.

"Ted! Come quick!" Molly shouted. "Momcat is gone!"

Chapter 43

They followed Molly. "She's gone. Something bad is happening. She's gone," the woman wailed. "She went out the cat door a while ago—you know—like she does when she has to pee. She'd fed the babies and licked them and cuddled with them like she does, then she just went out the cat door. I was helping with the dinner cleanup when I heard this god-awful yowling from outside." She wiped her eyes, standing over the box where the four kittens lay. "I opened the door and she wasn't there. I've been walking around out there calling her for the longest time, but she hasn't come back. I don't know what to do."

Ted put a comforting arm around Molly's shoulders, leading her to the chair in his office area. "We'll find her, Molly. Something's spooked her. That's all. She's feral, not used to being around people. She won't leave her kittens for long, even if she's scared. You'll see. She'll come creeping back in through that cat door in no time."

Molly wiped her eyes with the edge of her apron. "Do you really think so?"

"He's right, Molly," Maureen said. "You know what a good mother Momcat is. She'd never leave her babies, no matter what. Do you want us to wait here with you?"

"Would you?"

Maureen and Ted spoke simultaneously. "Yes." Ted pulled three folding chairs from the stack used for extra seating, and the three sat in the very clean, well-organized kitchen, each of them concentrating on the big blanket-lined FedEx box where Meg, Jo, Beth, and Amy had begun to wake up. A faint, persistent, and somehow pitiful mewling issued from the tiger-striped huddle of furry babies. Molly began to cry.

"They're hungry," she said. "They're always hungry. How are we going to feed them if she doesn't come back?"

"Hush, don't cry. There's such a thing as kitten formula. I've seen it in the pet food aisle at Walmart when I buy food for Bogie and Bacall." Maureen tried to comfort the woman. "They even have tiny nursing bottles. The kittens are going to be fine."

"Is it open now?" Molly wailed. "They're hungry now."

"It's open all night," Maureen said. "We'll send one of the boys to get some. George is probably still awake watching the sports channel."

"I'll get him." Ted hurried to the dining room exit, as the chorus of mews from the box became louder.

George was, in fact, awake and willing to make a quick trip to the store. "I needed toothpaste anyway," he told Molly. "It's no problem." He gave her an awkward hug. "Don't cry, Moll. The kittens will be fine, and the mother cat will come home soon. You'll see."

Maureen hoped he was right. While Ted made coffee and Molly petted the kittens one at a time, Maureen turned on the outside light and, stepping just outside the back door, called softly, "Here, kitty, kitty, kitty. Come home, Momcat. Come, kitty, kitty, kitty." She waited for a long moment, hoping for a response, then came inside, turning the light off and locking the door behind her.

On George's return, directions read, formula heated, and

four little nursing bottles filled, Molly, George, Ted, and Maureen each picked up a kitten, and each in his or her own way, figured out how to convince Meg, Jo, Beth, and Amy to take nourishment.

With kittens fed and re-bedded and the foursome on caffeine overload, no one seemed anxious to leave. George pointed to the kitchen clock. "Hey. guys, it's almost one o'clock. The first tournament day has already started."

"He's right," Maureen said. "All of the boat captains plan to meet here at about five for final instructions. Lines can be in the water by six thirty."

"My morning crew will be checking in to get breakfast started at four." Ted folded his chair and put it back onto the stack. "I might as well get things going. Want to get the muffins started, Molly?"

"Sure. Might as well. The kittens have to be fed every two hours anyway, so there's no point in trying to go to sleep now. The morning kids can help feed them." She folded her chair. "Blueberry or chocolate chip?"

"A couple dozen of each. Maureen, I'll call you as soon as the morning crew gets organized so you can bring Finn down."

"Okay." She added her chair to the stack. "I'll see you all at breakfast."

The hallway was quiet when Maureen reached the third floor. She unlocked the door, turned on the kitchen light, tiptoed past the cat tower, through the kitchen, and into the bedroom. Finn raised his head, uttered a sleepy "woof," and went back to sleep.

She sat at the kitchen table, wide awake, looking out the window into the darkness. *If he's out there, can he see me? Every time I turn on a light, does he know what room I'm in?*

Was her fear of Harvey becoming obsessive? She tried to shake the bad thoughts away. Maybe as soon as the tournament was over she *should* consider going to see her parents in California. Let Hubbard deal with it. *What about Kim? What about the inn? What about Ted?*

She knew she wasn't going to California or anywhere else. She folded her arms, put her head down on the table, and slept until exactly four o'clock. She'd just showered and changed clothes when Ted called. She leashed Finn, and walking as quietly as she could, hurried down the two flights to the lobby where there was more activity than usual at that early hour.

Finn woofed happily when he saw Ted, probably knowing he was going to have a faster than usual beach run. Gert and Sam were there, having arrived in time to relieve Molly and George in the kitchen, and were receiving instructions on kitten feeding. Ron Treadwell, with full camera gear, smilingly received congratulations from everyone who'd seen his work displayed on the local TV channel. "One of the captains let me climb up into his Bimini tower to get that shot," he explained. "What a nice bunch of guys."

"Most of the captains are here for the meeting right now, Ron," Sam said. "The parking lot is full of party-boat trucks and fishing gear vehicles and even a bait truck, all with signs about the tournament plastered all over them. Some of them even had to park in the overflow lot out back."

Kim, now wearing the black wrist brace, listened intently as Gert and Molly talked excitedly about the disappearance of Momcat, emphasizing the importance of the feedings every two hours. "I'll be happy to help. I bottle-fed a baby goat once up in New Hampshire," she offered. "Maybe it works the same way."

"I'd give you a quick lesson, Kim," Maureen said, "but it's time for me to get over to the bar and welcome the captains. I'll catch up with you later." She joined the group of men and the one female captain—Tommy Manuel—in the bar area.

Trent, who'd volunteered to help at the weigh-in station, joined her. She introduced herself, wished them all good luck, and sat beside Trent while one of the captains announced the weigh-in rules. She made a mental note that on all three days, weigh-in would begin at three o'clock each afternoon and end at five. *Perfect*, she thought. *That leaves plenty of time for Kim and me to finish weaving our spiderweb under the oak tree.*

Chapter 44

Day one of the Eddie Manuel Memorial Kingfishing Tournament was rated by all concerned as an unqualified success. When the five o'clock weigh-in was completed, and the scores had been posted on the big new chalk board at the front of the charter boat dock, it seemed as though all of Haven was in a celebratory frame of mind—fishermen and non-fishermen alike.

Maureen and Ted shared a brief moment together in the kitchen, while he supervised the preparation of dinner and she checked on the progress of the still-orphaned kittens. "Not bad for a one-week, tossed-together promotion," she said.

"It was a true what-have-we-got-to-lose crapshoot," he admitted, "and it definitely worked."

"The inn is full, the bar is packed, the gift shop is a hit," she said, "and we even got a mention on the *Today* show this morning. Haven is on the map as more than a drive-by on the way to Disney World. I'm thinking this will be an annual event in Haven for sure."

"It was all your idea," he said.

"No. It was Penelope Josephine's idea. She practically handed it to me from that old trunk of hers."

"Well, you made it work," he told her. "Tomorrow is day

two, and it might get even busier. Can you relax for a little while? Grab a little rest before it starts all over again?"

"Yep. Kim and I are going to sit outdoors and watch the sunset as usual," she promised. "There's nothing like watching a Florida sunset to relax a person."

Especially when you have a push button to the police at your fingertips, and you're looking over your shoulder for a might-be killer.

"I'm glad you have your hotline to Hubbard ready while you two are out there," he said. "Not that Album is likely to get that close to the inn with all that's going on here. He'd be walking into a buzz saw of your friends."

"True that," she said, while contemplating Album getting exactly that close to the inn. "I'm going upstairs to slip into something more comfortable. See you in the dining room later." She visited with the kittens for a moment longer, encouraging the current bottle brigade, and noting that the tiny tiger cats looked bigger every day.

Kim was already standing at the side entrance with the folded beach chairs, one under each arm, when Maureen arrived. "I went over and watched the weigh-in," she said. "I felt safe because there were so many people around me. I almost expected to see you-know-who in the crowd."

"I know the feeling." Maureen carried the champagne bottle filled with ginger ale and the wineglasses. "I jump every time I see a bearded guy with horn-rimmed glasses."

They set up the chairs in the usual spot, Maureen poured their drinks, and they sat facing the sunset, backs to the tree. Under any other circumstances, Maureen thought, this would have been a welcome oasis of quiet after a hectic day.

"I enjoy feeding the kittens," Kim said. "It's relaxing."

"I know. Sort of like watching the angelfish swimming."

"Someday we should spend a vacation here when we're not walking on eggshells most of the time."

272   *Carol J. Perry*

Maureen raised her glass in a toast. "To kittens and angel-fish."

Kim's glass met hers with a clink. "And to reeling in a very big fish."

Together they played out what had become a familiar charade—chatting, smiling, laughing, posing, and at the same time wondering, dreading, anticipating. Was he watching them at that very minute? They each smiled and pointed when Bogie strolled past, then turned and came back and lay down in front of Maureen's chair.

Does Bogie know that Harvey hates cats?

Kim answered the unspoken question. "Your cat is protecting you. Sometimes I wish I had a cat."

"I'm pretty sure I know where you can get a kitten."

"I'm thinking about that."

When the sun had almost completely faded into the gulf, they picked up their chairs and bottle and Penelope Josephine's second-best stemware and hurried inside. Bogie followed, but used his cat door.

After dinner Ted and Maureen considered the usual late date in the bar, but with Haven's present mellow mood, the bar would surely be full of paying customers far into the night. "I'll meet you and Finn in the lobby in the morning," Ted promised. "Try to get some sleep. You've earned it."

A bit regretfully, because of the missed time with Ted, but looking forward to donning pajamas, Maureen rode the elevator to the third floor. Tucked into the blond Heywood-Wakefield bed, with Finn beside her, she turned on the Channel Nine evening news. Perfect weather was in the forecast, and after a video from one of the station's livestream cameras on St. Pete Beach, there was an excellent overhead view of the Haven Inn's parking lot, filled with the colorful assortment of trucks the captains and tradespeople had driven to the morning meeting—each one prominently displaying a message promoting the tournament, along with another video of the weigh-in. Both were credited to Ron Treadwell of Haven.

"Look at that, Finn," she said. "Our friend Ron is almost famous."

"Woof," Finn agreed.

Sleep came surprisingly easily, considering the many things—good, bad, and downright frightening—crowding into her life at that moment. When she awoke, the room was still dark, but Finn seemed to know that it was time for a run on the beach. She could hear his toenails on the kitchen floor as he ran from the bedroom through the kitchen to the front door and back, until she climbed out of bed and prepared his breakfast. Yawning, she donned shorts and T-shirt and picked up the leash, and the two started down the stairs to the lobby.

Ted greeted her with a side hug and a whispered "I missed you last night."

"Me too." She handed him the leash. "Any word on Momcat?"

"Not a peep." He frowned. "Poor Molly is beside herself—walking around outside calling for her at all hours. She's convinced that she can hear the poor cat crying in the woodlot."

"It doesn't look hopeful, does it? I mean, if she could, Momcat would be back with those kittens if she was able, don't you think so?"

"Everyone is holding out hope, but it's been a little while. It doesn't look good." He clipped Finn's leash onto the collar. "The kittens are thriving, though. All the surrogate moms are doing a good job."

Maureen knelt on the floor and gave Finn a hug. He responded with a face lick and a happy woof. "Have a good run, you two," she said.

"I wish you were coming with us," Ted said. "You'll have another busy day, I guess."

"I wish I was coming with you too," she said, meaning it sincerely. "Things are going along as planned for the tournament, and the inn business is the best it's been for a long time." She smiled up at him. "But you know that. It's largely due to your magic in the kitchen."

"We're a good team." He extended his hand, pulling her toward him. "I'd spend all day, every day, with you if I could. Maureen, I worry about you all the time. You're being careful, aren't you? You're sure Hubbard has your back? He's tracking Album somehow?"

"Hubbard is doing everything he lawfully can," she assured him. "I'm not leaving this property alone for even a minute. I promise. Actually, between the full house, the tournament, and the new shop, I couldn't go very far even if I wanted to. Enjoy your run."

"We will. See you at breakfast?"

"Absolutely." She followed them onto the porch and watched as they started down the boulevard toward the beach—Ted in an easy jog and Finn in his happiest prancing mode.

Was someone else watching from the shadows? Watching them? Watching her?

The second day of the Eddie Manuel Memorial Kingfish Tournament began in such an orderly way that Maureen was pleasantly surprised. "You'd think we'd been running these things for years," she told Trent, also an early riser. "Everybody involved—the captains, the merchants, the customers— everybody gets along, everybody is having a good time."

"You're right," Trent said. "Pierre is having a ball fishing. Even the kingfish are cooperating. I'll bet next year's tournament will be even bigger."

"I wouldn't be surprised," she said. "So far, so good." Her phone buzzed, altering her lighthearted mood. Caller ID showed Frank Hubbard. She spoke a tentative "Hello?"

"Why didn't you tell me about the damned bag?" he growled.

"The yellow bag?" Confused, she said, "I did."

"Sure. And that one never even showed up. No. I'm talking about a raggedy-ass old canvas bag your girlfriend apparently found in the Forest. I got a call from some big shot at Fish and Wildlife because this bag you didn't bother to tell me about has bloodstains on it." He cleared his throat. "The blood DNA matches up to some samples from an old cold case—an old murder case from Haven."

She knew without his saying the name. The blood on the bag had come from Everett Sherman's body—the man who'd fished at Haven's first tournament, and who'd died beside an Indian mound.

All thought of an "orderly" day flew out the window. Had Fish and Wildlife notified Kim of what they'd found on the bag? Or was information about an unsolved murder what the doctor had laughingly called "above her pay grade"?

It was early, but Maureen went into her office and buzzed Kim's room anyway. "Sorry to wake you so early, Kim," she said. "Has Fish and Wildlife contacted you about—about what they found on the canvas bag they picked up?" She tried to keep her voice steady.

"They sent me a text," she said. "Wait a minute. I'll read it to you. They believe it once contained some Tocobaga artifacts." Short pause. "Here it is. **Minute shards of Native pottery found in the lining were identified as a type known to be from the Haven, Florida area. A portion of an eating utensil made from bone was also found in the bag.** See? Harvey—if it was Harvey—robbed the mound over twenty years ago and got interrupted—probably by poor Mr. Sherman—so he stashed the stuff in the canvas bag and put it back into the mound and beat it out of Haven—meaning to come back for it some day when things cooled off."

"They didn't say anything about—about—any kind of stains on the bag?" Maureen asked.

"Stains? No. It was old and probably stained from being in the ground with mud and all. Why?" Kim asked. "The important thing is, Harvey took things from that bag and put them into the yellow bag. Simple."

Frank Hubbard hadn't asked Maureen to keep the news from Kim. "Fish and Wildlife notified the police that there are bloodstains on the canvas bag," she said. "They tie the bag to a Haven cold case. A murder."

Kim caught on just as fast as Maureen had. "The man who was killed next to the mound during the first tournament. Sherman."

"Right."

"Does Harvey know they've discovered that?"

"I don't know how he could, unless he's listening to my phone calls."

"It's so aggravating," Kim said, "how everything points to Harvey but nothing actually sticks to him. We know he had the yellow bag. We know he's been digging in the mound. We know he took something out of the canvas bag. We're even pretty sure he killed Eddie."

"If he gets caught trying to grab one or both of us, that'll stick for sure." Maureen assured her, "and it's not as if Hubbard doesn't agree with us, it's just that he hasn't got actual proof of any of it. And we're supposed to leave it up to him and to mind our own business."

"Oh, sure." Kim snorted. "As if knowing we're the only things standing in the way of him getting away with all of it—including a couple of murders—isn't our business."

"We'll stick to the pattern," Maureen promised. "Harvey likes patterns."

"Yes, we will. We'll stay inside today until it's time to walk Finn, right?"

"I have to keep an eye on the tournament. I'm going to watch the weigh-in again. I hope the second day is going to be as good as the first one was," Maureen wished aloud.

She watched the lobby from her vantage point inside the office and at the same time listened to messages from the fishing vessels throughout the day. Within minutes of the time the lines were officially in the water at six thirty that morning she'd heard the words, "Kingfish on" from at least a dozen boats. It appeared that the second day of Eddie's tournament was going to be a success.

Chapter 45

The scene at the weigh-in on Saturday was exciting and joyous and a little bit chaotic. So far, the smallest kid in the youth category had caught by far the biggest fish. Maureen's friends, Dick and Ethel were leaders in the outboard motorboat competition, and one after another, fishermen and captains, shop owners, and even city officials wanted to shake Maureen's hand—wanted to thank her for lifting Haven out of its midyear financial slump. Even Ron Treadwell's fortunes had taken a big turn for the better. The TV station had contacted with him to do the full half-hour coverage of the fireworks show at the close of the tournament.

Maureen herself had ambitious plans for bringing some more of Trent's watercolor dream sketches to reality—maybe beginning with the yellow-and-white wicker office and lobby space where she spent so much of her time. She'd promised herself a redo of the guest laundry too, and maybe the construction of an outdoor tiki bar at the edge of the woodlot.

She'd felt secure enough to increase the orders for merchandise for the gift shop, confident that Haven House Inn could afford the larger inventory. She was, in spite of the ever-present current of fear beneath it all, having fun.

After the day-two weigh-in, as she dressed carefully in shorts, top, and hotline necklace in preparation to meet Kim for their sunset ritual, it occurred to her that they—she and Kim—had perhaps become too comfortable in the routine. Perhaps Harvey had in fact become the spider. Perhaps they'd wandered too far into *his* parlor.

"Do you think Harvey is falling for our little reality show?" she asked when Kim arrived in the long corridor leading to the side yard. "Or have we set ourselves up for him too well?"

Kim was thoughtful as they passed the guest laundry and the vending machines. "It doesn't actually matter much," she said. "Either way, he has to meet us face-to-face."

Maureen had just pushed the outer door open when Jolene burst into the corridor. "Hey, everybody! Momcat is back. Where's Molly?"

The two women turned abruptly. Sunset could wait. Harvey could wait. Momcat was back. They ran, following Jolene to the lobby. George and Gert were already there, on their way to the kitchen. "Somebody find Molly!" George yelled. "She should be there!"

"I'll check the third floor." Maureen ran for the stairs. "Somebody check the second floor. She may be changing linens." If Momcat had come home, Molly shouldn't miss the excitement. The hall leading to Maureen's suite was empty. Finn looked up from a napping position near the door. No Molly. With a quick apology to the golden, Maureen retraced her steps and joined the growing crowd headed for the kitchen.

It was true. Momcat was home, safely snuggled into the FedEx box surrounded by hungry kittens, crowding each other for feeding positions. Sam and Shelley and four of the self-named "bottle brigade" surrounded the box. "Give her space," Sam instructed, holding his arms out wide. "Don't get too close. Where the hell is Molly? She should be seeing this. And why the hell does Momcat smell like she's been rolling in fish bait?"

"I'll look outside," Shelly offered. "She's been out there looking for the cat at all hours."

Maureen and Kim moved closer to the action. Maureen, keenly aware that dinner preparations were in progress, attempted to steer the oohing-and-aahing gathering of onlookers to the edge of the room where Ted warned them away from hot stoves, open refrigerators, and kitchen staff workers chopping and peeling and stirring while at the same time trying to sneak a peek at the returning prodigal cat.

Kim tugged on Maureen's arm, pointing to the kitchen window. "The sun's going down. We'd better get out there."

What to do? Should she help maintain order in the kitchen? Look for Molly, who deserved to be with Momcat right now? Or should she sit in the yard, pretending to relax, drinking fake wine while chaos reigned inside her inn? This was no time to break the pattern they'd established.

"Let's go," she said, and the two women, moving against the flow of indoor traffic, raced for the side door.

"We're only a tiny bit late," Kim whispered as they adjusted their chairs and Maureen managed to keep her hand from shaking as she poured the ginger ale. "Maybe he won't notice."

"Maybe," Maureen said, knowing that Harvey liked things orderly and on time. She barely had time to reach under her shirt for the button when a familiar white bait-and-tackle truck with a red-lettered EDDIE MANUEL MEMORIAL KINGFISH TOURNAMENT sign rolled past the tree and stopped a few feet from the chairs. That same truck had been in the parking lot and at the weigh-in station every day since the captain's meeting. She stopped short of pressing the button. Was there a bait problem with the tournament? That could be serious. The dark-haired man stepped out of the driver's seat and slid open the side door.

The woman was blindfolded and a gag covered her mouth, rope bound her arms behind her back. The man pulled her out of the truck so roughly that she nearly fell. "You two," he said. "Get into the truck or I'll shoot her where she stands." He waved a gun. "Get in and I'll let her go." The man, clean-shaven, hair dyed black, wearing gold-rimmed glasses, was Harvey Album, his eyes bright with excitement. "I traded the cat for her," he said. "Now it's your turn to be traded. Get in."

Maureen pushed her button and was sure that Kim had pushed hers.

"All right." Maureen raised her hands above her head. She kept her voice level, knowing she was speaking to a madman. "Let Molly go. I'll come with you."

"Both of you." He pressed the gun against Molly's head and moved aside. "Get in."

They did as they were told, standing inside the truck next to plastic buckets of smelly bait, watching as he gave Molly a vicious shove, sending her sprawling to the ground while he reached to close the sliding door on the captive women.

The three looked up at a sound. It was a trilling, "hoot, hoot, hoot." Maureen recognized a fair imitation of the cry of Eastern Screech owl she'd heard on the porch of the casino—just before it had pounced on a hapless mouse.

Ron Treadwell, helmeted, with full climbing gear, his shin protectors with their sharp pointed spikes at his ankles flashing in the fading sunlight like talons and a yellow rope coiled over one arm, plummeted from the tree above directly onto a flailing, helpless Harvey Album, kicking the gun out of the way and effectively hog-tying his ex-boss while sirens wailed nearby.

It didn't take long for the police to make order out of the chaotic scene. While a deputy handcuffed the already dis-abled Harvey Album, Frank Hubbard read him his rights from a well-worn card. Maureen and Kim dashed to Molly's side, removing the blindfold, the cruelly tight gag over her mouth, and the rope bruising her wrists. Her first words were, predictably, "Is Momcat all right?"

Assured that cat and kittens were fine, Molly began to cry. "He had Momcat by the scruff of her neck. He had a knife. He said he'd kill her if I didn't get in the truck. What could I do? At least he let her go." She threw her arms around Ron. "Then he was going to shoot me! You're a hero! You saved my life." She stood back then, her hands on his shoulders. "But what the hell were you doing up in that tree?"

With Harvey safely secured in the back seat of a cruiser, loudly demanding a lawyer, Frank turned his attention to the photographer. "That's what I'd like to know too," he said. "Just what the hell *were* you doing up there?"

Ron, his face coloring slightly—perhaps from the "hero" designation—gave a dismissive shrug. "I've been hired to cover the fireworks display tomorrow night for TV. It's the biggest assignment I've ever had." He lifted the camera on its leather strap. "I was practicing for it—figuring distance, light variation, focus. You know."

The sirens and the commotion in the side yard had drawn a crowd from inside Haven House and passersby on the boulevard. Molly, embraced by staff members and guests alike, was on her way to the kitchen to see for herself that Momcat was well and happy to be home.

Ted dashed from the side door and pulled Maureen close. "He had a gun," he murmured, kissing her face, her eyes, her throat. "I could have lost you."

Maureen, fully aware of the audience surrounding them, wholeheartedly kissed him back.

Epilogue

Harvey Album's many years of staying outside of the law had come to an end. However, he refused to admit to any of the thefts of artifacts from the Haven mounds, and he firmly denied killing Eddie with a blow to the head when Eddie had surprised him digging in the mound, then pushing his body from the Jet Ski.

Ron Treadwell was questioned thoroughly about his association with Album, and his part—if any—in the artifact thefts. It was determined that although he'd used poor judgment in letting his boss use the yellow bag, he'd had no actual knowledge of what it was used for.

Ron's camera had recorded Harvey's admission that he'd kidnapped Molly, abused her, threatened her life, and attempted to kidnap Maureen and Kim, providing Frank Hubbard with sufficient grounds to arrest him. He'd actually stolen the white truck when he'd abandoned his van back in Georgia and was found guilty of grand theft auto, so that crime was added to his sentence. The circumstantial evidence of Harvey removing the bloodstained canvas bag from the mound, along with the dashcam video of the car with Utah plates led to a thorough investigation of his ties to a nationwide ring of artifact robbers that could very likely result in an extremely long jail term for both Harvey and the Utah mastermind who'd told him to clean up his mess. Excavating and removing archaeological resources located on designated historic public lands is in violation of the Archaeological Resources Protection Act and carries severe penalties, both in terms of fines and prison time. Hubbard reopened the case of Everett Sherman's murder and was not giving up on proving Harvey guilty of Eddie's death as well, but Harvey's well-established pattern of keeping everything he touched spotlessly clean had so far precluded any fingerprints or DNA that could be brought into evidence. Ron Treadwell joined the staff of the local TV station in addition to being the inn's official photographer, and could finally, happily, afford to pay his own rent. *Watching Birds* magazine closed shop.

The first Eddie Manuel Memorial Kingfish Tournament was a rousing success on every level. It was immediately scheduled by the city of Haven for every June in the foreseeable future. The lucky youngster who'd caught the biggest fish on Saturday was voted the King of the Beach, and announced that he would put his thousand-dollar reward toward college—where he planned to study marine biology.

Tommy Manuel's tournament crew won two of the Revere bowls, and galley guy Alan was promoted to first mate. The Quic Shop had news of Maureen and Ted's kissing scene before they'd even gone indoors, but it seemed that nobody was surprised.

Meg, Amy, Beth, and Jo were all spoken for before it was time for them to leave Momcat, who'd been lovingly shampooed and crème rinsed after her imprisonment in the bait truck. Beth and Jo were claimed by Molly and Gert. Erle Stanley gained new baby sister Amy and Frank Hubbard's mom was gifted with Meg. Momcat was attended to by Maureen's vet, and chose to return to her outdoor life, but still visited the kitchen occasionally. Dr. Kim Salter left for a new teaching position in Colorado, promising to return for a Florida vacation the following June in time to celebrate Trent's next birthday party. Maureen looked forward to having a new office and lobby to show off by then, along with a paint job and new machines for the guest laundry.

She had reason to believe that she might also soon be showing off a new diamond ring.

On the last night of the tournament, while everyone in Haven was outside watching the best fireworks display the city had ever seen, Maureen lingered for a moment in the empty dining room, admiring the area with its carved woodwork and lazily swimming angelfish. A shimmering motion at the end scat of the bar caught her eye.

The woman, dressed entirely in black, smiled and lifted a tall glass—the contents glowing green—in a silent toast.

Acknowledgments

What would a writer do without research? Writing mysteries requires much more information than simply figuring out new ways to kill somebody—though I sometimes wonder if someone, somewhere, is keeping track of my frequent searches for information on poisons, garottes, arrows, bullets, and other means of termination!

Haunting License required me to learn a little bit about a lot of things: Native American artifacts, various species of birds, how to care for newborn kittens, how arborists work, tree-climbing equipment, cameras, Florida history, Joe DiMaggio, archaeology, Jet Skis, high-end fashions, vintage arcade machines, tournament fishing, charter boats and more—besides how to murder someone.

The information on the 1930s vintage "Grandmother's Prophecies" amusement arcade machine is accurate. The fortune cards are the real thing too. (I have played the Lotto numbers several times and haven't won a cent, but you're welcome to try them.)

I sincerely want to thank the authors, experts, and researchers of the many topics that writers like me have to learn about in order to make our own stories ring true.

RECIPES

Ted's Giant Blueberry Muffins

(Makes 6 giant muffins)

½ cup of softened butter
1 cup of sugar
2 large eggs
½ cup buttermilk
1 teaspoon good quality vanilla extract
2 cups flour
2 teaspoons baking powder
¼ teaspoon salt
2 cups fresh blueberries

For the topping:
3 tablespoons brown sugar
⅛ teaspoon ground cinnamon
⅛ teaspoon ground nutmeg

   Preheat the oven to 400 degrees F. In a large bowl, cream the butter and sugar until light and fluffy—5 to 7 minutes. Add the eggs one at a time, beating well after each addition. Beat in the buttermilk and vanilla. In another bowl, whisk flour, baking powder, and salt. Add to the creamed mixture and stir until just moistened. Fold in the blueberries.

Fill greased or paper-lined jumbo-sized muffin cups ⅔ full. Mix the topping and sprinkle it evenly over the tops. Bake 20 to 25 minutes or until a toothpick inserted in center of muffin comes out clean. Cool 5 minutes before removing from the pan to a wire rack. Best served warm.

Aster's Easy Meatball-Vegetable Soup

(Almost as good as Ted's and much easier!)

(Makes 4 servings)

1 can (18.5 ounces) ready-to-eat French onion soup
1 can (14.5 ounces) sliced potatoes, drained
1 can (14.5 ounces) diced tomatoes with basil, garlic, and
    oregano
1 package (10 ounces) frozen mixed vegetables
12 frozen cocktail-sized meatballs, halved

In a large pot, combine soup, potatoes, 1½ cups of water, tomatoes with liquid, vegetables, meatballs, and ⅛ teaspoon of pepper. Cover. Over high heat bring to a boil. Cook on medium heat until meatballs are heated through and flavors have blended (about 15 minutes). Ted sprinkles his with chopped parsley. You can if you want to.

Maureen's Grandmother's 7UP Cake

2 sticks butter
½ cup Crisco
3 cups sugar
5 eggs
1 teaspoon vanilla extract
1 teaspoon lemon juice
3½ cups flour
7 ounces 7UP at room temperature

Mix butter and Crisco. Mix in sugar gradually. Add the eggs, one at a time. Mix in the vanilla, lemon juice, flour and 7UP. Bake at 350 degrees F in a greased and floured tube pan, one to one and a half hours.

Ron's Grandmother's 7UP Cake

1 package lemon cake mix
1 package instant lemon pudding
¾ cup vegetable oil
1 (10-ounce) bottle of 7UP
4 eggs

Mix the cake mix, instant pudding mix, oil, 7UP, and eggs in a large bowl. Beat for 4 minutes. Pour into a greased and floured 13-x-9-inch pan and bake for 1 hour at 325 degrees F. (Ron's grandmother says the cake may shrink slightly in the center as it cools.) Frost as you like.

Visit our website at
KensingtonBooks.com
to sign up for our newsletters, read
more from your favorite authors, see
books by series, view reading group
guides, and more!

Become a Part of Our
Between the Chapters Book Club
Community and Join the Conversation

Submit your book review for a chance to win exclusive
Between the Chapters swag you can't get anywhere else!
https://www.kensingtonbooks.com/pages/review/